The
W...n

Elizabeth r... I was thinking," she said, "about y... to have this. You can sell it. It's worth mo... pound, five shillings."

Michael looked, ... heavy gold locket on a thin gold chain. For a moment, his love for Elizabeth surged, then his pride took over.

"Keep your gold," he said coldly. "I don't need it."

"But Michael…"

He turned and walked quickly away. He did not want her to see how red his face was, how ashamed he was to be in such a position that he needed her charity. In his dreams, he wanted to be the one to give her gold, whatever she wanted or needed.

She began to walk after him. "Michael?"

"Go away, Elizabeth. Go back to your castle."

She followed him, but he broke into a run, easily out-pacing her.

Elizabeth faltered then stopped, tears running down her cheeks.

Also available in the Forget Me Not series:

VAMPIRES AT MIDNIGHT

Vampires at Midnight

formerly titled *The Midnight People*

*Seventeen brilliant and chilling tales
of the ghastly bloodsucking Undead*

Edited by PETER HAINING

WARNER BOOKS

For
Geoff Waring
From
'The Man of the Macabre'

A *Warner* Book

First published in Great Britain in 1968
by Leslie Frewin Publishers
under the title *The Midnight People*
Published in the United States in
1970 by Grosset & Dunlap
This edition published by Warner in 1993

Copyright © 1968 Peter Haining

The moral right of the author has been asserted

A CIP catalogue for this book
is available from the British Library

ISBN 0 7515 0146 8

Printed in England by Clays Ltd, St Ives plc

Warner
A Division of
Little, Brown and Company (UK) Limited
165 Great Dover Street
London SE1 4YA

ACKNOWLEDGMENT

The Editor is grateful to the following authors, agents and publishers for permission to include copyright material in this collection: The Hutchinson Publishing Group for THREE YOUNG LADIES by Bram Stoker; Edward Arnold (Publishers) Ltd. for AN EPISODE OF CATHEDRAL HISTORY by M. R. James; The Scott Meredith Literary Agency for BAT'S BELFRY by August Derleth and THE DRIFTING SNOW by Stephen Grendon; the author's executors and The Hutchinson Publishing Group for 'AND NO BIRD SINGS' by E. F. Benson; Hodder and Stoughton for THE BELIEVER by Sidney Horler; the author and his agent for WHEN IT WAS MOONLIGHT by Manly Wade Wellman; the author and his agent for OVER THE RIVER by P. Schuyler Miller; Messrs. A. D. Peters and Co., Ltd. for DRINK MY BLOOD by Richard Matheson and PILLAR OF FIRE by Ray Bradbury; the author for DOCTOR PORTHOS by Basil Copper; B. P. Singer Features for THE LIVING DEAD by Robert Bloch; the author and his agent for THE GIRL WITH THE HUNGRY EYES by Fritz Leiber.

But see, amid the human round
A crawling shape intrude!
A blood-red thing that writhes from out
The scenic solitude!
It writhes! – it writhes! – with mortal pangs
And man becomes its food,
The angels sob at vermin fangs
In human gore imbrued.

— EDGAR ALLAN POE

Contents

CONTENTS

Foreword

MY GREAT FRIEND, the late Boris Karloff, and I were once discussing the art of acting in horror movies, or "graveyard films" as I prefer to call them. The secret, he said, was to "leave it to the audience". He believed it was what people conjured up in their minds rather than what they saw on the screen which provided the real *frisson* of horror. I think the same is true of the horror story, for no matter how good the writing, it can never quite match the inventive power of the human imagination.

But why *do* we react in this way? I believe it has something to do with what Shakespeare called "the secret, black and midnight" aspects of our character: the part of our nature which makes us react to the supernatural in the ways we do. I don't believe we watch these films or read these stories out of any kind of morbid urge. It is simply because we enjoy them.

During my life I have met a number of the leading names in supernatural fiction. I was interviewed by M. R. James, the Provost of Eton, in 1935 when I sat my scholarship exam for that famous school. I can still clearly remember his learned manner, his strong, dignified face and resonant voice which so enraptured those lucky enough to have listened to him telling his ghost stories. I did actually hear some ghost stories being told by that other fine writer, E. F. Benson, who read a number to the boys of Wellington College while I was studying there. I can hear his quiet voice chilling the blood of every single person in the room – I don't think anyone, master or pupil, slept a wink that night! Unfortunately, I never had the opportunity of meeting Bram Stoker, but I did meet some members of his family while making the first of my Dracula films.

I am now friendly with a number of the current writers of macabre fiction, including Robert Bloch, Ray Bradbury, Richard Matheson and Fritz Leiber, and have appeared on the screen in stories scripted by most of them. I shall always remember the night in 1964 when I was staying with Robert Bloch in Los Angeles while filming an episode for the Alfred Hitchcock TV series. Bob took me along to a house in the city where Ray Bradbury and Fritz Leiber were also guests. It was the home of a Dr Doolittle from the University of California and he kept us completely spellbound for three hours talking about genetic surgery. I must confess that I didn't understand a word he said – and I don't think that the others did, either, although all of us knew the Frankenstein story and had been involved with it, in one way or another, for our work. It was a case of science surpassing art, I decided!

I have always liked the story that Bram Stoker once claimed – with his tongue in his cheek, I suspect – that he dreamed the story of Dracula after a particularly heavy supper of lobster. Whether he already had the idea in his mind nobody can be quite sure, but it certainly must have evolved from some kind of subconscious working – for, in the words of that other famous story by Richard Matheson, there is "No Such Thing As A Vampire". *Is there?*

Christopher Lee

(talking to Peter Haining)

Introduction

Vampire – *a dead body which continues to live in the grave; which it leaves, however, by night, for the purpose of sucking the blood of the living, whereby it is nourished and preserved in good condition, instead of becoming decomposed like other dead bodies.*

George Conrad Horst,
German philosopher and occultist.

THROUGHOUT the whole of macabre literature there is no creature more feared, more dreadful and more fascinating than the Vampire. No other monster, succubus, or ephemeral spirit has commanded so much studied attention from the great masters of the *genre* – and no other horror from the dark has inspired so many outstanding nightmare tales.

Unlike many of the ghastly creations of macabre writers and artists, the Vampire has its roots firmly based in fact: in legends and folk tales that date back to antiquity. Vampires appear in the histories of countries as far apart as China and Germany, India and Mexico, and accounts of their nefarious activities have even come to hand from the more remote parts of Europe, Greece and Malaya in quite recent times. While these reports are often detailed in their account of what the creature caused to happen, they are rarely either clear or definite about what it looked like.

To get a picture, then, it is necessary to turn to the works of the famed Occultist, the Reverend Montague Summers, and in particular his two classic studies of the Vampire, *The Vampire: His Kith and Kin*, and *The Vampire in Europe*. In the former he analyses all the existing material and comes up with as complete a picture as we could wish for.

He defines the Vampire as 'one who has led a life of more than ordinary immortality and unbridled wickedness; a man of foul, gross and selfish passions, of evil ambitions, delighting in cruelty and blood'.

Turning to physical appearance he writes: 'A Vampire is generally described as being exceedingly gaunt and lean with a hideous countenance and eyes wherein are glinting the red fire of perdition. When, however, he has satiated his lust for warm human blood his body becomes horribly puffed and bloated, as though he were some great leech gorged and replete to bursting. Cold as ice, or it may be fevered and burning as a hot coal, the skin is deathly pale, but the lips are very full and rich, blub and red; the teeth white and gleaming, and the canine teeth wherewith he bites deep into the neck of his prey to suck thence the vital streams which re-animate his body and invigorate all his forces appear notably sharp and pointed. Often his mouth curls back in a vulpine snarl which bares these fangs, "a gaping mouth and gleaming teeth", says Leone Allacci, and so in many districts the hare-lipped are avoided as being certainly Vampires. In Bulgaria, it is thought that the Vampire who returns from the tomb has only one nostril; and in certain districts of Poland he is supposed to have a sharp point at the end of his tongue, like the sting of a bee. It is said that the palms of a Vampire's hands are downy with hair, and the nails are always curved and crooked, often well-nigh the length of a great bird's claw, the quicks dirty and foul with glots and gouts of black blood. His breath is unbearably fetid and rank with corruption, the stench of the charnel.'

Whether or not you, the general reader, taking up this book for the sake of reading pleasure, are prepared to accept the existence of Vampires, let alone a 'run-down' on their appearance and character, is not important to its enjoyment. If, however, you do wish to investigate these phenomena more fully I can only recommend Mr Summers' two books to you.

The story of the Vampire in fiction is of a considerably newer date. It begins in 1819 with John William Polidori's *The Vampyre* which is included in this book, and progresses to the present day in numerous striking, highly inventive and well-written stories. It is necessary for me to state here and now that there are several noteworthy omissions from this collection – and they have been left out for the simple reason that they have already been anthologised numerous times and would therefore be familiar to all keen readers of horror stories. Particularly outstanding tales such as Sheridan Le Fanu's *Carmilla*, Edgar Allan Poe's *Berenice*, Theophile Gautier's *The Beautiful Vampire*, E. F. Benson's *Mrs Amworth* and *The Room in the Tower*, ought to be included as they are landmarks in the development of Vampire stories – but their inclusion would have prevented me using some of the other extremely rare and interesting stories I unearthed during my research. To any reader not familiar with the tales I have mentioned, I can only refer him to the collected works of the author in question. I should also add that the stories in this anthology are placed in chronological order so that the development of styles, themes and approach can be clearly seen.

To begin the book, I have quoted the two best modern *authenticated* stories of real Vampires I have been able to find – Montague Summers' incredible tale of Fritz Haarmann The Hanover Vampire and an equally convincing account of events at mysterious Croglin Grange by Augustus Hare. I think they admirably set off what is to follow. If they cause a fluttering of the nerves, be warned!

Finally, I would like to give particular thanks to the following people for their help and encouragement in compiling this work: Leslie Frewin, my publisher, who set the whole thing

13

off; Basil Copper, who was an invaluable source for reference material; the various publishers and agents who went to considerable trouble on my behalf tracking down stories and who are regrettably too numerous to mention; Kurt Singer for assistance in locating American material; Miss Pearl Lowry, my secretary, who typed a great deal of material in a very short space of time; and last, but by no means least, my wife, Philippa, who shared the compiling of the anthology right from the start and should by rights be credited as co-editor. To you all, my sincere thanks.

P H

Broxbourne, Hertfordshire
October 1968

Fritz Haarmann – 'The Hanover Vampire'

MONTAGUE SUMMERS

On the morning of 17th April 1925, the London *Daily Express* printed the following incredible story on its front page:

VAMPIRE BRAIN. PLAN TO PRESERVE IT FOR SCIENCE.

Berlin. Thursday, April 16th. The body of Fritz Haarmann, executed yesterday at Hanover for twenty-seven murders, will not be buried until it has been examined at Gottingen University.

Owing to the exceptional character of the crimes – most of Haarmann's victims were bitten to death – the case aroused tremendous interest among German scientists. It is probable that Haarmann's brain will be removed and preserved by the University authorities. – Central News.

Fritz Haarmann, who was dubbed 'The Hanover Vampire' was born in Hanover, 25th October 1879. His father, 'Olle Haarmann', a locomotive-stoker, was well-known as a rough, cross-grained choleric man, whom Fritz, his youngest son, both hated and feared. As a youth, Fritz Haarmann was educated at a Church School, and then at a preparatory school for non-commissioned officers at New Breisach. It is significant that he was always dull and stupid, unable to learn; but it appears a good soldier. When released from military service owing to ill-health he returned home, only to be accused in a short while of offences against children. Being considered irresponsible for his actions the Court sent him to an asylum at Hildesheim, whence however he managed to escape and took refuge in Switzerland. Later he returned to Hanover, but the house became unbearable owing to the violent quarrels which were of daily occurrence between him and his father. Accordingly he enlisted and was sent to the crack 10th Jager Battalion, at Colmar in Alsace. Here he won golden opinions, and when released owing to illness, with a pension, his papers were marked 'Recht gut'. When he reached home there were fresh scenes of rancour whilst blows were not infrequently exchanged, and in 1903 he was examined by a medical expert, Dr Andrae, who considered him morally lacking but yet there were no grounds for sending him to an asylum. Before long he sank to the status of a tramp; a street hawker, at times; a pilferer and a thief. Again and again he was sent to jail, now charged with larceny, now with burglary, now with indecency, now with fraud. In 1918, he was released after a long stretch to find another Germany. He returned to Hanover, and was able to open a small cook shop in the old quarter of the town, where he also hawked meat which was eagerly sought at a time of general hunger and scarcity. He drove yet another trade, that of 'copper's nark', an old lag who had turned spy and informer, and gave secret tips to the police as to the whereabouts of men they wanted. 'Detective Haarmann' he was nick-named by the women who thronged his shop because he always had plenty of fresh meat in store, and he invariably contrived to undersell the other butchers and victuallers of the quarter.

The centre of Hanover was the Great Railway Station, and Hanover was thronged especially at its centre with a vast ever-moving population, fugitives, wanderers and homeless from all parts of dislocated Germany. Runaway lads from towns in every direction made their way here, looking for work, looking for food, idly tramping without any definite object, without any definite goal, because they had nothing else to do. It can well be imagined that the police, a hopelessly inadequate force, kept as sharp a watch as possible on the Station and its purlieus, and Haarmann used to help them in their surveyance. At midnight, or in the early morning, he would walk up and down among the rows of huddled sleeping forms in the third-class waiting halls and suddenly waking up some frightened youngster demand to see his ticket, ask to know whence he had come and where he was going. Some sad story would be sobbed out, and the kindly Haarmann was wont to offer a mattress and a meal in his own place down town.

So far as could be traced the first boy he so charitably took to his rooms was a lad of seventeen named Friedel Rothe, who had run away from home. On 29th September 1918, his mother received a postcard, and it so happened the very same day his father returned from the war. The parents were not going to let their son disappear without a search, and they soon began to hunt for him in real earnest. One of Friedel's pals told them that the missing boy had met a detective who offered him shelter. Other clues were traced and with extraordinary trouble, for the authorities had more pressing matters in hand than tracking truant schoolboys, the family obliged the police to search Cellarstrasse 27, where Haarmann lived. When a sudden entry was made Haarmann was found with another boy in such an unequivocal situation that his friends, the police, were obliged to arrest him there and then, and he received nine months' imprisonment for gross indecency under Section 175 of the German Code. Four years later when Haarmann was awaiting trial for twenty-four murders he remarked: 'At the time when the policeman arrested me the head of the boy Friedel Rothe was hidden under a newspaper behind the oven. Later on, I threw it into the canal.'

In September 1919, Haarmann first met Hans Grans, the handsome lad who was to stand beside him in the dock. Grans, the type of abnormal and dangerous decadent which is only too common today, was one of the foulest parasites of society, pilferer and thief, bully, informer, spy, agent provocateur, murderer, renter, prostitute, and what is lower and fouler than all, blackmailer. The influence of this Ganymede over Haarmann was complete. It was he who instigated many of the murders – Adolf Hannappel a lad of seventeen was killed in November 1923, because Grans wanted his pair of trousers; Ernst Spiecker, likewise aged seventeen, was killed on 5th January 1924, because Grans coveted his 'toff shirt' – it was he who arranged the details, he who very often trapped the prey.

It may be said that in 1918 Hanover, a town of 450,000 inhabitants, was well known as being markedly homosexual. There were inscribed on the police lists no less than 500 'Männliche Prostituierten' of whom the comeliest and best-dressed, the mannered and well-behaved elegants, frequented the Café Kropcke in the Georgstrasse, one of the first boulevards of New Hanover; whilst others met their friends at the androgynous balls in the Kalenberger Vorstadt, or in the old Assembly Rooms; and lowest of all there was a tiny dancing-place, 'Zur schwulen Guste', 'Hot-Stuff Guissie's' where poor boys found their clientele. It was here, for example, that Grans picked up young Ernst Spiecker, whose tawdry shirt cost him his life.

With regards to his demeanour at the trial the contemporary newspapers write: 'Throughout the long ordeal Haarmann was utterly impassive and complacent. . . . The details of the atrocious crimes for which Haarmann will shortly pay with his life were extremely revolting. All his victims were between 12 and 18 years of age, and it was proved that the accused actually sold the flesh for human consumption. He once made sausages in his kitchen, and, together with the purchaser, cooked and ate them. . . . Some alienists hold that even then the twenty-four murders cannot possibly exhaust the full toll of Haarmann's atrocious crimes, and estimate the total as high as fifty. With the exception of a few counts, the prisoner made minutely detailed confessions and for days the court listened to his grim narrative of how he cut up the bodies of his victims and disposed of the fragments in various ways. He consistently repudiated the imputation of insanity, but at the same time maintained unhesitatingly that all the murders were committed when he was in a state of trance, and unaware of what he was doing. This contention was specifically brushed aside by the Bench, which in its judgement pointed out that according to his own account of what happened, it was necessary for him to hold down his victims by hand in a peculiar way before it was possible for him to inflict a fatal bite on their throats. Such action necessarily involved some degree of deliberation and conscious purpose.'

Another account says with regard to Haarmann: 'The killing of altogether twenty-seven young men is laid at his door, the horror of the deeds being magnified by the allegation that he sold to customers for consumption the flesh of those he did not himself eat. . . . With Haarmann in the dock appeared a younger man, his friend Hans Grans, first accused of assisting in the actual murders but now charged with inciting to commit them and with receiving stolen property. The police are still hunting for a third man, Charles, also a butcher, who is alleged to have completed the monstrous trio . . . the prosecuting attorney has an array of nearly 200 witnesses to prove that all the missing youths were done to death in the same horrible way. . . . He would take them to his rooms, and after a copious meal would praise the looks of his young guests. Then he would kill them after the fashion of a vampire. Their clothes he would put up on sale in his shop, and the bodies would be cut up and disposed of with the assistance of Charles.'

In open court, however, Haarmann admitted that Grans often used to select his victims for him. More than once, he alleged, Grans beat him for failing to kill the 'game' brought in, and Haarmann would keep the corpses in a cupboard actually in his rooms when there was a body awaiting dismemberment. The back of the place abutted on the river, and the bones and skulls were thrown into the water. Some of them were discovered, but their origin was a mystery until a police inspector paid a surprise visit to the prisoner's home to inquire into a dispute between Haarmann and an intended victim who escaped.

Suspicion had at last fallen upon him principally, owing to the skulls and bones found in the river Leine during May, June, and July 1924. The newspapers said that during 1924, no less than 600 persons had disappeared, for the most part lads between 14 and 18. On the night of 22nd June at the railway station, sometime after midnight, a quarrel broke out between Haarmann and a young fellow named Fromm, who accused him of indecency. Both were taken to the central station, and meanwhile Haarmann's room in the Red Row was thoroughly examined with the result that damning evidence came to light. Before long he accused Grans as his accomplice, since at the moment they happened to be on bad terms. Haarmann was sentenced to be decapitated, a sentence executed with a heavy sword. Grans was condemned to imprisonment for life, afterwards commuted to twelve years' penal servitude. In accordance with the law, Haarmann was put to death on Wednesday, 15th April 1925.

This is probably one of the most extraordinary cases of vampirism known. The violent eroticism, the fatal bite in the throat, are typical of the vampire, and it was perhaps something more than mere coincidence that the mode of execution should be the severing of the head from the body, since this was one of the efficacious methods of destroying a vampire.

Certainly in the extended sense of the word, as it is now so commonly used, Fritz Haarmann was a vampire in every particular.

The Vampire of Croglin Grange

As told by CAPTAIN FISHER
to AUGUSTUS HARE

'FISHER,' said the Captain, 'may sound a very plebeian name, but this family is of a very ancient lineage, and for many hundreds of years they have possessed a very curious old place in Cumberland, which bears the weird name of Croglin Grange. The great characteristic of the house is that never at any period of its very long existence has it been more than one storey high, but it has a terrace from which large grounds sweep away towards the church in the hollow, and a fine distant view.

'When, in lapse of years, the Fishers outgrew Croglin Grange in family and fortune, they were wise enough not to destroy the long-standing characteristic of the place by adding another storey to the house, but they went away to the south, to reside at Thorncombe near Guildford, and they let Croglin Grange.

'They were extremely fortunate in their tenants, two brothers and a sister. They heard their praises from all quarters. To their poorer neighbours they were all that is most kind and beneficent, and their neighbours of a higher class spoke of them as a most welcome addition to the little society of the neighbourhood. On their part, the tenants were greatly delighted with their new residence. The arrangement of the house, which would have been a trial to many, was not so to them. In every respect Croglin Grange was exactly suited to them.

'The winter was spent most happily by the new inmates of Croglin Grange, who shared in all the little social pleasures of the district, and made themselves very popular. In the following summer there was one day which was dreadfully, annihilatingly hot. The brothers lay under the trees with their books, for it was too hot for any active occupation. The sister sat on the veranda and worked, or tried to work, for in the intense sultriness of that summer day, work was next to impossible. They dined early, and after dinner they still sat out on the veranda, enjoying the cool air which came with the evening, and they watched the sun set, and the moon rise over the belt of trees which separated the grounds from the church-yard, seeing it mount the heavens till the whole lawn was bathed in silver light, across which the long shadows from the shrubbery fell as if embossed, so vivid and distinct were they.

'When they separated for the night, all retiring to their rooms on the ground floor (for, as I said, there was no upstairs in that house), the sister felt that the heat was still so great that she could not sleep, and having fastened her window, she did not close the shutters—in that very quiet place it was not necessary—and, propped against the pillows, she still watched the wonderful, the marvellous beauty of that summer night. Gradually she became aware of two lights, two lights which flickered in and out in the belt of trees which separated the lawn from the churchyard, and, as her gaze became fixed upon them, she saw them emerge, fixed in a dark substance, a definite ghastly something, which seemed every moment to become nearer, increasing in size and substance as it approached. Every now and then it was lost for a moment in the long shadows which stretched across the lawn from the trees, and then it emerged larger than ever, and still coming on. As she watched it, the most uncontrollable horror seized her. She longed to get away, but the door was close to the window, and the door was locked on the inside, and while she was unlocking it she must be for an instant nearer to it. She longed to scream, but her voice seemed paralysed, her tongue glued to the roof of her mouth.

'Suddenly – she could never explain why afterwards – the terrible object seemed to turn to one side, seemed to be going round the house, not to be coming to her at all, and immediately she jumped out of bed and rushed to the door, but as she was unlocking it she heard scratch, scratch, scratch upon the window. She felt a sort of mental comfort in the knowledge that the window was securely fastened on the inside. Suddenly the scratching sound ceased, and a kind of pecking sound took its place. Then, in her agony, she became aware that the creature was unpicking the lead! The noise continued, and a diamond pane of glass fell into the room. Then a long bony finger of the creature came in and turned the handle of the window, and the window opened, and the creature came in; and it came across the room, and her terror was so great that she could not scream, and it came up to the bed, and it twisted its long, bony fingers into her hair, and it dragged her head over the side of the bed, and – it bit her violently in the throat.

'As it bit her, her voice was released, and she screamed with all her might and main. Her brothers rushed out of their rooms, but the door was locked on the inside. A moment was lost while they got a poker and broke it open. Then the creature had already escaped through the window, and the sister, bleeding violently from a wound in the throat, was lying un-conscious over the side of the bed. One brother pursued the creature, which fled before him through the moonlight with gigantic strides, and eventually seemed to disappear over the wall into the churchyard. Then he rejoined his brother by the sister's bedside. She was dreadfully hurt, and her wound was a very definite one, but she was of strong disposition, not even given to romance or superstition, and when she came to herself she said, "What has happened is most extraordinary and I am very much hurt. It seems inexplicable, but of course there is an explanation, and we must wait for it. It will turn out that a lunatic has escaped from some asylum and found his way here." The wound healed, and she appeared to get well, but the doctor who was sent for to her would not believe that she could bear so terrible a shock so easily, and insisted that she must have change, mental and physical; so her brothers took her to Switzerland.

'Being a sensible girl, when she went abroad she threw herself at once into the interests of the country she was in. She dried plants, she made sketches, she went up mountains, and, as autumn came on, she was the person who urged that they should return to Croglin Grange. "We have taken it," she said, "for seven years, and we have only been there one; and we shall always find it difficult to let a house which is only one storey high, so we had better return there; lunatics do not escape every day." As she urged it, her brothers wished nothing better, and the family returned to Cumberland. From there being no upstairs in the house it was impossible to make any great change in their arrangements. The sister occupied the same room, but it is unnecessary to say she always closed the shutters, which, however, as in many old houses, always left one top pane of the window uncovered. The brothers moved, and occupied a room together, exactly opposite that of their sister, and they always kept loaded pistols in their room.

'The winter passed most peacefully and happily. In the following March, the sister was suddenly awakened by a sound she remembered only too well – scratch, scratch, scratch upon the window, and, looking up, she saw climbed up to the topmost pane of the window, the same hideous brown shrivelled face, with glaring eyes, looking in at her. This time she screamed as loud as she could. Her brothers rushed out of their room with pistols, and out of the front door. The creature was already scudding away across the lawn. One of the brothers fired and hit it in the leg, but still with the other leg it continued to make way, scrambled over the wall into the churchyard, and seemed to disappear into a vault which belonged to a family long extinct.

'The next day the brothers summoned all the tenants of Croglin Grange, and in their presence the vault was opened. A horrible scene revealed itself. The vault was full of coffins; they had been broken open, and their contents, horribly mangled and distorted, were scattered over the floor. One coffin alone remained intact. Of that the lid had been lifted, but still lay loose upon the coffin. They raised it, and there – brown, withered, shrivelled, mummified, but quite entire – was the same hideous figure which had looked in at the windows of Croglin Grange, with the marks of a recent pistol-shot in the leg: and they did the only thing that can lay a vampire – they burnt it.'

The Vampyre

JOHN POLIDORI

*This is the story which introduced the Vampire into modern
literature and thereby became the model for all the myriad
stories to follow. Conceived at that amazing literary gathering
in 1819 of Lord Byron, Polidori (who was Byron's secretary),
Mary Godwin and the poet Shelley – which produced the
immortal horror classic* Frankenstein – The Vampyre
*created a sensation on its publication. Firstly because it gave
reality to a subject that had always been dismissed by the
intelligentsia as mere folk myth, and secondly because it was
published under the name of Lord Byron. This sales gimmick
was allowed to continue for several reprints before the publishers finally gave the versatile Dr Polidori his due credit.*
The Vampyre *is a beautifully executed story, moving to its
dreadful climax with leisurely and compelling style.*

IT HAPPENED THAT in the midst of the dissipations attendant
upon a London winter, there appeared at the various parties of
the leaders of the *ton* a nobleman, more remarkable for his
singularities, than his rank. He gazed upon the mirth around
him, as if he could not participate therein. Apparently, the light
laughter of the fair only attracted his attention, that he might
by a look quell it, and throw fear into those breasts where
thoughtlessness reigned. Those who felt this sensation of awe,
could not explain whence it arose: some attributed it to the dead
grey eye, which fixing upon the object's face, did not seem to
penetrate, and at one glance to pierce through to the inward
workings of the heart; but fell upon the cheek with a leaden ray
that weighed upon the skin it could not pass. His peculiarities
caused him to be invited to every house; all wished to see him,

and those who had been accustomed to violent excitement, and now felt the weight of *ennui*, were pleased at having something in their presence capable of engaging their attention. In spite of the deadly hue of his face, which never gained a warmer tint, either from the blush of modesty, or from the strong emotion of passion, though its form and outline were beautiful, many of the female hunters after notoriety attempted to win his attentions, and gain, at least, some marks of what they might term affection: Lady Mercer, who had been the mockery of every monster shewn in drawing-rooms since her marriage, threw herself in his way, and did all but put on the dress of a mountebank, to attract his notice – though in vain – when she stood before him, though his eyes were apparently fixed upon hers, still it seemed as if they were unperceived – even her un-appalled impudence was baffled, and she left the field. But though the common adultress could not influence even the guid-ance of his eyes, it was not that the female sex was indifferent to him: yet such was the apparent caution with which he spoke to the virtuous wife and innocent daughter, that few knew he ever addressed himself to females. He had, however, the reputation of a winning tongue; and whether it was that it even overcame the dread of his singular character, or that they were moved by his apparent hatred of vice, he was as often among those females who form the boast of their sex from their domestic virtues, as among those who sully it by their vices.

About the same time, there came to London a young gentle-man of the name of Aubrey: he was an orphan left with an only sister in the possession of great wealth, by parents who died while he was yet in childhood. Left also to himself by guardians, who thought it their duty merely to take care of his fortune, while they relinquished the more important charge of his mind to the care of mercenary subalterns, he cultivated more his imagination than his judgment. He had, hence, that high romantic feeling of honour and candour, which daily ruins so many milliners' apprentices. He believed all to sympathise with virtue, and thought that vice was thrown in by Providence merely for the picturesque effect of the scene, as we see in romances: he thought that the misery of a cottage merely consisted in the vesting of clothes, which were warm, but which were better adapted to the painter's eye by their irregular folds and various coloured patches. He thought, in fine, that the dreams of poets were the realities of life. He was handsome, frank, and rich: for these reasons, upon his entering into the gay circles, many mothers surrounded him, striving which should describe with least truth their languishing or romping favourites: the daughters at the same time, by their brightening countenances when he approached, and by their sparkling eyes, when he opened his lips, soon led him into false notions of his talents and his merit. Attached as he was to the romance of his solitary hours, he was startled at finding, that, except in the tallow and wax candles that flickered, not from the presence of a ghost, but from want of snuffing, there was no foundation in real life for any of that congeries of pleasing pictures and descriptions contained in those volumes, from which he had formed his study. Finding, however, some compensation in his gratified vanity, he was about to relinquish his dreams, when the extraordinary being we have above described, crossed him in his career.

He watched him; and the very impossibility of forming an idea of the character of a man entirely absorbed in himself, who gave few other signs of his observation of external objects, than the tacit assent of their existence, implied by the avoidance of their contact: allowing his imagination to picture every thing that flattered its propensity to extravagant ideas, he soon formed this object into the hero of a romance, and determined to observe the offspring of his fancy, rather than the person before him. He became acquainted with him, paid him attentions, and so far advanced upon his notice, that his presence was always recognised. He gradually learnt that Lord Ruthven's affairs were embarrassed, and soon found, from the notes of preparation in —— Street, that he was about to travel. Desirous of gaining some information respecting this singular character, who, till now, had only whetted his curiosity, he hinted to his guardians, that it was time for him to perform the tour, which for many generations has been thought necessary to enable the young to take some rapid steps in the career of vice towards putting themselves upon an equality with the aged, and not allowing them to appear as if fallen from the skies, whenever scandalous intrigues are mentioned as the subjects of pleasantry or of praise, according to the degree of skill shewn in carrying them on. They consented: and Aubrey immediately mentioning his intentions to Lord Ruthven, was surprised to receive from him a proposal to join him. Flattered by such a mark of esteem from him, who, apparently, had nothing in common with other men, he gladly accepted it, and in a few days they had passed the circling waters.

Hitherto, Aubrey had had no opportunity of studying Lord Ruthven's character, and now he found, that, though many more of his actions were exposed to his view, the results offered different conclusions from the apparent motives to his conduct. His companion was profuse in his liberality – the idle, the vagabond, and the beggar, received from his hand more than enough to relieve their immediate wants. But Aubrey could not avoid remarking, that it was not upon the virtuous, reduced to indigence by the misfortunes attendant even upon virtue, that he bestowed his alms – these were sent from the door with hardly suppressed sneers; but when the profligate came to ask something, not to relieve his wants, but to allow him to wallow in his lust, or to sink him still deeper in his iniquity, he was sent away with rich charity. This was, however, attributed by him to the greater importunity of the vicious, which generally prevails over the retiring bashfulness of the virtuous indigent.

There was one circumstance about the charity of his Lordship, which was still more impressed upon his mind: all those upon whom it was bestowed, inevitably found that there was a curse upon it, for they were all either led to the scaffold, or sunk to the lowest and the most abject misery. At Brussels and other towns through which they passed, Aubrey was surprised at the apparent eagerness with which his companion sought for the centres of all fashionable vice; there he entered into all the spirit of the faro table: he betted, and always gambled with success, except where the known sharper was his antagonist, and then he lost even more than he gained; but it was always with the same unchanging face, with which he generally watched the society around: it was not, however, so when he encountered the rash youthful novice, or the luckless father of a numerous family; then his very wish seemed fortune's law – this apparent abstractedness of mind was laid aside, and his eyes sparkled with more fire than that of the cat whilst dallying with the half-dead mouse. In every town, he left the formerly affluent youth, torn from the circle he adorned, cursing, in the solitude of a dungeon, the fate that had drawn him within the reach of this fiend; whilst many a father sat frantic, amidst the speaking looks of mute hungry children, without a single farthing of his late immense wealth, wherewith to buy even sufficient to satisfy their present craving. Yet he took no money from the gambling table; but immediately lost, to the ruiner of many, the last gilder he had just snatched from the convulsive grasp of the innocent: this might but be the result of a certain degree of knowledge, which was not, however, capable of combating the cunning of the more experienced. Aubrey often wished to represent this to his friend, and beg him to resign that charity and pleasure which proved the ruin of all, and did not tend to his own profit; but he delayed it – for each day he hoped his friend would give him some opportunity of speaking frankly and openly to him; however, this never occurred. Lord

Ruthven in his carriage, and amidst the various wild and rich scenes of nature, was always the same: his eye spoke less than his lip; and though Aubrey was near the object of his curiosity, he obtained no greater gratification from it than the constant excitement of vainly wishing to break that mystery, which to his exalted imagination began to assume the appearance of something supernatural.

They soon arrived at Rome, and Aubrey for a time lost sight of his companion; he left him in daily attendance upon the morning circle of an Italian countess, whilst he went in search of the memorials of another almost deserted city. Whilst he was thus engaged, letters arrived from England, which he opened with eager impatience; the first was from his sister, breathing nothing but affection; the others were from his guardians, the latter astonished him; if it had before entered into his imagination that there was an evil power resident in his companion, these seemed to give him almost sufficient reason for the belief. His guardians insisted upon his immediately leaving his friend, and urged, that his character was dreadfully vicious, for that the possession of irresistible powers of seduction, rendered his licentious habits more dangerous to society. It had been discovered, that his contempt for the adultress had not originated in hatred of her character; but that he had required, to enhance his gratification, that his victim, the partner of his guilt, should be hurled from the pinnacle of unsullied virtue, down to the lowest abyss of infamy and degradation: in fine, that all those females whom he had sought, apparently on account of their virtue, had, since his departure, thrown even the mask aside, and had not scrupled to expose the whole deformity of their vices to the public gaze.

Aubrey determined upon leaving one, whose character had not yet shown a single bright point on which to rest the eye. He resolved to invent some plausible pretext for abandoning him altogether, purposing, in the meanwhile, to watch him more

31

closely, and to let no slight circumstances pass by unnoticed. He entered into the same circle, and soon perceived, that his Lordship was endeavouring to work upon the inexperience of the daughter of the lady whose house he chiefly frequented. In Italy, it is seldom that an unmarried female is met with in society; he was therefore obliged to carry on his plans in secret; but Aubrey's eye followed him in all his windings, and soon discovered that an assignation had been appointed, which would most likely end in the ruin of an innocent, though thoughtless girl. Losing no time, he entered the apartment of Lord Ruthven, and abruptly asked him his intentions with respect to the lady, informing him at the same time that he was aware of his being about to meet her that very night. Lord Ruthven answered, that his intentions were such as he supposed all would have upon such an occasion; and upon being pressed whether he intended to marry her, merely laughed. Aubrey retired; and, immediately writing a note, to say, that from that moment he must decline accompanying his Lordship in the remainder of their proposed tour, he ordered his servant to seek other apartments, and calling upon the mother of the lady, informed her of all he knew, not only with regard to her daughter, but also concerning the character of his Lordship. The assignation was prevented. Lord Ruthven next day merely sent his servant to notify his complete assent to a separation; but did not hint any suspicion of his plans having been foiled by Aubrey's interposition.

Having left Rome, Aubrey directed his steps towards Greece, and crossing the Peninsula, soon found himself in Athens. He then fixed his residence in the house of a Greek; and soon occupied himself in tracing the faded records of ancient glory upon monuments that apparently, ashamed of chronicling the deeds of freemen only before slaves, had hidden themselves beneath the sheltering soil or many coloured lichen. Under the same roof as himself, existed a being, so beautiful and delicate, that she might have formed the model for a painter, wishing to portray on canvass the promised hope of the faithful in Mahomet's paradise, save that her eyes spoke too much mind for any one to think she could belong to those who had no souls. As she danced upon the plain, or tripped along the mountain's side, one would have thought the gazelle a poor type of her beauties; for who would have exchanged her eye, apparently the eye of animated nature, for that sleepy luxurious look of the animal suited but to the taste of an epicure. The light step of Ianthe often accompanied Aubrey in his search after antiquities, and often would the unconscious girl, engaged in the pursuit of a Kashmere butterfly, show the whole beauty of her form, floating as it were upon the wind, to the eager gaze of him, who forgot the letters he had just deciphered upon an almost effaced tablet, in the contemplation of her sylph-like figure. Often would her tresses falling, as she flitted around, exhibit in the sun's ray such delicately brilliant and swiftly fading hues, as might well excuse the forgetfulness of the antiquary, who let escape from his mind the very object he had before thought of vital importance to the proper interpretation of a passage in Pausanias. But why attempt to describe charms which all feel, but none can appreciate? It was innocence, youth, and beauty, unaffected by crowded drawing-rooms and stifling balls. Whilst he drew those remains of which he wished to preserve a memorial for his future hours, she would stand by, and watch the magic effects of his pencil, in tracing the scenes of her native place; she would then describe to him the circling dance upon the open plain, would paint to him in all the glowing colours of youthful memory, the marriage pomp she remembered viewing in her infancy; and then, turning to subjects that had evidently made a greater impression upon her mind, would tell him all the supernatural tales of her nurse. Her earnestness and apparent belief of what she narrated, excited the interest even of Aubrey; and often as she told him the tale of the living

Vampyre, who had passed years amidst his friends, and dearest ties, forced every year, by feeding upon the life of a lovely female to prolong his existence for the ensuing months, his blood would run cold, whilst he attempted to laugh her out of such idle and horrible fantasies; but Ianthe cited to him the names of old men, who had at last detected one living among themselves, after several of their near relatives and children had been found marked with the stamp of the fiend's appetite; and when she found him so incredulous, she begged of him to believe her, for it had been remarked, that those who had dared to question their existence, always had some proof given, which obliged them, with grief and heartbreaking, to confess it was true. She detailed to him the traditional appearance of these monsters, and his horror was increased, by hearing a pretty accurate description of Lord Ruthven; he, however, still persisted in persuading her, that there could be no truth in her fears, though at the same time he wondered at the many coincidences which had all tended to excite a belief in the supernatural power of Lord Ruthven.

Aubrey began to attach himself more and more to Ianthe; her innocence, so contrasted with all the affected virtues of the women among whom he had sought for his vision of romance, won his heart; and while he ridiculed the idea of a young man of English habits, marrying an uneducated Greek girl, still he found himself more and more attached to the almost fairy form before him. He would tear himself at times from her, and, forming a plan for some antiquarian research, he would depart, determined not to return until his object was attained; but he always found it impossible to fix his attention upon the ruins around him, whilst in his mind he retained an image that seemed alone the rightful possessor of his thoughts. Ianthe was unconscious of his love, and was ever the same frank infantile being he had first known. She always seemed to part from him with reluctance; but it was because she had no longer anyone with whom she could visit her favourite haunts, whilst her guardian was occupied in sketching or uncovering some fragment which had yet escaped the destructive hand of time. She had appealed to her parents on the subject of Vampyres, and they both, with several present, affirmed their existence, pale with horror at the very name. Soon after, Aubrey determined to proceed upon one of his excursions, which was to detain him for a few hours; when they heard the name of the place, they all at once begged of him not to return at night, as he must necessarily pass through a wood, where no Greek would ever remain, after the day had closed, upon any consideration. They described it as the resort of the vampyres in their nocturnal orgies, and denounced the most heavy evils as impending upon him who dared to cross their path. Aubrey made light of their representations, and tried to laugh them out of the idea; but when he saw them shudder at his daring thus to mock a superior, infernal power, the very name of which apparently made their blood freeze, he was silent.

Next morning Aubrey set off upon his excursion unattended; he was surprised to observe the melancholy face of his host, and was concerned to find that his words, mocking the belief of those horrible fiends, had inspired them with such terror. When he was about to depart, Ianthe came to the side of his horse, and earnestly begged of him to return, ere night allowed the power of these beings to be put in action – he promised. He was, however, so occupied in his research that he did not perceive that daylight would soon end, and that in the horizon there was one of those specks which, in the warmer climates, so rapidly gather into a tremendous mass, and pour all their rage upon the devoted country. He at last, however, mounted his horse, determined to make up by speed for his delay: but it was too late. Twilight, in these southern climates, is almost unknown; immediately the sun sets, night begins: and ere he had advanced far, the power of the storm was above – its echoing thunders

35

had scarcely an interval of rest – its thick heavy rain forced its way through the canopying foliage, whilst the blue forked lightning seemed to fall and radiate at his very feet. Suddenly his horse took fright, and he was carried with dreadful rapidity through the entangled forest. The animal at last, through fatigue, stopped, and he found, by the glare of lightning, that he was in the neighbourhood of a hovel that hardly lifted itself up from the masses of dead leaves and brushwood which surrounded it. Dismounting, he approached, hoping to find someone to guide him to the town, or at least trusting to obtain shelter from the pelting storm. As he approached, the thunders, for a moment silent, allowed him to hear the dreadful shrieks of a woman mingling with the stifled, exultant mockery of a laugh, continued in one almost unbroken sound – he was startled: but, roused by the thunder which again rolled over his head, he, with a sudden effort, forced open the door of the hut. He found himself in utter darkness: the sound, however, guided him. He was apparently unperceived; for, though he called, still the sounds continued, and no notice was taken of him. He found himself in contact with someone, whom he immediately seized; when a voice cried, 'Again baffled!' to which a loud laugh succeeded; and he felt himself grappled by one whose strength seemed superhuman: determined to sell his life as dearly as he could, he struggled; but it was in vain: he was lifted from his feet and hurled with enormous force against the ground – his enemy threw himself upon him, and kneeling upon his breast, had placed his hands upon his throat – when the glare of many torches penetrating through the hole that gave light in the day, disturbed him – he instantly rose, and, leaving his prey, rushed through the door, and in a moment the crashing of the branches, as he broke through the wood, was no longer heard. The storm was now still; and Aubrey, incapable of moving, was soon heard by those without. They entered; the light of their torches fell upon the mud walls, and the thatch loaded on every individual straw with heavy flakes of soot. At the desire of Aubrey they searched for her who had attracted him by her cries; he was again left in darkness; but what was his horror, when the light of the torches once more burst upon him, to perceive the airy form of his fair conductress brought in a lifeless corpse. He shut his eyes, hoping that it was but a vision arising from his disturbed imagination; but he again saw the same form, when he unclosed them, stretched by his side. There was no colour upon her cheek, not even upon her lip; yet there was a stillness about her face that seemed almost as attaching as the life that once dwelt there – upon her neck and breast was blood, and upon her throat were the marks of teeth having opened the vein – to this the men pointed, crying simultaneously struck with horror, 'A Vampyre! a Vampyre!' A litter was quickly formed, and Aubrey was laid by the side of her who had lately been to him the object of so many bright and fairy visions, now fallen with the flower of life that had died within her. He knew not what his thoughts were – his mind was benumbed and seemed to shun reflection, and take refuge in vacancy – he held almost unconsciously in his hand a naked dagger of a particular construction, which had been found in the hut. They were soon met by different parties who had been engaged in the search of her whom a mother had missed. Their lamentable cries, as they approached the city, forewarned the parents of some dreadful catastrophe. To describe their grief would be impossible; but when they ascertained the cause of their child's death, they looked at Aubrey, and pointed to the corpse. They were inconsolable; both died broken-hearted.

Aubrey being put to bed was seized with a most violent fever, and was often delirious; in these intervals he would call upon Lord Ruthven and upon Ianthe – by some unaccountable combination he seemed to beg of his former companion to spare the being he loved. At other times he would imprecate maledictions upon his head, and curse him as her destroyer. Lord Ruthven chanced at this time to arrive at Athens, and, from whatever motive, upon hearing of the state of Aubrey, immediately placed himself in the same house, and became his constant attendant. When the latter recovered from his delirium, he was horrified and startled at the sight of him whose image he had now combined with that of a Vampyre; but Lord Ruthven, by his kind words, implying almost repentance for the fault that had caused their separation, and still more by the attention, anxiety, and care which he showed, soon reconciled him to his presence. His lordship seemed quite changed; he no longer appeared that apathetic being who had so astonished Aubrey; but as his convalescence began to be rapid, he again gradually retired into the same state of mind, and Aubrey perceived no difference from the former man, except that at times he was surprised to meet his gaze fixed intently upon him, with a smile of malicious exultation playing upon his lips: he knew not why, but this smile haunted him. During the last stage of the invalid's recovery, Lord Ruthven was apparently engaged in watching the tideless waves raised by the cooling breeze, or in marking the progress of those orbs, circling, like our world, the moveless sun – indeed, he appeared to wish to avoid the eyes of all.

Aubrey's mind, by this shock, was much weakened, and that elasticity of spirit which had once so distinguished him now seemed to have fled forever. He was now as much a lover of solitude and silence as Lord Ruthven; but much as he wished for solitude, his mind could not find it in the neighbourhood of Athens; if he sought it amidst the ruins he had formerly frequented, Ianthe's form stood by his side – if he sought it in the woods, her light step would appear wandering amidst the underwood, in quest of the modest violet; then suddenly turning round, would show, to his wild imagination, her pale face and wounded throat, with a meek smile upon her lips. He determined to fly scenes, every feature of which created such bitter associations in his mind. He proposed to Lord Ruthven, to whom he held himself bound by the tender care he had taken of him during his illness, that they should visit those parts of Greece neither had yet seen. They travelled in every direction, and sought every spot to which a recollection could be attached: but though they thus hastened from place to place, yet they seemed not to heed what they gazed upon. They heard much of robbers, but they gradually began to slight these reports, which they imagined were only the invention of individuals, whose interest it was to excite the generosity of those whom they defended from pretended dangers. In consequence of thus neglecting the advice of the inhabitants, on one occasion they travelled with only a few guards, more to serve as guides than as a defence. Upon entering, however, a narrow defile, at the bottom of which was the bed of a torrent, with large masses of rock brought down from the neighbouring precipices, they had reason to repent their negligence; for scarcely were the whole of the party engaged in the narrow pass, when they were startled by the whistling of bullets close to their heads, and by the echoed report of several guns. In an instant their guards had left them, and, placing themselves behind rocks, had begun to fire in the direction whence the report came. Lord Ruthven and Aubrey, imitating their example, retired for a moment behind the sheltering turn of the defile: but ashamed of being thus detained by a foe, who with insulting shouts bade them advance, and being exposed to unresisting slaughter, if any of the robbers should climb above and take them in the rear, they determined at once to rush forward in search of the enemy. Hardly had they lost the shelter of the rock, when Lord Ruthven received a shot in the shoulder, which brought him to the ground. Aubrey hastened to his assistance; and, no longer heeding the contest of his own peril, was soon surprised by seeing the robbers' faces around him – his guards having, upon Lord

Ruthven's being wounded, immediately thrown up their arms and surrendered.

By promises of great reward, Aubrey soon induced them to convey his wounded friend to a neighbouring cabin; and having agreed upon a ransom, he was no more disturbed by their presence – they being content merely to guard the entrance till their comrade should return with the promised sum, for which he had an order. Lord Ruthven's strength rapidly decreased; in two days mortification ensued, and death seemed advancing with hasty steps. His conduct and appearance had not changed; he seemed as unconscious of pain as he had been of the objects about him: but towards the close of the last evening, his mind became apparently uneasy, and his eye often fixed upon Aubrey, who was induced to offer his assistance with more than usual earnestness – 'Assist me! you may save me – you may do more than that – I mean not my life, I heed the death of my existence as little as that of the passing day; but you may save my honour, your friend's honour.' 'How? tell me how? I would do anything,' replied Aubrey. 'I need but little – my life ebbs apace – I cannot explain the whole – but if you would conceal all you know of me, my honour were free from stain in the world's mouth – and if my death were unknown for some time in England – I – I – but life.' 'It shall not be known.' 'Swear!' cried the dying man, raising himself with exultant violence, 'Swear by all your soul reveres, by all your nature fears, swear that for a year and a day you will not impart your knowledge of my crimes or death to any living being in any way, whatever may happen, or whatever you may see.' His eyes seemed bursting from their sockets: 'I swear!' said Aubrey; he sunk laughing upon his pillow, and breathed no more.

Aubrey retired to rest, but did not sleep; the many circumstances attending his acquaintance with this man rose upon his mind, and he knew not why; when he remembered his oath a cold shivering came over him, as if from the presentiment of something horrible awaiting him. Rising early in the morning, he was about to enter the hovel in which he had left the corpse, when a robber met him, and informed him that it was no longer there, having been conveyed by himself and comrades, upon his retiring, to the pinnacle of a neighbouring mount, according to a promise they had given his lordship, that it should be exposed to the first cold ray of the moon that rose after his death. Aubrey was astonished, and taking several of the men, determined to go and bury it upon the spot where it lay. But, when he had mounted to the summit he found no trace of either the corpse or the clothes, though the robbers swore they pointed out the identical rock on which they had laid the body. For a time his mind was bewildered in conjectures, but he at last returned, convinced that they had buried the corpse for the sake of the clothes.

Weary of a country in which he had met with such terrible misfortunes, and in which all apparently conspired to heighten that superstitious melancholy that had seized upon his mind, he resolved to leave it, and soon arrived at Smyrna. While waiting for a vessel to convey him to Otranto, or to Naples, he occupied himself in arranging those effects he had with him belonging to Lord Ruthven. Amongst other things there was a case containing several weapons of offence, more or less adapted to ensure the death of the victim. There were several daggers and ataghans. Whilst turning them over, and examining their curious forms, what was his surprise at finding a sheath apparently ornamented in the same style as the dagger discovered in the fatal hut – he shuddered – hastening to gain further proof, he found the weapon, and his horror may be imagined when he discovered that it fitted, though peculiarly shaped, the sheath he held in his hand. His eyes seemed to need no further certainty – they seemed gazing to be bound to the dagger; yet still he wished to disbelieve; but the particular form, the same varying tints upon the haft and sheath were alike in splendour on both, and left no room for doubt; there were also drops of blood on each.

He left Smyrna, and on his way home, at Rome, his first inquiries were concerning the lady he had attempted to snatch from Lord Ruthven's seductive arts. Her parents were in distress, their fortune ruined, and she had not been heard of since the departure of his lordship. Aubrey's mind became almost broken under so many repeated horrors; he was afraid that this lady had fallen a victim to the destroyer of Ianthe. He became morose and silent; and his only occupation consisted in urging the speed of the postilions, as if he were going to save the life of someone he held dear. He arrived at Calais; a breeze, which seemed obedient to his will, soon wafted him to the English shores; and he hastened to the mansion of his fathers, and there, for a moment, appeared to lose, in the embraces and caresses of his sister, all memory of the past. If she before, by her infantine caresses, had gained his affection, now that the woman began to appear, she was still more attaching as a companion.

Miss Aubrey had not that winning grace which gains the gaze and applause of the drawing-room assemblies. There was none of that light brilliancy which only exists in the heated atmosphere of a crowded apartment. Her blue eye was never lit up by the levity of the mind beneath. There was a melancholy charm about it which did not seem to arise from misfortune, but from some feeling within, that appeared to indicate a soul conscious of a brighter realm. Her step was not that light footing, which strays where'er a butterfly or a colour may attract – it was sedate and pensive. When alone, her face was never brightened by the smile of joy; but when her brother breathed to her his affection, and would in her presence forget those griefs she knew destroyed his rest, who would have exchanged her smile for that of the voluptuary? It seemed as if those eyes, that face were then playing in the light of their own native sphere. She was yet only eighteen, and had not been presented to the world, it having been thought by her guardians more fit that her presentation should be delayed until her brother's return from the continent, when he might be her protector. It was now, therefore, resolved that the next drawing-room, which was fast approaching, should be the epoch of her entry into the 'busy scene'. Aubrey would rather have remained in the mansion of his fathers, and fed upon the melancholy which overpowered him. He could not feel interest about the frivolities of fashionable strangers, when his mind had been so torn by the events he had witnessed; but he determined to sacrifice his own comfort to the protection of his sister. They soon arrived in town, and prepared for the next day, which had been announced as a drawing-room.

The crowd was excessive – a drawing-room had not been held for a long time, and all who were anxious to bask in the smile of royalty, hastened thither. Aubrey was there with his sister. While he was standing in a corner by himself, heedless of all around him, engaged in the remembrance that the first time he had seen Lord Ruthven was in that very place – he felt himself suddenly seized by the arm, and a voice he recognised too well, sounded in his ear – 'Remember your oath.' He had hardly courage to turn, fearful of seeing a spectre that would blast him, when he perceived, at a little distance, the same figure which had attracted his notice on this spot upon his first entry into society. He gazed till his limbs almost refusing to bear their weight, he was obliged to take the arm of a friend, and forcing a passage through the crowd, he threw himself into his carriage, and was driven home. He paced the room with hurried steps, and fixed his hands upon his head, as if he were afraid his thoughts were bursting from his brain. Lord Ruthven again before him – circumstances started up in dreadful array – the dagger – his oath. He roused himself, he could not believe it possible – the dead rise again! He thought his imagination had conjured up the image his mind was resting upon. It was impossible that it could be real – he determined, therefore, to go again into society; for though he attempted to ask concerning Lord Ruthven, the name hung upon his lips, and he could not succeed in gaining information. He went a few nights after with his sister to the assembly of a near relation. Leaving her under the protection of a matron, he retired into a recess, and there gave himself up to his own devouring thoughts. Perceiving, at last, that many were leaving, he roused himself, and entering another room, found his sister surrounded by several apparently in earnest conversation; he attempted to pass and get near her, when one, whom he requested to move, turned round, and revealed to him those features he most abhorred. He sprang forward, seized his sister's arm, and, with hurried step, forced her towards the street: at the door he found himself impeded by the crowd of servants who were waiting for their lords; and while he was engaged in passing them, he again heard that voice whisper close to him – 'Remember your oath!' He did not dare to turn, but, hurrying his sister, soon reached home.

Aubrey became almost distracted. If before his mind had been absorbed by one subject, how much more completely was it engrossed, now that the certainty of the monster's living again pressed upon his thoughts. His sister's attentions were now unheeded, and it was in vain that she entreated him to explain to her what had caused his abrupt conduct. He only uttered a few words, and those terrified her. The more he thought, the more he was bewildered. His oath startled him – was he then to allow this monster to roam, bearing ruin upon his breath, amidst all he held dear, and not avert its progress? His very sister might have been touched by him. But even if he were to break his oath, and disclose his suspicions, who would believe him? He thought of employing his own hand to free the world from such a wretch; but death, he remembered, had been already mocked. For days he remained in this state; shut

44

up in his room, he saw no one, and ate only when his sister came, who, with eyes streaming with tears, besought him, for her sake, to support nature. At last, no longer capable of bearing stillness and solitude, he left his house, roamed from street to street, anxious to fly that image which haunted him. His dress became neglected, and he wandered, as often exposed to the noon-day sun as to the midnight damps. He was no longer to be recognised; at first he returned with the evening to the house; but at last he laid himself down to rest wherever fatigue overtook him. His sister, anxious for his safety, employed people to follow him; but they were soon distanced by him who fled from a pursuer swifter than any – from thought. His conduct, however, suddenly changed. Struck with the idea that he left by his absence the whole of his friends, with a fiend amongst them, of whose presence they were unconscious, he determined to enter again into society, and watch him closely, anxious to forewarn, in spite of his oath, all whom Lord Ruthven approached with intimacy. But when he entered into a room, his haggard and suspicious looks were so striking, his inward shudderings so visible, that his sister was at last obliged to beg of him to abstain from seeking, for her sake, a society which affected him so strongly. When, however, remonstrance proved unavailing, the guardians thought proper to interpose, and, fearing that his mind was becoming alienated, they thought it high time to resume again that trust which had been before imposed upon them by Aubrey's parents.

Desirous of saving him from the injuries and sufferings he had daily encountered in his wanderings, and of preventing him from exposing to the general eye those marks of what they considered folly, they engaged a physician to reside in the house, and take constant care of him. He hardly appeared to notice it, so completely was his mind absorbed by one terrible subject. His incoherence became at last so great, that he was confined to his chamber. There he would often lie for days, incapable of being roused. He had become emaciated, his eyes had attained a glassy lustre – the only sign of affection and recollection remaining displayed itself upon the entry of his sister; then he would sometimes start, and, seizing her hands, with looks that severely afflicted her, he would desire her not to touch him. 'Oh, do not touch him—if your love for me is aught, do not go near him!' When, however, she enquired to whom he referred, his only answer was, 'True! true!' and again he sank into a state, whence not even she could rouse him. This lasted many months: gradually, however, as the year was passing, his incoherences became less frequent, and his mind threw off a portion of its gloom, whilst his guardians observed, that several times in the day he would count upon his fingers a definite number, and then smile.

The time had nearly elapsed, when, upon the last day of the year, one of his guardians entering his room, began to converse with his physician upon the melancholy circumstance of Aubrey's being in so awful a situation, when his sister was going next day to be married. Instantly Aubrey's attention was at racted; he asked anxiously to whom. Glad of this mark of returning intellect, of which they feared he had been deprived, they mentioned the name of the Earl of Marsden. Thinking this was a young Earl whom he had met with in society, Aubrey seemed pleased, and astonished them still more by his expressing his intention to be present at the nuptials, and desiring to see his sister. They answered not, but in a few minutes his sister was with him. He was apparently again capable of being affected by the influence of her lovely smile; for he pressed her to his breast, and kissed her cheek, wet with tears, flowing at the thought of her brother's being once more alive to the feelings of affection. He began to speak with all his wonted warmth, and to congratulate her upon her marriage with a person so distinguished for rank and every accomplishment; when he suddenly perceived a locket upon her breast; opening it, what was his surprise at beholding the features of the monster who had so long influenced his life. He seized the portrait in a paroxysm of rage, and trampled it under foot. Upon her asking him why he thus destroyed the resemblance of her future husband, he looked as if he did not understand her – then seizing her hands, and gazing on her with a frantic expression of countenance, he bade her swear that she would never wed this monster, for he – But he could not advance – it seemed as if that voice again bade him remember his oath – he turned suddenly round, thinking Lord Ruthven was near him but saw no one. In the meantime the guardians and physician, who had heard the whole, and thought this was but a return of his disorder, entered, and forcing him from Miss Aubrey, desired her to leave him. He fell upon his knees to them, he implored, he begged of them to delay but one day. They, attributing this to the insanity they imagined had taken possession of his mind, endeavoured to pacify him, and retired.

Lord Ruthven had called the morning after the drawing-room, and had been refused with everyone else. When he heard of Aubrey's ill health, he readily understood himself to be the cause of it; but when he learned that he was deemed insane, his exultation and pleasure could hardly be concealed from those among whom he had gained this information. He hastened to the house of his former companion, and, by constant attendance, and the pretence of great affection for the brother and interest in his fate, he gradually won the ear of Miss Aubrey. Who could resist his power? His tongue had dangers and toils to recount – could speak of himself as of an individual having no sympathy with any being on the crowded earth, save with her to whom he addressed himself – could tell how, since he knew her, his existence had begun to seem worthy of preservation, if it were merely that he might listen to her soothing accents – in fine, he knew so well how to use the serpent's art, or such was the will of fate, that he gained her affections. The title of the elder branch falling at length to him, he obtained an important embassy, which served as an excuse for hastening the marriage (in spite of her brother's deranged state), which was to take place the very day before his departure for the continent.

Aubrey, when he was left by the physician and his guardians, attempted to bribe the servants, but in vain. He asked for pen and paper; it was given him; he wrote a letter to his sister, conjuring her, as she valued her own happiness, her own honour, and the honour of those now in the grave, who once held her in their arms as their hope and the hope of their house, to delay but for a few hours that marriage, on which he denounced the most heavy curses. The servants promised they would deliver it; but giving it to the physician, he thought it better not to harass any more the mind of Miss Aubrey by, what he considered, the ravings of a maniac. Night passed on without rest to the busy inmates of the house; and Aubrey heard, with a horror that may more easily be conceived than described, the notes of busy preparation. Morning came, and the sound of carriages broke upon his ear. Aubrey grew almost frantic. The curiosity of the servants at last overcame their vigilance, they gradually stole away, leaving him in the custody of a helpless old woman. He seized the opportunity, with one bound was out of the room, and in a moment found himself in the apartment where all were nearly assembled. Lord Ruthven was the first to perceive him: he immediately approached, and, taking his arm by force, hurried him from the room, speechless with rage. When on the staircase, Lord Ruthven whispered in his ear – 'Remember your oath, and know, if not my bride today, your sister is dishonoured. Women are frail!' So saying, he pushed him towards his attendants, who, roused by the old woman, had come in search of him. Aubrey could no longer support himself; his rage not finding vent, had broken a blood-vessel, and he was conveyed to bed. This was not mentioned to his sister, who was not present when he entered, as the physician was afraid of agitating her. The marriage was solemnised, and the bride and bridegroom left London.

Aubrey's weakness increased; the effusion of blood produced symptoms of the near approach of death. He desired his sister's guardians might be called, and when the midnight hour had struck, he related composedly what the reader has perused – he died immediately after.

The guardians hastened to protect Miss Aubrey; but when they arrived, it was too late. Lord Ruthven had disappeared, and Aubrey's sister had glutted the thirst of a VAMPYRE!

The Storm Visitor

THOMAS PRESKETT PREST

Of all the flood of Vampire tales, stories and even stage plays, which inevitably followed the publication of The Vampyre, *none was to have a wider success than Thomas Preskett Prest's* Varney the Vampire: or The Feast of Blood. *Prest was an incredibly prolific writer of blood and thunder melodramas, and packed into all his tales every conceivable element of horror and bloodshed.* Varney *was undoubtedly one of the high points of his writing career and with its epic length (over 800 pages), the meticulously drawn and ghastly vampire and his gruesome adventures, achieved a classic stature which it has never lost despite being impossibly rare today. After its publication in 1847,* Varney *was widely plagiarised but still remained infinitely more popular because of its authenticity – Prest had undoubtedly done his research carefully and painstakingly. Of the many vivid incidents which crowd one upon another in the book, the section which I have reprinted here is probably particularly noteworthy for its atmosphere and description of a vampire. It can still raise a shudder well over a century after it was written.*

THE SOLEMN TONES of the old cathedral clock have announced midnight – the air is thick and heavy – a strange death-like stillness pervades all nature. All is as still as the very grave.

But in a while there is a change – hail begins to fall – yes, a hailstorm has burst over the city. Leaves are dashed from the trees, mingled with small boughs; windows that lie most opposed to the direct fury of the pelting particles of ice are broken, and the rapt repose that before was so remarkable in its intensity, is exchanged for a noise which, in its accumulation, drowns every cry of surprise or consternation which here and there arose from persons who found their houses invaded by the storm.

Oh, how the storm raged! Hail – rain – wind. It was, in very truth, an awful night.

There is an antique chamber in an ancient house. Curious and quaint carvings adorn the walls, and the large chimney-piece is a curiosity of itself. The ceiling is low, and a large bay window, from roof to floor, looks to the west. The window is latticed, and filled with curiously painted glass and rich stained pieces, which send in a strange, yet beautiful light, when sun or moon shines into the apartment.

There is a stately bed in the room, of carved walnut-wood is it made, rich in design and elaborate in execution; one of those works of art which owe their existence to the Elizabethan era. It is hung with heavy silken and damask furnishing; nodding feathers are at its corners – covered with dust are they, and they lend a funereal aspect to the room. The floor is of polished oak.

God! how the hail dashes on the old bay window! Like an occasional discharge of mimic musketry, it comes dashing, beating, and cracking upon the small panes; but they resist it – their small size saves them: the wind, the hail, the rain, expend their fury in vain.

The bed in that old chamber is occupied. A creature formed in all fashions of loveliness lies in a half sleep upon that ancient couch – a girl young and beautiful as a spring morning. Her long hair has escaped from its confinement and streams over the various coverings of the bedstead; she has been restless in her sleep, for the clothing of the bed is in much confusion. One arm is over her head, the other hangs nearly off the side of the bed near to which she lies. A neck and a bosom that would have formed a study for the rarest sculptor that ever Providence gave genius to, were half disclosed. She moaned slightly in her sleep, and once or twice the lips moved as if in prayer – at least one might judge so, for the name of Him who suffered for all came once faintly from them.

She has endured much fatigue, and the storm does not awaken her; but it can disturb the slumbers it does not possess the power to destroy entirely. The turmoil of the elements wakes the senses, although it cannot entirely break the repose they have lapsed into.

Oh, what a world of witchery was in that mouth, slightly parted, and exhibiting within the pearly teeth that glistened even in the faint light that came from that bay window. How sweetly the long silken eyelashes lay upon the cheek. Now she moves, and one shoulder is entirely visible – whiter, fairer than the spotless clothing of the bed on which she lies, is the smooth skin of that fair creature, just budding into womanhood, and in that transition state which presents to us all the charms of the girl – almost of the child, with the more matured beauty and gentleness of advancing years.

Was that lightning? Yes – an awful, vivid, terrifying flash – then a roaring peal of thunder, as if a thousand mountains were rolling one over the other in the blue vault of Heaven! Who sleeps now in that ancient city? Not one living soul. The dread trumpet of eternity could not more effectively have awakened anyone.

The hail continues. The wind continues. The uproar of the elements seems at its height. Now she awakens – that beautiful girl on the antique bed; she opens those eyes of celestial blue, and a faint cry of alarm bursts from her lips. At least it is a cry which, amid the noise and turmoil without, sounds but faint and weak. She sits upon the bed and presses her hands upon her eyes.

Another flash – a wild, blue, bewildering flash of lightning streams across that bay window, for an instant bringing out every colour in it with terrible distinctness. A shriek bursts from the lips of the young girl, and then, with eyes fixed upon that window, which, in another moment, is all darkness, and with such an expression of terror upon her face as it had never before known, she trembled, and the perspiration of intense fear stood upon her brow.

'What – what was it?' she gasped; 'real, or a delusion? Oh, God, what was it? A figure tall and gaunt, endeavouring from the outside to unclasp the window. I saw it. That flash of lightning revealed it to me. It stood the whole length of the window.'

There was a lull of the wind. The hail was not falling so thickly – moreover, it now fell, what there was of it, straight, and yet a strange clattering sound came upon the glass of that long window. It could not be a delusion – she is awake, and she hears it. What can produce it? Another flash of lightning – another shriek – there could be now no delusion.

A tall figure is standing on the ledge immediately outside the window. It is its finger-nails upon the glass that produce the sound so like the hail, now that the hail has ceased. Intense fear paralysed the limbs of that beautiful girl. That one shriek is all she can utter – with hands clasped, a face of marble, a heart beating so wildly in her bosom, that each moment it seems as if it would break its confines, eyes distended and fixed upon the window, she waits, frozen with horror.

The pattering and clattering of the nails continues. No word is spoken, and now she fancies she can trace the darker form of that figure against the window, and she can see the long arms moving to and from, feeling for some mode of entrance. What strange light is that which now gradually creeps up into the air? red and terrible – brighter and brighter it grows. The lightning has set fire to a mill, and the reflection of the rapidly consuming building falls upon that long window. There can be no mistake. The figure is there, still feeling for an entrance, and clattering against the glass with its long nails, that appear as if the growth of many years had been untouched.

She tries to scream again but a choking sensation comes over her, and she cannot. It is too dreadful – she tries to move – each limb seems wedged down by tons of lead – she can but in a hoarse faint whisper cry –

'Help – help – help – help!'

And that one word she repeats like a person in a dream. The red glare of the fire continues. It throws up the tall gaunt figure in hideous relief against the long window.

A small pane of glass is broken, and the form from without introduces a long gaunt hand, which seems utterly destitute of flesh. The fastening is removed, and one-half of the window, which opens like folding doors, is swung wide open upon its hinges.

And yet now she could not scream – she could not move. 'Help! – help! – help! –' was all she could say. But, oh, that look of terror that sat upon her face, it was dreadful – a look to haunt the memory for a life-time – a look to obtrude itself upon the happiest moments, and turn them to bitterness.

The figure turns half round, and the light falls upon the face. It is perfectly white – perfectly bloodless. The eyes look like polished tin; the lips are drawn back, and the principal feature next to those dreadful eyes is the teeth – the fearful looking teeth – projecting like those of some wild animal, hideously, glaringly white, and fang-like.

It approaches the bed with a strange, gliding movement. It clashes together the long nails that literally appear to hang from the finger ends. No sound comes from its lips. Is she going mad? that young, beautiful girl exposed to so much terror; she has drawn up all her limbs; she cannot even now say help. The power of articulation is gone, but the power of movement has returned to her; she can draw herself slowly along to the other side of the bed from that towards which the hideous appearance is coming.

But her eyes are fascinated. The glance of a serpent could not have produced a greater effect upon her than did the fixed gaze of those awful, metallic-looking eyes that were bent on her face. Crouching down so that the gigantic height was lost, and the horrible, protruding, white face was the most prominent object, came on the figure. What was it? – what did it want there? – what made it look so hideous – so unlike an inhabitant of the earth, and yet to be on it?

Now she has got to the verge of the bed, and the figure pauses. It seemed as if when it paused she lost the power to proceed. The clothing of the bed was now clutched in her hands with unconscious power. She drew her breath short and thick. Her bosom heaves, and her limbs tremble, yet she cannot withdraw her eyes from that marble-looking face. He holds her with his glittering eye.

The storm has ceased – all is still. The winds are hushed; the church clock proclaims the hour of one: a hissing sound comes from the throat of the hideous being, and he raises his long, gaunt arms – the lips move. He advances. The girl places one small foot from the bed on to the floor. She is unconsciously dragging the clothing with her. The door of the room is in that direction – can she reach it? Has she power to walk? – can she withdraw her eyes from the face of the intruder, and so break the hideous charm? God of Heaven! is it real, or some dream so like reality as to nearly overturn the judgment for ever?

The figure has paused again, and half on the bed and half out of it that young girl lies trembling. Her long hair streams across the entire width of the bed. As she has slowly moved along she has left it streaming across the pillows. The pause lasted about a minute – oh, what an age of agony. The minute was, indeed, enough for madness to do its full work in.

With a sudden rush that could not be foreseen – with a

strange howling cry that was enough to awaken terror in every breast, the figure seized the long tresses of her hair, and twining them round his bony hands he held her to the bed.

Then she screamed – Heaven granted her that power to scream. Shriek followed shriek in rapid succession. The bed-clothes fell in a heap by the side of the bed – she was dragged by her long silken hair completely on to it again. Her beautiful rounded limbs quivered with the agony of her soul. The glassy, horrible eyes of the figure ran over that angelic form with a hideous satisfaction – horrible profanation. He drags her head to the bed's edge. He forces it back by the long hair still entwined in his grasp.

With a plunge he seizes her neck in his fang-like teeth – a gush of blood, and a hideous sucking noise follows. *The girl has swooned, and the vampire is at his hideous repast!*

Three Young Ladies

BRAM STOKER

Only one story has ever really surpassed Varney the Vampire
in immediate popularity – Bram Stoker's Dracula *which was
first published in 1897. There is no doubt that Stoker had read
and been delighted by the work of Prest, but in his venture into
the realms of the vampire he brought to bear a far more literary
style and this has no doubt been the reason why* Dracula *has
never been long out of print ever since. The story of the vampire
Count and his evil castle, told through the diaries of one
Jonathan Harker, is probably familiar to a great many
readers of this book, but because of its place of eminence in the
development of the vampire story, I feel a short extract is called
for. In the episode I have selected, Harker is already a prisoner
in the castle and has been warned by the Count of the terrible
dangers he faces if he tries to escape. To soothe himself to sleep
he begins to write in his diary – and in a while encounters
three young ladies with the most unpredictable tastes. . . .*

GOD PRESERVE MY sanity, for I am reduced to near insanity.
Safety and the assurance of safety are things of the past. Whilst
I live on here there is but one thing to hope for, that I may not
go mad, if, indeed, I be not mad already.

If I be sane, then surely it is maddening to think that of all
the foul things that lurk in this hateful place the Count is the
least dreadful to me; that to him alone I can look for safety,
even though this be only whilst I can serve his purpose. Great
God! merciful God! Let me be calm, for out of that way lies
madness indeed.

I begin to get new lights on certain things which have
puzzled me. Up to now I never quite knew what Shakespeare
meant when he made Hamlet say:

> 'My tablets, quick, my tablets!
> 'Tis meet that I put it down,' etc.,

for now, feeling as though my own brain were unhinged or as if the shock had come which must end in its undoing, I turn to my diary for repose. The habit of entering accurately must help to soothe me.

When I had written in my diary and had fortunately replaced the book and pen in my pocket I felt sleepy. The Count's warning came into my mind, but I was now too tired to think any more about it. The sense of sleep was upon me, and with it the obstinacy which sleep brings as outrider.

The soft moonlight soothed, and the wide expanse without gave a sense of freedom which refreshed me. I determined not to return tonight to the gloom-haunted rooms, but to sleep here, where, of old, ladies had sat and sung and lived sweet lives whilst their gentle breasts were sad for their menfolk away in the midst of remorseless wars. I drew a great couch out of its place near the corner, so that as I lay, I could look at the lovely view to east and south, and unthinking of and uncaring for the dust, composed myself for sleep. I suppose I must have fallen asleep; I hope so, but I fear, for all that followed was startlingly real – so real that now sitting here in the broad, full sunlight of the morning, I cannot in the least believe that it was all sleep.

I was not alone. The room was the same, unchanged in any way since I came into it; I could see along the floor, in the brilliant moonlight, my own footsteps marked where I had disturbed the long accumulation of dust. In the moonlight opposite me were three young women, ladies by their dress and manner. I thought at the time that I must be dreaming when I saw them, for though the moonlight was behind them, they threw no shadow on the floor. They came close to me, and looked at me for some time, and then whispered together.

Two were dark, and had high aquiline noses, like the Count, and great dark, piercing eyes, that seemed to be almost red when contrasted with the pale yellow moon. The other was fair, as fair as can be, with great wavy masses of golden hair and eyes like pale sapphires. I seemed somehow to know her face, and to know it in connection with some dreamy fear, but I could not recollect at the moment how or where. All three had brilliant white teeth that shone like pearls against the ruby of their voluptuous lips.

There was something about them that made me uneasy, some longing and at the same time some deadly fear. I felt in my heart a wicked burning desire that they would kiss me with those red lips. It is not good to note this down; lest some day it should meet my wife's eyes and cause her pain; but it is the truth. They whispered together, and then they all three laughed – such a silvery, musical laugh, but as hard as though the sound never could have come through the softness of human lips. It was like the intolerable, tingling sweetness of water-glasses when played on by a cunning hand. The fair girl shook her head coquettishly, and the other two urged her on. One said:

'Go on! You are first, and we shall follow; yours is the right to begin.' The other added:

'He is young and strong; there are kisses for us all.' I lay quiet, looking out under my eyelashes in an agony of delightful anticipation. The fair girl advanced and bent over me till I could feel the movement of her breath upon me. Sweet it was in one sense, honey-sweet, and sent the same tingling through the nerves as her voice, but with a bitter underlying the sweet, a bitter offensiveness, as one smells in blood.

I was afraid to raise my eyelids, but looked out and saw perfectly under the lashes. The girl went on her knees, and bent over me, simply gloating. There was a deliberate voluptuousness which was both thrilling and repulsive, and as she arched her neck she actually licked her lips like an animal, till I could see in the moonlight the moisture shining on the scarlet lips and on the red tongue as it lapped the white sharp teeth.

Lower and lower went her head as the lips went below the range of my mouth and chin and seemed about to fasten on my throat. Then she paused, and I could hear the churning sound of her tongue as it licked her teeth and lips, and could feel the hot breath on my neck. Then the skin of my throat began to tingle as one's flesh does when the hand that is to tickle it approaches nearer – nearer. I could feel the soft, shivering touch of the lips on the super-sensitive skin of my throat, and the hard dents of two sharp teeth, just touching and pausing there. I closed my eyes in a languorous ecstasy and waited – waited with beating heart.

But at that instant, another sensation swept through me as quick as lightning. I was conscious of the presence of the Count, and of his being as if lapped in a storm of fury. As my eyes opened involuntarily I saw his strong hand grasp the slender neck of the fair woman and with giant's power draw it back, the blue eyes transformed with fury, the white teeth champing with rage, and the fair cheeks blazing with passion. But the Count! Never did I imagine such wrath and fury, even from the demons of the pit.

His eyes were positively blazing. The red light in them was lurid, as if the flames of hell-fire blazed behind them. His face was deathly pale, and the lines of it were hard like drawn wires; the thick eyebrows that met over the nose now seemed like a heaving bar of white-hot metal. With a fierce sweep of his arm, he hurled the woman from him, and then motioned to the others, as though he were beating them back; it was the same imperious gesture that I had seen used to the wolves. In a voice which, though low and almost in a whisper, seemed to cut through the air and then ring round the room he said:

'How dare you touch him, any of you? How dare you cast

eyes on him when I had forbidden it? Back, I tell you all! This man belongs to me! Beware how you meddle with him, or you'll have to deal with me.' The fair girl, with a laugh of ribald coquetry, turned to answer him:

'You yourself never loved; you never love!' On this the other women joined, and such mirthless, hard, soulless laughter rang through the room that it almost made me faint to hear; it seemed like the pleasure of fiends. Then the Count turned, after looking at my face attentively, and said in a soft whisper:

'Yes, I too can love; you yourselves can tell it from the past. Is it not so? Well, now I promise you that when I am done with him you shall kiss him at your will. Now go! go! I must awaken him, for there is work to be done.'

'Are we to have nothing tonight?' said one of them, with a low laugh, as she pointed to the bag which he had thrown upon the floor, and which moved as though there were some living thing within it. For answer he nodded his head. One of the women jumped forward and opened it. If my ears did not deceive me there was a gasp and a low wail, as of a half smothered child. The women closed round, whilst I was aghast with horror; but as I looked they disappeared, and with them the dreadful bag. There was no door near them, and they could not have passed me without my noticing. They simply seemed to fade into the rays of the moonlight and pass out through the window, for I could see outside the dim, shadowy forms for a moment before they entirely faded away.

Then the horror overcame me, and I sank down unconscious.

An Episode of Cathedral History

M. R. JAMES

M. R. James has an assured position in the front rank of English ghost story writers. His collection Ghost Stories of an Antiquary *is one of the most distinguished in the language and is always rewardingly discovered by each new generation of readers. A man of tremendous scholarship, he had a life-long interest in the macabre and wrote widely on the subject. This particular story – for years hard to obtain – introduces a somewhat different kind of vampire – not one of flesh and blood, but an ephemeral being nonetheless capable of creating fear and terror. Even the strongest-nerved reader may well find himself feeling a little uneasy about ever visiting a Cathedral again!*

THERE was once a learned gentleman who was deputed to examine and report upon the archives of the Cathedral of Southminster. The examination of these records demanded a very considerable expenditure of time: hence it became advisable for him to engage lodgings in the city: for though the Cathedral body were profuse in their offers of hospitality, Mr Lake felt that he would prefer to be master of his day. This was recognised as reasonable. The Dean eventually wrote advising Mr Lake, if he were not already suited, to communicate with Mr Worby, the principal Verger, who occupied a house convenient to the church and was prepared to take in a quiet lodger for three or four weeks. Such an arrangement was precisely what Mr Lake desired. Terms were easily agreed upon, and early in December, like another Mr Datchery (as he remarked to himself), the investigator found himself in the occupation of a very comfortable room in an ancient and 'cathedraly' house.

One so familiar with the customs of Cathedral Churches, and trusted with such obvious consideration by the Dean and Chapter of this Cathedral in particular, could not fail to command the respect of the Head Verger. Mr Worby even acquiesced in certain modifications of statements he had been accustomed to offer for years to parties of visitors. Mr Lake, on his part, found the Verger a very cheery companion, and took advantage of any occasion that presented itself for enjoying his conversation when the day's work was over.

One evening, about nine o'clock, Mr Worby knocked at his lodger's door. 'I've occasion,' he said, 'to go across to the Cathedral, Mr Lake, and I think I made you a promise when I did so next I would give you the opportunity to see what it looked like at night time. It's quite fine and dry outside, if you care to come.'

'To be sure I will; very much obliged to you, Mr Worby, for thinking of it, but let me get my coat.'

'Here it is, sir, and I've another lantern here that you'll find advisable for the steps, as there's no moon.'

'Anyone might think we were Jasper and Durdles, over again, mightn't they?' said Lake, as they crossed the close, for he had ascertained that the Verger had read *Edwin Drood*.

'Well, so they might,' said Mr Worby, with a short laugh, 'though I don't know whether we ought to take it as a compliment. Odd ways, I often think, they had at that Cathedral, don't it seem so to you, sir? Full choral matins at seven o'clock in the morning all the year round. Wouldn't suit our boys' voices nowadays, and I think there's one or two of the men would be applying for a rise if the Chapter was to bring it in – particular the alltoes.'

They were now at the south-west door. As Mr Worby was unlocking it, Lake said, 'Did you ever find anybody locked in here by accident?'

'Twice I did. One was a drunk sailor; however he got in I

don't know. I s'pose he went to sleep in the service, but by the time I got to him he was praying fit to bring the roof in. Lor'! what a noise that man did make! said it was the first time he'd been inside a church for ten years, and blest if ever he'd try it again. The other was an old sheep: them boys it was, up to their games. That was the last time they tried it on, though. There, sir, now you see what we look like; our late Dean used now and again to bring parties in, but he preferred a moonlight night, and there was a piece of verse he'd say to 'em, relating to a Scotch cathedral, I understand; but I don't know; I almost think the effect's better when it's all dark-like. Seems to add to the size and height. Now if you won't mind stopping somewhere in the nave while I go up into the choir where my business lays, you'll see what I mean.'

Accordingly Lake waited, leaning against a pillar, and watched the light wavering along the length of the church, and up the steps into the choir, until it was intercepted by some screen or other furniture, which only allowed the reflection to be seen on the piers and roof. Not many minutes had passed before Worby reappeared at the door of the choir and by waving his lantern signalled to Lake to rejoin him.

'I suppose it *is* Worby, and not a substitute,' thought Lake to himself, as he walked up the nave. There was, in fact, nothing untoward. Worby showed him the papers which he had come to fetch out of the Dean's stall, and asked him what he thought of the spectacle: Lake agreed that it was well worth seeing. 'I suppose,' he said, as they walked towards the altar-steps together, 'that you're too much used to going about here at night to feel nervous – but you must get a start every now and then, don't you, when a book falls down or a door swings to?'

'No, Mr Lake, I can't say I think much about noises, not nowadays: I'm much more afraid of finding an escape of gas or a burst in the stove pipes than anything else. Still there have been times, years ago. Did you notice that plain altar-tomb there – fifteenth century we say it is, I don't know if you agree to that? Well, if you didn't look at it, just come back and give it a glance, if you'd be so good.' It was on the north side of the choir, and rather awkwardly placed: only about three feet from the enclosing stone screen. Quite plain, as the Verger had said, but for some ordinary stone panelling. A metal cross of some size on the northern side (that next to the screen) was the solitary feature of any interest.

Lake agreed that it was not earlier than the Perpendicular period: 'But,' he said, 'unless it's the tomb of some remarkable person, you'll forgive me for saying that I don't think it's particularly noteworthy.'

'Well, I can't say as it is the tomb of anybody noted in 'istory,' said Worby, who had a dry smile on his face, 'for we don't own any record whatsoever of who it was put up to. For all that, if you've half an hour to spare, sir, when we get back to the house, Mr Lake, I could tell you a tale about that tomb. I won't begin on it now; it strikes cold here, and we don't want to be dawdling about all night.'

'Of course I should like to hear it immensely.'

'Very well, sir, you shall. Now if I might put a question to you,' he went on, as they passed down the choir aisle, 'in our little local guide – and not only there, but in the little book on our Cathedral in the series – you'll find it stated that this portion of the building was erected previous to the twelfth century. Now of course I should be glad enough to take that view, but – mind the step, sir – but, I put it to you – does the lay of the stone 'ere in this portion of the wall' (which he tapped with his key), 'does it to your eye carry the flavour of what you might call Saxon masonry? No, I thought not; no more it does to me: now, if you'll believe me, I've said as much to those men – one's the librarian of our Free Library here, and the other came down from London on purpose – fifty times, if I have once, but I might just as well have talked to that bit of stonework. But there it is, I suppose everyone's got their opinions.'

The discussion of this peculiar trait of human nature occupied Mr Worby almost up to the moment when he and Lake re-entered the former's house. The condition of the fire in Lake's sitting-room led to a suggestion from Mr Worby that they should finish the evening in his own parlour. We find them accordingly settled there some short time afterwards.

Mr Worby made his story a long one, and I will not undertake to tell it wholly in his own words, or in his own order. Lake committed the substance of it to paper immediately after hearing it, together with some few passages of the narrative which had fixed themselves *verbatim* in his mind; I shall probably find it expedient to condense Lake's record to some extent.

Mr Worby was born, it appeared, about the year 1828. His father before him had been connected with the Cathedral, and likewise his grandfather. One or both had been choristers, and in later life both had done work as mason and carpenter respectively about the fabric. Worby himself, though possessed, as he frankly acknowledged, of an indifferent voice, had been drafted into the choir at about ten years of age.

It was in 1840 that the wave of the Gothic revival smote the Cathedral of Southminster. 'There was a lot of lovely stuff went then, sir,' said Worby, with a sigh. 'My father couldn't hardly believe it when he got his orders to clear out the choir. There was a new dean just come in – Dean Burscough it was – and my father had been 'prenticed to a good firm of joiners in the city, and knew what good work was when he saw it. Crool it was, he used to say: all that beautiful wainscot oak, as good as the day it was put up, and garlands-like of foliage and fruit, and lovely old gilding work on the coats of arms and the organ pipes. All went to the timber yard – every bit except some little pieces worked up in the Lady Chapel, and 'ere in this overmantel. Well – I may be mistook, but I say our choir never looked as well since. Still there was a lot found out about the history of the church, and no doubt but what it did stand in need of repair. There was very few winters passed but what we'd lose a pinnacle.' Mr Lake expressed his concurrence with Worby's views of restoration, but owns to a fear about this point lest the story proper should never be reached. Possibly this was perceptible in his manner.

Worby hastened to reassure him, 'Not but what I could carry on about that topic for hours at a time, and do so when I see my opportunity. But Dean Burscough he was very set on the Gothic period, and nothing would serve him but everything must be made agreeable to that. And one morning after service he appointed for my father to meet him in the choir, and he came back after he'd taken off his robes in the vestry, and he'd got a roll of paper with him, and the verger that was then brought in a table, and they begun spreading it out on the table with prayer books to keep it down, and my father helped 'em, and he saw it was a picture of the inside of a choir in a Cathedral; and the Dean – he was a quick-spoken gentleman – he says, "Well, Worby, what do you think of that?" "Why," says my father, "I don't think I 'ave the pleasure of knowing that view. Would that be Hereford Cathedral, Mr Dean?" "No, Worby," says the Dean, "that's Southminster Cathedral as we hope to see it before many years." "Indeed, sir," says my father, and that was all he did say – leastways to the Dean – but he used to tell me he felt really faint in himself when he looked round our choir as I can remember it, all comfortable and furnished-like, and then see this nasty little dry picter, as he called it, drawn out by some London architect. Well, there I am again. But you'll see what I mean if you look at this old view.'

Worby reached down a framed print from the wall. 'Well, the long and the short of it was that the Dean he handed over to my father a copy of an order of the Chapter that he was to clear out every bit of the choir – make a clean sweep – ready for the new work that was being designed up in town, and he was to put it in hand as soon as ever he could get the breakers together. Now then, sir, if you look at that view, you'll see where the pulpit used to stand: that's what I want you to notice, if you please.' It was, indeed, easily seen; an unusually large structure of timber with a domed sounding-board, standing at the east end of the stalls on the north side of the choir, facing the bishop's throne. Worby proceeded to explain that during the alterations, services were held in the nave, the members of the choir being thereby disappointed of an anticipated holiday, and the organist in particular incurring the suspicion of having wilfully damaged the mechanism of the temporary organ that was hired at considerable expense from London.

The work of demolition began with the choir screens and organ loft, and proceeded gradually eastwards, disclosing, as Worby said, many interesting features of older work. While this was going on, the members of the Chapter were, naturally, in and about the choir a great deal, and it soon became apparent to the elder Worby – who could not help overhearing some of their talk – that, on the part of the senior Canons especially, there must have been a good deal of disagreement before the policy now being carried out had been adopted. Some were of opinion that they should catch their deaths of cold in the return-stalls, unprotected by a screen from the draughts in the nave: others objected to being exposed to the view of persons in the choir aisles, especially, they said, during the sermons, when they found it helpful to listen in a posture which was liable to misconstruction. The strongest opposition, however, came from the oldest of the body, who up to the last moment objected to the removal of the pulpit. 'You ought not to touch it, Mr Dean,' he said with great emphasis one morning, when the two were standing before it: 'you don't know what mischief you may do.' 'Mischief? it's not a work of any particular merit, Canon.' 'Don't call me Canon,' said the old man with great asperity, 'that is, for thirty years I've been known as Dr Ayloff, and I shall be obliged, Mr Dean, if you would kindly humour me in that matter. And as to the pulpit (which I've preached from for thirty years, though I don't insist on that), all I'll say is, I *know* you're doing wrong in moving it.' 'But what sense could there be, my dear Doctor, in leaving it where it is, when we're fitting up the rest of the choir in a totally different *style*? What reason could be given – apart from the look of the thing?' 'Reason! reason!' said old Dr Ayloff; 'if you young men – if I may say so without any disrespect, Mr Dean – if you'd only listen to reason a little, and not be always asking for it, we should get on better. But there, I've said my say.' The old gentleman hobbled off, and as it proved, never entered the Cathedral again. The season – it was a hot summer – turned sickly on a sudden. Dr Ayloff was one of the first to go, with some affection of the muscles of the thorax, which took him painfully at night. And at many services the number of choirmen and boys was very thin.

Meanwhile the pulpit had been done away with. In fact, the sounding-board (part of which still exists as a table in a summerhouse in the palace garden) was taken down within an hour or two of Dr Ayloff's protest. The removal of the base – not effected without considerable trouble – disclosed to view, greatly to the exultation of the restoring party, an altar-tomb – the tomb, of course, to which Worby had attracted Lake's attention that same evening. Much fruitless research was expended in attempts to identify the occupant; from that day to this he has never had a name put to him. The structure had been most carefully boxed in under the pulpit-base, so that such slight ornament as it possessed was not defaced; only on the north side of it there was what looked like an injury; a gap between two of the slabs composing the side. It might be two or three inches across. Palmer, the mason, was directed to fill it up in a week's time, when he came to do some other small jobs near that part of the choir.

The season was undoubtedly a very trying one. Whether the church was built on a site that had once been a marsh, as was suggested, or for whatever reason, the residents in its immediate neighbourhood had, many of them, but little enjoyment of the exquisite sunny days and the calm nights of August and September. To several of the older people – Dr Ayloff, among others, as we have seen – the summer proved downright fatal, but even among the younger, few escaped either a sojourn in bed for a matter of weeks, or at the least, a brooding sense of oppression, accompanied by hateful nightmares. Gradually there formulated itself a suspicion – which grew into a conviction – that the alterations in the Cathedral had something to say in the matter. The widow of a former old verger, a pensioner of the Chapter of Southminster, was visited by dreams, which she retailed to her friends, of a shape that slipped out of the little door of the south transept as the dark fell in, and flitted – taking a fresh direction every night – about the Close, disappearing for a while in house after house, and finally emerging again when the night sky was paling. She could see nothing of it, she said, but that it was a moving form: only she had an impression that when it returned to the church, as it seemed to do in the end of the dream, it turned its head: and then, she could not tell why, but she thought it had red eyes. Worby remembered hearing the old lady tell this dream at a tea-party in the house of the chapter clerk. Its recurrence might, perhaps, he said, be taken as a symptom of approaching illness; at any rate before the end of September the old lady was in her grave.

The interest excited by the restoration of this great church was not confined to its own county. One day that summer an F.S.A., of some celebrity, visited the place. His business was to write an account of the discoveries that had been made, for the Society of Antiquaries, and his wife, who accompanied him, was to make a series of illustrative drawings for his report. In the morning she employed herself in making a general sketch of the choir; in the afternoon she devoted herself to details. She first drew the newly-exposed altar-tomb, and when that was finished, she called her husband's attention to a beautiful piece of diaper-ornament on the screen just behind it, which had, like the tomb itself, been completely concealed by the pulpit. Of course, he said, an illustration of that must be made; so she seated herself on the tomb and began a careful drawing which occupied her till dusk.

Her husband had by this time finished his work of measuring and description, and they agreed that it was time to be getting back to their hotel. 'You may as well brush my skirt, Frank,' said the lady, 'it must have got covered with dust, I'm sure.' He obeyed dutifully; but, after a moment, he said, 'I don't know whether you value this dress particularly, my dear, but I'm inclined to think it's seen its best days. There's a great bit of it gone.' 'Gone? Where?' said she. 'I don't know where it's gone, but it's off at the bottom edge behind here.' She pulled it hastily into sight, and was horrified to find a jagged tear extending some way into the substance of the stuff; very much, she said, as if a dog had rent it away. The dress was, in any case, hopelessly spoilt, to her great vexation, and though they looked everywhere, the missing piece could not be found. There were many ways, they concluded, in which the injury might have come about, for the choir was full of old bits of woodwork with nails sticking out of them. Finally, they could only suppose that one of these had caused the mischief, and that the workmen, who had been about all day, had carried off that particular piece with the fragment of dress still attached to it.

It was about this time, Worby thought, that his little dog began to wear an anxious expression when the hour for it to be put into the shed in the back yard approached. (For his mother had ordained that it must not sleep in the house.) One evening, he said, when he was just going to pick it up and carry it out, it looked at him 'like a Christian, and waved its 'and, and, I was going to say – well, you know 'ow they do carry on sometimes, and the end of it was I put it under my coat, and 'uddled it upstairs – and I'm afraid I as good as deceived my poor mother on the subject. After that the dog acted very artful with 'iding itself under the bed for half an hour or more before bedtime came, and we worked it so as my mother never found out what we'd done.' Of course Worby was glad of its company anyhow, but more particularly when the nuisance that is still remembered in Southminster as 'the crying' set in.

'Night after night,' said Worby, 'that dog seemed to know it was coming; he'd creep out, he would, and snuggle into the bed and cuddle right up to me shivering, and when the crying come he'd be like a wild thing, shoving his head under my arm, and I was fully near as bad. Six or seven times we'd hear it, not more, and when he'd dror out his 'ed again I'd know it was over for that night. What was it like, sir? Well, I never heard but one thing that seemed to hit it off. I happened to be playing about in the Close, and there was two of the Canons met and said "Good morning" one to another. "Sleep well last night?" says one – it was Mr Henslow that one, and Mr Lyall was the other. "Can't say I did," says Mr Lyall, "rather too much of Isaiah xxxiv. 14 for me." "xxxiv. 14," says Mr Henslow, "what's that?" "You call yourself a Bible reader!" says Mr Lyall. (Mr Henslow, you must know, he was one of what used to be termed Simeon's lot – pretty much what we should call the Evangelical party.) "You go and look it up." I wanted to know what he was getting at myself, and so off I ran home and got out my own Bible, and there it was: "the satyr shall cry to his fellow." Well, I thought, is that what we've been listening to these past nights? and I tell you it made me look over my shoulder a time or two. Of course I'd asked my father and mother about what it could be before that, but they both said it was most likely cats: but they spoke very short, and I could see they was troubled. My word! that was a noise – 'ungry-like, as if it was calling after someone that wouldn't come. If ever you felt you wanted company, it would be when you was waiting for it to begin again. I believe two or three nights there was men put on to watch in different parts of the Close; but they all used to get together in one corner, the nearest they could to the High Street, and nothing came of it.

'Well, the next thing was this. Me and another of the boys – he's in business in the city now as a grocer, like his father before him – we'd gone up in the choir after morning service was over, and we heard old Palmer the mason bellowing to some of his men. So we went up nearer, because we knew he was a rusty old chap and there might be some fun going. It appears Palmer 'd told this man to stop up the chink in that old tomb. Well, there was this man keeping on saying he'd done it the best he could, and there was Palmer carrying on like all possessed about it. "Call that making a job of it?" he says. "If you had your rights you'd get the sack for this. What do you suppose I pay you your wages for? What do you suppose I'm going to say to the Dean and Chapter when they come round, as come they may do any time, and see where you've been bungling about covering the 'ole place with mess and plaster and Lord knows what?" "Well, master, I done the best I could," says the man; "I don't know no more than what you do 'ow it come to fall out this way. I tamped it right in the 'ole," he says, "and now it's fell out," he says, "I never see."

' "Fell out?" says old Palmer, "why it's nowhere near the place. Blowed out, you mean"; and he picked up a bit of plaster, and so did I, that was laying up against the screen, three or four feet off, and not dry yet; and old Palmer he looked at it curious-like, and then he turned round on me and he says, "Now then, you boys, have you been up to some of your games here?"

"No," I says, "I haven't, Mr Palmer; there's none of us been about here till just this minute"; and while I was talking the other boy, Evans, he got looking in through the chink, and I heard him draw in his breath, and he came away sharp and up to us, and says he, "I believe there's something in there. I saw something shiny." "What! I dare say!" says old Palmer; "well, I ain't got time to stop about there. You, William, you go off and get some more stuff and make a job of it this time; if not, there'll be trouble in my yard," he says.

'So the man he went off, and Palmer too, and us boys stopped behind, and I says to Evans, "Did you really see anything in there?" "Yes," he says, "I did indeed." So then I says, "Let's shove something in and stir it up." And we tried several of the bits of wood that was laying about, but they were all too big. Then Evans he had a sheet of music he'd brought with him, an anthem or a service, I forget which it is now, and he rolled it up small and shoved it in the chink; two or three times he did it, and nothing happened. "Give it me, boy," I said, and I had a try. No, nothing happened. Then, I don't know why I thought of it, I'm sure, but I stooped down just opposite the chink and put my two fingers in my mouth and whistled – you know the way – and at that I seemed to think I heard something stirring, and I says to Evans, "Come away," I says; "I don't like this," "Oh, rot," he says, "give me that roll," and he took it and shoved it in. And I don't think ever I see anyone go so pale as he did. "I say, Worby," he says, "it's caught, or else someone's got hold of it." "Pull it out or leave it," I says. "Come and let's get off." So he gave a good pull, and it came away. Leastways most of it did, but the end was gone. Torn off it was, and Evans looked at it for a second and then he gave a sort of a croak and let it drop, and we both made off out of there as quick as ever we could. When we got outside Evans says to me, "Did you see the end of that paper?" "No," I says, "only it was torn." "Yes, it was," he says, "but it was wet too, and black!" Well, partly because of the fright we had, and partly because that music was wanted in a day or two, and we knew there'd be a set-out about it with the organist, we didn't say nothing to anyone else, and I suppose the workmen they swept up the bit that was left along with the rest of the rubbish. But Evans, if you were to ask him this very day about it, he'd stick to it he saw that paper wet and black at the end where it was torn.'

After that the boys gave the choir a wide berth, so that Worby was not sure what was the result of the mason's renewed mending of the tomb. Only he made out from fragments of conversation dropped by the workmen passing through the choir that some difficulty had been met with, and that the governor – Mr Palmer to wit – had tried his own hand at the job. A little later, he happened to see Mr Palmer himself knocking at the door of the Deanery and being admitted by the butler. A day or so after that, he gathered from a remark his father let fall at breakfast, that something a little out of the common was to be done in the Cathedral after morning service on the morrow. 'And I'd just as soon it was today,' his father added; 'I don't see the use of running risks.' ' "Father," I says, "what are you going to do in the Cathedral tomorrow?" And he turned on me as savage as I ever see him – he was a wonderful good-tempered man as a general thing, my poor father was. "My lad," he says, "I'll trouble you not to go picking up your elders' and betters' talk: it's not manners and it's not straight. What I'm going to do or not going to do in the Cathedral tomorrow is none of your business: and if I catch sight of you hanging about the place tomorrow after your work's done, I'll send you home with a flea in your ear. Now you mind that." Of course I said I was very sorry and that, and equally of course I went off and laid my plans with Evans. We knew there was a stair up in the corner of the transept which you can get up to the triforium, and in them days the door to it was pretty well always open, and even if it wasn't we knew the key usually laid under a bit of matting hard by. So we made up our minds we'd be putting away music and that, next morning, while the rest of the boys was clearing off, and then slip up the stairs and watch from the triforium if there was any signs of work going on.

'Well, that same night I dropped off asleep as sound as a boy does, and all of a sudden the dog woke me up, coming into the bed, and thought I, now we're going to get it sharp, for he seemed more frightened than usual. After about five minutes sure enough came this cry. I can't give you no idea what it was like; and so near too – nearer than I'd heard it yet – and a funny thing, Mr Lake, you know what a place this Close is for an echo, and particular if you stand this side of it. Well, this crying never made no sign of an echo at all. But, as I said, it was dreadful near this night; and on the top of the start I got with hearing it, I got another fright; for I heard something rustling outside in the passage. Now to be sure I thought I was done; but I noticed the dog seemed to perk up a bit, and next there was someone whispered outside the door, and I very near laughed out loud, for I knew it was my father and mother that had got out of bed with the noise. "Whatever is it?" says my mother. "Hush! I don't know," says my father, excited-like, "don't disturb the boy. I hope he didn't hear nothing."

'So, me knowing they were just outside, it made me bolder, and I slipped out of bed across to my little window – giving on the Close – but the dog he bored right down to the bottom of the bed – and I looked out. First go off I couldn't see anything. Then right down in the shadow under a buttress I made out what I shall always say was two spots of red – a dull red it was – nothing like a lamp or a fire, but just so as you could pick 'em out of the black shadow. I hadn't but just sighted 'em when it seemed we wasn't the only people that had been disturbed, because I see a window in a house on the left-hand side become lighted up, and the light moving. I just turned my head to make sure of it, and then looked back into the shadow for those two red things, and they were gone, and for all I peered about and stared, there was not a sign more of them. Then come my last fright that night – something come against my bare leg – but that was all right: that was my little dog had come out of bed, and prancing about making a great to-do, only holding his tongue, and me seeing he was quite in spirits again, I took him back to bed and we slept the night out!

'Next morning I made out to tell my mother I'd had the dog in my room, and I was surprised, after all she'd said about it before, how quiet she took it. "Did you?" she says. "Well, by good rights you ought to go without your breakfast for doing such a thing behind my back: but I don't know as there's any great harm done, only another time you ask my permission, do you hear?" A bit after that I said something to my father about having heard cats again "*Cats*" he says; and he looked over at my poor mother, and she coughed and he says, "Oh! ah! yes, cats. I believe I heard 'em myself."

'That was a funny morning altogether: nothing seemed to go right. The organist he stopped in bed, and the minor Canon he forgot it was the 19th day and waited for the *Venite*; and after a bit the deputy he set off playing the chant for evensong, which was a minor; and then the Decani boys were laughing so much they couldn't sing, and when it came to the anthem the solo boy he got took with the giggles, and made out his nose was bleeding, and shoved the book at me what hadn't practised the verse and wasn't much of a singer if I had known it. Well, things was rougher, you see, fifty years ago, and I got a nip from the counter-tenor behind me that I remembered.

'So we got through somehow, and neither the men nor the boys weren't by way of waiting to see whether the Canon in residence – Mr Henslow it was – would come to the vestries and fine 'em, but I don't believe he did: for one thing I fancy he'd read the wrong lesson for the first time in his life, and knew it. Anyhow, Evans and me didn't find no difficulty in slipping up the stairs as I told you, and when we got up we laid ourselves down flat on our stomachs where we could just stretch our heads out over the old tomb, and we hadn't but just done so when we heard the verger that was then, first shutting the iron porch-gates and locking the south-west door, and then the transept door, so we knew there was something up, and they meant to keep the public out for a bit.

'Next thing was, the Dean and the Canon come in by their door on the north, and then I see my father, and old Palmer, and a couple of their best men, and Palmer stood a talking for a bit with the Dean in the middle of the choir. He had a coil of rope and the men had crows. All of 'em looked a bit nervous. So there they stood talking, and at last I heard the Dean say, "Well, I've no time to waste, Palmer. If you think this'll satisfy Southminster people, I'll permit it to be done; but I must say this, that never in the whole course of my life have I heard such arrant nonsense from a practical man as I have from you. Don't you agree with me, Henslow?" As far as I could hear Mr Henslow said something like "Oh well! we're told, aren't we, Mr Dean, not to judge others?" And the Dean he gave a kind of sniff, and walked straight up to the tomb, and took his stand behind it with his back to the screen, and the others they come edging up rather gingerly. Henslow, he stopped on the south side and scratched on his chin, he did. Then the Dean spoke up: "Palmer," he says, "which can you do easiest, get the slab off the top, or shift one of the side slabs?"

'Old Palmer and his men they pottered about a bit looking round the edge of the top slab and sounding the sides on the south and east and west and everywhere but the north. Henslow said something about it being better to have a try at the south side, because there was more light and more room to move about in. Then my father, who'd been 'awatching of them, went round to the north side, and knelt down and felt the slab by the chink, and he got up and dusted his knees and says to the Dean: "Beg pardon, Mr Dean, but I think if Mr Palmer'll try this here slab he'll find it'll come out easy enough. Seems to me one of the men could prise it out with his crow by means of this chink." "Ah! thank you, Worby," says the Dean; "that's a good suggestion. Palmer, let one of your men do that, will you?"

'So the man come round, and put his bar in and bore on it, and just that minute when they were all bending over, and we boys got our heads well over the edge of the triforium, there came a most fearful crash down at the west end of the choir, as if a whole stack of big timber had fallen down a flight of stairs. Well, you can't expect me to tell you everything that happened all in a minute. Of course there was a terrible commotion. I heard the slab fall out, and the crowbar on the floor, and I heard the Dean say, "Good God!"

'When I looked down again I saw the Dean tumbled over on the floor, the men was making off down the choir, Henslow was just going to help the Dean up, Palmer was going to stop the men (as he said afterwards) and my father was sitting on the altar step with his face in his hands. The Dean he was very cross. "I wish to goodness you'd look where you're coming to, Henslow," he says. "Why you should all take to your heels when a stick of wood tumbles down I cannot imagine"; and all Henslow could do, explaining he was right away on the other side of the tomb, would not satisfy him.

'Then Palmer came back and reported there was nothing to account for this noise and nothing seemingly fallen down, and when the Dean finished feeling of himself they gathered round – except my father, he sat where he was – and someone lighted up a bit of candle and they looked into the tomb. "Nothing there," says the Dean, "what did I tell you? Stay! here's something. What's this? a bit of music paper, and a piece of torn stuff – part of a dress it looks like. Both quite modern – no interest whatever. Another time perhaps you'll take the advice of an educated man" – or something like that, and off he went, limping a bit, and out through the north door, only as he went he called back angry to Palmer for leaving the door standing open. Palmer called out "Very sorry, sir," but he shrugged his shoulders, and Henslow says, "I fancy Mr Dean's mistaken. I closed the door behind me, but he's a little upset." Then Palmer says, "Why, where's Worby?" and they saw him sitting on the step and went up to him. He was recovering himself, it seemed, and wiping his forehead, and Palmer helped him up on to his legs, as I was glad to see.

'They were too far off for me to hear what they said, but my father pointed to the north door in the aisle, and Palmer and Henslow both of them looked very surprised and scared. After a bit, my father and Henslow went out of the church, and the others made what haste they could to put the slab back and plaster it in. And about as the clock struck twelve the Cathedral was opened again and us boys made the best of our way home.

'I was in a great taking to know what it was had given my poor father such a turn, and when I got in and found him sitting in his chair taking a glass of spirits, and my mother standing looking anxious at him, I couldn't keep from bursting out and making confession where I'd been. But he didn't seem to take on, not in the way of losing his temper. "You was there, was you? Well, did you see it?" "I saw everything, father," I said, "except when the noise came." "Did you see what it was knocked the Dean over?" he says, "that what come out of the monument? You didn't? Well, that's a mercy." "Why, what was it, father?" I said. "Come, you must have seen it," he says. "*Didn't* you see? A thing like a man, all over hair, and two great eyes to it?"

'Well, that was all I could get out of him that time, and later on he seemed as if he was ashamed of being so frightened, and he used to put me off when I asked him about it. But years after when I was got to be a grown man, we had more talk now and again on the matter, and he always said the same thing. "Black it was," he'd say, "and a mass of hair, and two legs, and the light caught on its eyes."

'Well, that's the tale of that tomb, Mr Lake; it's one we don't tell to our visitors, and I should be obliged to you not to make any use of it till I'm out of the way. I doubt Mr Evans'll feel the same as I do, if you ask him.'

This proved to be the case. But over twenty years have passed by, and the grass is growing over both Worby and Evans; so Mr Lake felt no difficulty about communicating his notes – taken in 1890 – to me. He accompanied them with a sketch of the tomb and a copy of the short inscription on the metal cross which was affixed at the expense of Dr Lyall to the centre of the northern side. It was from the Vulgate of Isaiah xxiv., and consisted merely of the three words –

IBI CUBAVIT LAMIA.

Bat's Belfry

AUGUST DERLETH

August Derleth, whose work I have had the pleasure of present-
ing before, needs very little introduction to readers of horror
stories: as a writer of macabre tales and an anthologiser of the
best in the genre he has few equals. Among the hundreds of
stories he has written since he first put pen to paper in the early
twenties he has produced several with vampire themes. A few
are well-known, others Derleth would frankly prefer not to see
reprinted, but of them all Bat's Belfry *— one of his very first*
horror stories — still has a place in his affections. It has long
been out of print and while displaying certain elementary
mistakes which can be expected from any young writer, is
nevertheless a powerful and compelling piece of storytelling.

The following letter was found among the papers of the late Sir
Harry Everett Barclay, of Charing Cross, London.

June 10, 1925

My Dear Marc:

Having received no answer to my card, I can only surmise
that it did not reach you. I am writing from my summer home
here on the moor, a very secluded place. I am nursing the hope
that you will give me a pleasant surprise by dropping in on me
soon (as you hinted you might), for this is just the kind of
house that would intrigue you. It is very similar to the Basker-
ville home which Sir Arthur Conan Doyle describes in his
Hound of the Baskervilles. Vague rumours have it that the place
is the abode of evil spirits, which idea I promptly and emphatic-
ally pooh-poohed. You know that in the spiritual world I am
but slightly interested, and that it is in wizardry that I delight.

82

The thought that this quiet little building in the heart of England's peaceful moors should be the home of a multitude of evil spirits seems very foolish to me. However, the surroundings are exceedingly healthy and the house itself is partly an antique, which arouses my interest in archaeology. So you see there is enough to divert my attention from these foolish rumours. Leon, my valet, is here with me and so is old Mortimer. You remember Mortimer, who always prepared such excellent bachelor dinners for us?

I have been here just twelve days, and I have explored this old house from cellar to garret. In the latter I brought to light an aged trunk, which I searched, and in which I found nine old books, several of whose title pages were torn away. One of the books, which I took to the small garret window, I finally distinguished as *Dracula* by Bram Stoker, and this I at once decided was one of the first editions of the book ever printed.

At the cessation of the first three days a typical English fog descended with a vengeance upon the moor. At the first indication of this prank of the elements, which threatened completely to obscure the beautiful weather of the past, I had hauled out all the discoveries I had made in the garret of this building. Bram Stoker's *Dracula* I have already mentioned. There is also a book on the Black Art by De Rochas. Three books, by Orfilo, Swedenborg, and Cagliostro, I have laid temporarily aside. Then there are also Strindberg's *The Inferno*, Blavatsky's *Secret Doctrine*, Poe's *Eureka*, and Flammarion's *Atmosphere*. You, my dear friend, may well imagine with what excitement these books filled me, for you know I am inclined toward sorcery. Orfilo, you know, was but a chemist and physiologist; Swedenborg and Strindberg, two who might be called mystics; Poe, whose *Eureka* did not aid me much in the path of witchcraft, nevertheless fascinated me; but the remaining five were as gold to me. Cagliostro, court magician of France; Madame Blavatsky, the priestess of Isis and of the Occult

Doctrine; *Dracula*, with all its vampires; Flammarion's *Atmosphere*, with its diagnosis of the Gods of peoples; and De Rochas, of whom all I can say is to quote from August Strindberg's *The Inferno*, the following: 'I do not excuse myself, and only ask the reader to remember this fact, in case he should ever feel inclined to practise magic, especially those forms of it called wizardry, or more properly witchcraft: that its reality has been placed beyond all doubt by De Rochas.'

Truly, my friend, I wondered, for I had good reason to do so, what manner of man had resided here before my coming, who should be so fascinated by Poe, Orfilo, Strindberg, and De Rochas – four different types of authors. Fog or no fog, I determined to find out. There is not another dwelling near here and the nearest source of information is a village some miles away. This is rather odd, for this moor does not seem an undesirable place for a summer home. I stored the books away, and after informing my valet of my intentions to walk some miles to the village, I started out. I had not gone far, when Leon decided to accompany me, leaving Mortimer alone in the fog-surrounded house.

Leon and I established very little in the town. After a conversation with one of the grocers in the village, the only communicative person that we accosted, we found that the man who had last occupied the house was a Baronet Lohrville. It seemed that the people held the late baronet in awe, for they hesitated to speak of him. This grocer related a tale concerning the disappearance of four girls one dark night some years ago. Popular belief had and still has it that the baronet kidnapped them. This idea seems utterly ludicrous to me, for the superstitious villagers cannot substantiate their suspicions. By the way, this merchant also informed us that the Lohrville home is called the 'Bat's Belfry'. Personally I can see no connection between the residence and the ascribed title, as I have not noticed any bats around during my sojourn here.

My meditations on this matter were rudely interrupted by Mortimer, who complained of bats in the cellar – a rather queer coincidence. He said that he continually felt them brushing against his cheeks and that he feared they would become entangled in his hair. Of course, Leon and I went down to look for them, but we could not see any of them. However, Leon stated that one struck him, which I doubt. It is just possible that sudden draughts of air may have been the cause of the delusions.

This incident, Marc, was just the forerunner of the odd things that have been occurring since then. I am about to enumerate the most important of these incidents to you, and I hope you will be able to explain them.

Three days ago activities started in earnest. At that date Mortimer came to me and breathlessly informed me that no light could be kept in the cellar. Leon and I investigated and found that under no circumstances could a lamp or match be kept lit in the cellar, just as Mortimer had said. My only explanation of this is that it is due to the air currents in the cellar, which seemed disturbed. It is true a flashlight could be kept alight, but even that seemed dimmed. I cannot attempt to explain the latter fact.

Yesterday, Leon, who is a devout Catholic, took a few drops from a flask of holy water, which he continually carries with him, and descended into the cellar with the firm intention of driving out, if there were therein ensconced, any evil spirits. On the bottom of the steps I noticed, some time ago, a large stone tablet. As Leon came down the steps a large drop of the blessed fluid fell on this tablet. The drop of water actually sizzled while Leon muttered some incantations, in the midst of which he suddenly stopped and fled precipitantly, mumbling that the cellar was incontestably the very entrance to hell, guarded by the fiend incarnate himself! I confess to you, my dear Marc, that I was astounded at this remarkable occurrence.

Last night, while the three of us sat together in the spacious drawing-room of this building, the lamp was blown out. I say 'blown out' because there is no doubt that it was, and by some superhuman agency. There was not a breath of air stirring outside, yet I, who was sitting just across from the lamp, felt a cool draught. No one else noticed this draught. It was just as if someone directly opposite me had blown forcibly at the lamp, or as if the wing of a powerful bird had passed by it.

There can be no doubt there is something radically wrong in this house, and I am determined to find out what it is, regardless of consequences.

(Here the letter terminates abruptly, as if it were to be completed at a later date.)

The two doctors bending over the body of Sir Harry Barclay in Lohrville Manor at last ceased their examinations.

'I cannot account for this astounding loss of blood, Dr Mordaunt.'

'Neither can I, Dr Greene. He is so devoid of blood that some supernatural agency must have kept him alive!' He laughed lightly.

'About this loss of blood – I was figuring on internal haemorrhages as the cause, but there are absolutely no signs of anything of the sort. According to the expression of his features, which is too horrible for even me to gaze at——'

'And me.'

'——he died from some terrible fear of something, or else he witnessed some horrifying scene.'

'Most likely the latter.'

'I think we had better pronounce death due to internal hæmorrhage and apoplexy.'

'I agree.'

'Then we shall do so.'

The physicians bent over the open book on the table. Suddenly Dr Greene straightened up and his hand delved into his pocket and came out with a match.

'Here is a match, Dr Mordaunt. Scratch it and apply the flame to that book and say nothing to anyone.'

'It is for the best.'

Excerpts from the journal of Sir Harry E. Barclay, found beside his body in Lohrville Manor on July 17, 1925.

June 25 – Last night I had a curious nightmare. I dreamed that I met a beautiful girl in the wood around my father's castle in Lancaster. Without knowing why, we embraced, our lips meeting and remaining in the position for at least half an hour! Queer dream that! I must have had another nightmare of a different nature, although I cannot recall it; for, upon looking in the mirror this morning, I found my face devoid of all colour – rather drawn.

Later – Leon has told me that he had a similar dream, and as he is a confirmed misogynist, I cannot interpret it. Strange that it should be so parallel to mine in every way.

June 29 – Mortimer came to me early this morning and said he would not stay another instant, for he had certainly seen a ghost last night. A handsome old man, he said. He seemed horrified that the old man had kissed him. He must have dreamed it. I persuaded him to stay on these grounds and solemnly told him to say nothing about it. Leon remarked that the dream had returned in every particular to him the preceding night, and that he was not feeling well. I advised him to see a doctor, but he roundly refused to do so. He said, referring to the horrible nightmare (as he termed it), that tonight he would sprinkle a few drops of holy water on himself and that (he stated) would drive away any evil influence, if there were any,

87

connected with his dreams. Strange that he should attribute everything to evil entities!

Later – I made some enquiries today and I find that the description of the Baronet Lohrville fits to every detail the 'ghost' of Mortimer's dream. I also learned that several small children disappeared from the countryside during the life of the last of the Lohrvilles – not that they should be connected, but it seems the ignorant people ascribe their vanishing to the baronet.

June 30 – Leon claims he did not have the dream (which, by the way, revisited me last night), because of the potent effect of the holy water.

July 1 – Mortimer has left. He says he cannot live in the same house with the devil. It seems he must have actually seen the ghost of old Lohrville, although Leon scoffs at the idea.

July 4 – I had the same dream again last night. I felt very ill this morning, but was able to dispel the feeling easily during the day. Leon has used all the holy water, but as tomorrow is Sunday he will get some at the village parish when he attends mass.

July 5 – I tried to procure the services of another chef this morning in the village, but I am all at sea. No one in the town will enter the house, not even for one hundred pounds a week, they declare! I shall be forced to get along without one or send to London.

Leon experienced a misfortune today. Riding home after mass, almost all his holy water spilled from the bottle, and later the bottle, containing the remainder of it, fell to the ground and broke. Leon, nonplussed, remarked that he would get another as soon as possible from the parish priest.

July 6 – Both of us had the dream again last night. I feel rather weak, and Leon does, too. Leon went to a doctor, who asked him whether he had been cut, or severely injured so as to cause a heavy loss of blood, or if he had suffered from internal hæmorrhages. Leon said no, and the doctor prescribed raw onions and some other things for Leon to eat. Leon forgot his holy water.

July 9 – The dream again. Leon had a different nightmare – about an old man, who, he said, bit him. I asked him to show me where the man had bitten him in his dream, and when he loosened his collar to show me, sure enough, there were two tiny punctures on his throat. He and I are both feeling miserably weak.

July 15 – Leon left me today. I am firmly convinced that he went suddenly mad, for this morning he evinced an intense desire to invade the cellar again. He said that something seemed to draw him. I did not stop him, and some time later, as I was engrossed in a volume of Wells, he came shrieking up the cellar steps and dashed madly through the room in which I sat. I ran after him and, cornering him in his room, forcibly detained him. I asked for an explanation and all he could do was moan over and over.

'*Mon Dieu, Monsieur*, leave this accursed place at once. Leave it, *Monsieur*, I beg of you. *Le diable——le diable!*' At length he dashed away from me and ran at top speed from the house, I after him. In the road I shouted after him, and all I could catch of the words wafted back to me by the wind, were: '*Lamais—— le diable——Mon – Dieu——tablet——Book of Thoth.*' All very significant words, '*Le Diable*' and '*Mon Dieu*' – 'the devil' and 'my God' – I paid little attention to. But Lamais was a species of female vampire known intimately to a few select sorcerers only, and the *Book of Thoth* was the Egyptian book of magic. For a few minutes I entertained the rather wild fancy that the *Book of Thoth* was ensconced somewhere in this building, and as I racked my brains for a suitable connection between 'tablet' and *Book of Thoth* I at last became convinced that the book lay beneath the tablet at the foot of the cellar steps. I am going down to investigate.

July 16 – I have it! The *Book of Thoth!* It was below the stone tablet as I thought. The spirits guarding it evidently did not wish me to disturb its resting place, for they roused the air currents to a semblance of a gale while I worked to get the stone away. The book is secured by a heavy lock of antique pattern.

I had the dream again last night, but in addition I could almost swear that I saw the ghosts of old Lohrville and four beautiful girls. What a coincidence! I am very weak today, hardly able to walk around. There is no doubt that this house is infested, not by bats, but by vampires! Lamais! If I could only find their corpses I would drive sharp stakes through them.

Later – I made a new and shocking discovery today. I went down to the place where the tablet lay, and another rock below the cavity wherein the *Book of Thoth* had lain gave way below me and I found myself in a vault with about a score of skeletons – all of little children! If this house *is* inhabited by vampires, it is only too obvious that these skeletons are those of their unfortunate victims. However, I firmly believe that there is another cavern somewhere below, wherein the bodies of the vampires are hidden.

Later – I have been looking over the book by De Rochas and I have hit upon an excellent plan to discover the bodies of the vampires! I shall use the *Book of Thoth* to summon the vampires before me and force them to reveal the hiding place of their voluptuous bodies! De Rochas says that it can be done.

Nine o'clock – As the conditions are excellent at this time I am going to start to summon the vampires. Someone is passing and I hope he or she does not interrupt me in my work or tell anyone in the town to look in here. The book, as I mentioned before, is secured by a heavy seal, and I had trouble to loosen it. At last I succeeded in breaking it and I opened the book to find the place I need in my work of conjuring up the vampires.

I found it and I am beginning my incantations. The atmosphere in the room is changing slowly and it is becoming intolerably dark. The air currents in the room are swirling angrily, and the lamp has gone out . . . I am confident that the vampires will appear soon.

I am correct. There are some shades materialising in the room. They are becoming more distinct . . . there are five of them, four females and one male. Their features are very distinct. . . . They are casting covert glances in my direction. . . . Now they are glaring malevolently at me.

Good God! I have forgotten to place myself in a magic circle and I greatly fear the vampires will attack me! I am only too correct. They are moving in my direction. My God! . . . But stay! They are halting! The old baronet is gazing at me with his glittering eyes fiery with hate. The four female vampires smile voluptuously upon me.

Now, if ever, is my chance to break their evil spell. *Prayer!* But I cannot pray! I am forever banished from the sight of God for calling upon Satan to aid me. But even for that I cannot pray . . . I am hypnotised by the malefic leer disfiguring the countenance of the baronet. There is a sinister gleam in the eyes of the four beautiful ghouls. They glide towards me, arms outstretched. Their sinuous, obnoxious forms are before me; their crimson lips curved in a diabolically triumphant smile. I cannot bear to see the soft caress of their tongues on their red lips. I am resisting with all the power of my will, but what is one mere will against an infernal horde of ghouls?

God! Their foul presence taints my very soul! The baronet is moving forward. His mordacious propinquity casts a reviling sensation of obscenity about me. If I cannot appeal to God I must implore Satan to grant me time to construct the magic circle.

I cannot tolerate their virulence . . . I endeavoured to rise but I could not do so . . . I am no longer master of my own will!

The vampires are leering demonically at me . . I am doomed to die . . . and yet to live forever in the ranks of the Undead.

Their faces are approaching closer to mine and soon I shall sink into oblivion . . . but anything is better than this . . . to see the malignant Undead around me . . . A sharp stinging sensation in my throat . . . My God! . . . it is . . . .

'And No Bird Sings'

E. F. BENSON

Not all vampire stories are concerned with human blood-suckers; there are, as one explores the genre, tales of vampire flowers (H. G. Wells' The Flowering of the Strange Orchid), vampire plants (Fred White's The Purple Terror) and all manner of objects animate and inanimate which live on human blood. Of all the tales of this kind I have read, 'And No Bird Sings' strikes me as the most chillingly real – in fact I have avoided many a small copse of trees because of it! This particular story by Benson is almost completely unknown because of the great prominence given in anthology after anthology to his two classic vampire tales, Mrs Amworth and The Room in the Tower. I believe it is high time 'And No Bird Sings' was given the attention it so richly deserves.

THE red chimneys of the house for which I was bound were visible from just outside the station at which I had alighted, and, so the chauffeur told me, the distance was not more than a mile's walk if I took the path across the fields. It ran straight till it came to the edge of that wood yonder, which belonged to my host, and above which his chimneys were visible. I should find a gate in the paling of this wood, and a track traversing it, which debouched close to his garden. So, in this adorable afternoon of early May, it seemed a waste of time to do other than walk through the meadows and woods, and I set off on foot, while the motor carried my traps.

It was one of those golden days which every now and again leak out of Paradise and drip to earth. Spring had been late in coming, but now it was here with a burst, and the whole world was boiling with the sap of life. Never have I seen such a wealth of spring flowers, or such vividness of green, or heard such melodious business among the birds in the hedgerows; this walk through the meadows was a jubilee of festal ecstasy. And best of all, so I promised myself, would be the passage through the wood newly fledged with milky green that lay just ahead. There was the gate, just facing me, and I passed through it into the dappled lights and shadows of the grass-grown track.

Coming out of the brilliant sunshine was like entering a dim tunnel; one had the sense of being suddenly withdrawn from the brightness of the spring into some subaqueous cavern. The tree-tops formed a green roof overhead, excluding the light to a remarkable degree; I moved in a world of shifting obscurity. Presently, as the trees grew more scattered, their place was taken by a thick growth of hazels, which met over the path, and then, the ground sloping downwards, I came upon an open clearing, covered with bracken and heather and studded with birches. But though I now walked once more beneath the luminous sky, with the sunlight pouring down, it seemed to have lost its effulgence. The brightness – was it some odd optical illusion? – was veiled as if it came through crêpe. Yet there was the sun still well above the tree-tops in an unclouded heaven, but for all that the light was that of a stormy winter's day, without warmth or brilliance. It was oddly silent, too; I had thought that the bushes and trees would be ringing with the song of mating birds, but listening, I could hear no note of any sort, neither the fluting of thrush or blackbird, nor the cheerful whirr of the chaffinch, nor the cooing wood-pigeon, nor the strident clamour of the jay. I paused to verify this odd silence; there was no doubt about it. It was rather eerie, rather uncanny, but I supposed the birds knew their own business best, and if they were too busy to sing it was their affair.

As I went on it struck me also that since entering the wood I had not seen a bird of any kind; and now, as I crossed the clearing, I kept my eyes alert for them, but fruitlessly, and soon I entered the further belt of thick trees which surrounded it. Most of them I noticed were beeches, growing very close to each other, and the ground beneath them was bare but for the carpet of fallen leaves, and a few thin bramble-bushes. In this curious dimness and thickness of the trees, it was impossible to see far to right or left of the path, and now, for the first time since I had left the open, I heard some sound of life. There came the rustle of leaves from not far away, and I thought to myself that a rabbit, anyhow, was moving. But somehow it lacked the staccato patter of a small animal; there was a certain stealthy heaviness about it, as if something much larger were stealing along and desirous of not being heard. I paused again to see what might emerge, but instantly the sound ceased. Simultaneously I was conscious of some faint but very foul odour reaching me, a smell choking and corrupt, yet somehow pungent, more like the odour of something alive rather than rotting. It was peculiarly sickening, and not wanting to get any closer to its source I went on my way.

Before long I came to the edge of the wood; straight in front of me was a strip of meadow-land, and beyond an iron gate between two brick walls, through which I had a glimpse of lawn and flower-beds. To the left stood the house, and over house and garden there poured the amazing brightness of the declining afternoon.

Hugh Granger and his wife were sitting out on the lawn, with the usual pack of assorted dogs: a Welsh collie, a yellow retriever, a fox-terrier, and a Pekinese. Their protest at my intrusion gave way to the welcome of recognition, and I was admitted into the circle. There was much to say, for I had been out of England for the last three months, during which time Hugh had settled into this little estate left him by a recluse uncle, and he and Daisy had been busy during the Easter vacation with getting into the house. Certainly it was a most attractive legacy; the house, through which I was presently taken, was a delightful little Queen Anne manor, and its situation on the edge of this heather-clad Surrey ridge quite superb. We had tea in a small panelled parlour overlooking the garden, and soon the wider topics narrowed down to those of the day and the hour. I had walked, had I, asked Daisy, from the station: did I go through the wood, or follow the path outside it?

The question she thus put to me was given trivially enough; there was no hint in her voice that it mattered a straw to her which way I had come. But it was quite clearly borne in upon me that not only she but Hugh also listened intently for my reply. He had just lit a match for his cigarette, but held it unapplied till he heard my answer. Yes, I had gone through the wood; but now, though I had received some odd impressions in the wood, it seemed quite ridiculous to mention what they were. I could not soberly say that the sunshine there was of very poor quality, and that at one point in my traverse I had smelt a most iniquitous odour. I had walked through the wood; that was all I had to tell them.

I had known both my host and hostess for a tale of many years, and now, when I felt that there was nothing except purely fanciful stuff that I could volunteer about my experiences there, I noticed that they exchanged a swift glance, and could easily interpret it. Each of them signalled to the other an expression of relief; they told each other (so I construed their glance) that I, at any rate, had found nothing unusual in the wood, and they were pleased at that. But then, before any real pause had succeeded to my answer that I had gone through the wood, I remembered that strange absence of bird-song and birds, and as that seemed an innocuous observation in natural history, I thought I might as well mention it.

'One odd thing struck me,' I began (and instantly I saw the attention of both riveted again), 'I didn't see a single bird or hear one from the time I entered the wood to when I left it.'

Hugh lit his cigarette.

'I've noticed that too,' he said, 'and it's rather puzzling. The wood is certainly a bit of primeval forest, and one would have thought that hosts of birds would have nested in it from time immemorial. But, like you, I've never heard or seen one in it. And I've never seen a rabbit there either.'

'I thought I heard one this afternoon,' said I. 'Something was moving in the fallen beech leaves.'

'Did you see it?' he asked.

I recollected that I had decided that the noise was not quite the patter of a rabbit.

'No, I didn't see it,' I said, 'and perhaps it wasn't one. It sounded, I remember, more like something larger.'

Once again and unmistakingly a glance passed between Hugh and his wife, and she rose.

'I must be off,' she said. 'Post goes out at seven, and I lazed all morning. What are you two going to do?'

'Something out of doors, please,' said I. 'I want to see the domain.'

Hugh and I accordingly strolled out again with the cohort of dogs. The domain was certainly very charming; a small lake lay beyond the garden, with a reed bed vocal with warblers, and a tufted margin into which coots and moorhens scudded at our approach. Rising from the end of that was a high heathery knoll full of rabbit holes, which the dogs nosed at with joyful expectations, and there we sat for a while overlooking the wood which covered the rest of the estate. Even now in the blaze of the sun near to its setting, it seemed to be in shadow, though like the rest of the view it should have basked in brilliance, for not a cloud flecked the sky and the level rays enveloped the world in a crimson splendour. But the wood was grey and darkling. Hugh, also, I was aware, had been looking at it, and now, with an air of breaking into a disagreeable topic, he turned to me.

'Tell me,' he said, 'does anything strike you about that wood?'

'Yes: it seems to lie in shadow.'

He frowned.

'But it can't, you know,' he said. 'Where does the shadow come from? Not from outside, for sky and land are on fire.'

'From inside, then?' I asked.

He was silent a moment.

'There's something queer about it,' he said at length. 'There's something there, and I don't know what it is. Daisy feels it too; she won't ever go into the wood, and it appears that birds won't either. Is it just the fact that, for some unexplained reason, there are no birds in it that has set all our imaginations at work?'

I jumped up.

'Oh, it's all rubbish,' I said. 'Let's go through it now and find a bird. I bet you I find a bird.'

'Sixpence for every bird you see,' said Hugh.

We went down the hillside and walked round the wood till we came to the gate where I had entered that afternoon. I held it open after I had gone in for the dogs to follow. But there they stood, a yard or so away, and none of them moved.

'Come on, dogs,' I said, and Fifi, the fox-terrier, came a step nearer and then with a little whine retreated again.

'They always do that,' said Hugh, 'not one of them will set foot inside the wood. Look!'

He whistled and called, he cajoled and scolded, but it was no use. There the dogs remained, with little apologetic grins and signallings of tails, but quite determined not to come.

'But why?' I asked.

'Same reason as the birds, I suppose, whatever that happens to be. There's Fifi, for instance, the sweetest-tempered little lady; once I tried to pick her up and carry her in, and she snapped at me. They'll have nothing to do with the wood; they'll trot round outside it and go home.'

We left them there, and in the sunset light which was now beginning to fade began the passage. Usually the sense of eeriness disappears if one has a companion, but now to me, even with Hugh walking by my side, the place seemed even more uncanny than it had done that afternoon, and a sense of intolerable uneasiness, that grew into a sort of waking nightmare, obsessed me. I had thought before that the silence and loneliness of it had played tricks with my nerves; but with Hugh here it could not be that, and indeed I felt that it was not any such notion that lay at the root of this fear, but rather the conviction that there was some presence lurking there, invisible as yet, but permeating the gathered gloom. I could not form the slightest idea of what it might be, or whether it was material or ghostly; all I could diagnose of it from my own sensations was that it was evil and antique.

As we came to the open ground in the middle of the wood, Hugh stopped, and though the evening was cool I noticed that he mopped his forehead.

'Pretty nasty,' he said. 'No wonder the dogs don't like it. How do you feel about it?'

Before I could answer, he shot out his hand, pointing to the belt of trees that lay beyond.

'What's that?' he said in a whisper.

I followed his finger, and for one half-second thought I saw against the black of the wood some vague flicker, grey or faintly luminous. It waved as if it had been the head and forepart of some huge snake rearing itself, but it instantly disappeared, and my glimpse had been so momentary that I could not trust my impression.

'It's gone,' said Hugh, still looking in the direction he had pointed; and as we stood there, I heard again what I had heard that afternoon, a rustle among the fallen beech-leaves. But there was no wind nor breath of breeze astir.

He turned to me.

'What on earth was it?' he said. 'It looked like some enormous slug standing up. Did you see it?'

'I'm not sure whether I did or not,' I said. 'I think I just caught sight of what you saw.'

'But what was it?' he said again. 'Was it a real material creature, or was it——'

'Something ghostly, do you mean?' I asked.

'Something halfway between the two,' he said. 'I'll tell you what I mean afterwards, when we've got out of this place.'

The thing, whatever it was, had vanished among the trees to the left of where our path lay, and in silence we walked across the open till we came to where it entered tunnel-like among the trees. Frankly I hated and feared the thought of plunging into that darkness with the knowledge that not so far off there was something the nature of which I could not ever so faintly conjecture, but which, I now made no doubt, was that which filled the wood with some nameless terror. Was it material, was it ghostly, or was it (and now some inkling of what Hugh meant began to form itself into my mind) some being that lay on the borderline between the two? Of all the sinister possibilities that appeared the most terrifying.

As we entered the trees again I perceived that reek, alive and yet corrupt, which I had smelt before, but now it was far more potent, and we hurried on, choking with the odour that I now guessed to be not the putrescence of decay, but the living substance of that which crawled and reared itself in the darkness of the wood where no bird would shelter. Somewhere among those trees lurked the reptilian thing that defied and yet compelled credence.

It was a blessed relief to get out of that dim tunnel into the wholesome air of the open and the clear light of evening. Within doors, when we returned, windows were curtained and lamps lit. There was a hint of frost, and Hugh put a match to the fire in his room, where the dogs, still a little apologetic, hailed us with thumpings of drowsy tails.

'And now we've got to talk,' said he, 'and lay our plans, for whatever it is that is in the wood, we've got to make an end of it. And, if you want to know what I think it is, I'll tell you.'

'Go ahead,' said I.

'You may laugh at me, if you like,' he said, 'but I believe it's an elemental. That's what I meant when I said it was a being halfway between the material and the ghostly. I never caught a glimpse of it till this afternoon; I only felt there was something horrible there. But now I've seen it, and it's like what spiritualists and that sort of folk describe as an elemental. A huge phosphorescent slug is what they tell us of it, which at will can surround itself with darkness.'

Somehow, now safe within doors, in the cheerful light and warmth of the room, the suggestion appeared merely grotesque. Out there in the darkness of that uncomfortable wood something within me had quaked, and I was prepared to believe any horror, but now commonsense revolted.

'But you don't mean to tell me you believe in such rubbish?' I said. 'You might as well say it was a unicorn. What *is* an elemental, anyway? Who has ever seen one except the people who listen to raps in the darkness and say they are made by their aunts?'

'What is it then?' he asked.

'I should think it is chiefly our own nerves,' I said. 'I frankly acknowledge I got the creeps when I went through the wood first, and I got them much worse when I went through it with you. But it was just nerves; we are frightening ourselves and each other.'

'And are the dogs frightening themselves and each other?' he asked. 'And the birds?'

That was rather harder to answer; in fact I gave it up.

Hugh continued.

'Well, just for the moment we'll suppose that something else, not ourselves, frightened us and the dogs and the birds,' he said, 'and that we did see something like a huge phosphorescent slug. I won't call it an elemental, if you object to that; I'll call it It. There's another thing, too, which the existence of It would explain.'

'What's that?' I asked.

'Well, It is supposed to be some incarnation of evil; it is a corporeal form of the devil. It is not only spiritual, it is material to this extent that it can be seen bodily in form, and heard, and, as you noticed, smelt, and, God forbid, handled. It has to be kept alive by nourishment. And that explains perhaps why, every day since I have been here, I've found on that knoll we went up some half-dozen dead rabbits.'

'Stoats and weasels,' said I.

'No, not stoats and weasels. Stoats kill their prey and eat it. These rabbits have not been eaten; they've been drunk.'

'What on earth do you mean?' I asked.

'I examined several of them. There was just a small hole in their throats, and they were drained of blood. Just skin and bones, and a sort of grey mash of fibre, like, like the fibre of an orange which has been sucked. Also there was a horrible smell lingering on them. And was the thing you had a glimpse of like a stoat or a weasel?'

There came a rattle at the handle of the door.

'Not a word to Daisy,' said Hugh as she entered.

'I heard you come in,' she said. 'Where did you go?'

'All round the place,' said I, 'and came back through the wood. It is odd; not a bird did we see, but that is partly accounted for because it was dark.'

I saw her eyes search Hugh's, but she found no communication there. I guessed that he was planning some attack on It next day, and he did not wish her to know that anything was afoot.

'The wood's unpopular,' he said. 'Birds won't go there, dogs won't go there, and Daisy won't go there. I'm bound to say I share the feeling too, but having braved its terrors in the dark I've broken the spell.'

'All quiet, was it?' asked she.

'Quiet wasn't the word for it. The smallest pin could have been heard dropping half a mile off.'

We talked over our plans that night after she had gone up to bed. Hugh's story about the sucked rabbits was rather horrible, and though there was no certain connection between those empty rinds of animals and what we had seen, there seemed a certain reasonableness about it. But anything, as he pointed out, which could feed like that was clearly not without its material side – ghosts did not have dinner, and if it was material it was vulnerable.

Our plans, therefore, were very simple; we were going to tramp through the wood, as one walks up partridges in a field of turnips, each with a shot-gun and a supply of cartridges. I cannot say that I looked forward to the expedition, for I hated the thought of getting into closer quarters with that mysterious denizen of the woods; but there was a certain excitement about it, sufficient to keep me awake a long time, and when I got to sleep to cause very vivid and awful dreams.

The morning failed to fulfil the promise of the clear sunset; the sky was lowering and cloudy and a fine rain was falling. Daisy had shopping-errands which took her into the little town, and as soon as she had set off we started on our business. The yellow retriever, mad with joy at the sight of guns, came bounding with us across the garden, but on our entering the wood he slunk back home again.

The wood was roughly circular in shape, with a diameter perhaps of half a mile. In the centre, as I have said, there was an open clearing about a quarter of a mile across, which was thus surrounded by a belt of thick trees and copse a couple of hundred yards in breadth. Our plan was first to walk together up the path which led through the wood, with all possible stealth, hoping to hear some movement on the part of what we had come to seek. Failing that, we had settled to tramp through the wood at the distance of some fifty yards from each other in a circular track; two or three of these circuits would cover the whole ground pretty thoroughly. Of the nature of our quarry, whether it would try to steal away from us, or possibly attack, we had no idea; it seemed, however, yesterday to have avoided us.

Rain had been falling steadily for an hour when we entered to wood; it hissed a little in the tree-tops overhead; but so thick was the cover that the ground below was still not more than damp. It was a dark morning outside; here you would say that the sun had already set and that night was falling. Very quietly we moved up the grassy path, where our footfalls were noiseless, and once we caught a whiff of that odour of live corruption; but though we stayed and listened not a sound of anything stirred except the sibilant rain over our heads. We went across the clearing and through to the far gate, and still there was no sign.

'We'll be getting into the trees then,' said Hugh. 'We had better start where we got that whiff of it.'

We went back to the place, which was towards the middle of the encompassing trees. The odour still lingered on the windless air.

'Go on about fifty yards,' he said, 'and then we'll go in. If either of us comes on the track of it we'll shout to each other.'

I walked on down the path till I had gone the right distance, signalled to him, and we stepped in among the trees.

I have never known the sensation of such utter loneliness. I knew that Hugh was walking parallel with me, only fifty yards away, and if I hung on my step I could faintly hear his tread among the beech leaves. But I felt as if I was quite sundered in this dim place from all companionship of man; the only live thing that lurked here was that monstrous mysterious creature of evil. So thick were the trees that I could not see more than a dozen yards in any direction; all places outside the wood seemed infinitely remote, and infinitely remote also everything that had occurred to me in normal human life. I had been whisked out of all wholesome experiences into this antique and evil place. The rain had ceased, it whispered no longer in the tree-tops, testifying that there did exist a world and a sky outside, and only a few drops from above pattered on the beech leaves.

Suddenly I heard the report of Hugh's gun, followed by his shouting voice.

'I've missed it,' he shouted, 'it's coming in your direction.'

I heard him running towards me, the beech-leaves rustling, and no doubt his footsteps drowned a stealthier noise that was close to me. All that happened now, until once more I heard the report of Hugh's gun, happened, I suppose, in less than a minute. If it had taken much longer I do not imagine I should be telling it today.

I stood there then, having heard Hugh's shout, with my gun cocked, and ready to put to my shoulder, and I listened to his running footsteps. But still I saw nothing to shoot at and heard nothing. Then between two beech trees, quite close to me, I saw what I can only describe as a ball of darkness. It rolled very swiftly towards me over the few yards that separated me from it, and then, too late, I heard the dead beech-leaves rustling below it. Just before it reached me, my brain realised what it was, or what it might be, but before I could raise my gun to shoot at that nothingness, it was upon me. My gun was twitched out of my hand, and I was enveloped in this blackness, which was the very essence of corruption. It knocked me off my feet, and I sprawled flat on my back, and upon me, as I lay there, I felt the weight of this invisible assailant.

I groped wildly with my hands and they clutched something cold and slimy and hairy. They slipped off it, and next moment there was laid across my shoulder and neck something which felt like an india-rubber tube. The end of it fastened on to my neck like a snake, and I felt the skin rise beneath it. Again, with clutching hands, I tried to tear that obscene strength away from me, and as I struggled with it, I heard Hugh's footsteps close to me through this layer of darkness that hid everything.

My mouth was free, and I shouted at him.

'Here, here!' I yelled. 'Close to you, where it is darkest.'

I felt his hands on mine, and that added strength detached from my neck that sucker that pulled at it. The coil that lay heavy on my legs and chest writhed and struggled and relaxed. Whatever it was that our four hands held, slipped out of them and I saw Hugh standing close to me. A yard or two off, vanishing among the beech trunks, was that darkness which had poured over me. Hugh put up his gun, and with his second barrel fired at it.

The blackness dispersed, and there, wriggling and twisting like a huge worm lay what we had come to find. It was alive still, and I picked up my gun which lay by my side and fired two more barrels into it. The writhings dwindled into mere shudderings and shakings, and then it lay still.

With Hugh's help I got to my feet, and we both reloaded before going nearer. On the ground there lay a monstrous thing, half slug, half worm. There was no head to it; it ended in a blunt point with an orifice. In colour it was grey covered with sparse black hairs; its length I suppose was some four feet, its thickness at the broadest part was that of a man's thigh, tapering towards each end. It was shattered by shot at its middle. There were stray pellets which had hit it elsewhere, and from the holes they had made there oozed not blood, but some grey viscous matter.

As we stood there some swift process of disintegration and decay began. It lost outline, it melted, it liquefied, and in a minute more we were looking at a mass of stained and coagulated beech leaves. Again and quickly that liquor of corruption faded, and there lay at our feet no trace of what had been there. The overpowering odour passed away, and there came from the ground just the sweet savour of wet earth in springtime, and from above the glint of a sunbeam piercing the clouds. Then a sudden pattering among the dead leaves sent my heart into my mouth again, and I cocked my gun. But it was only Hugh's yellow retriever who had joined us.

We looked at each other.

'You're not hurt?' he said.

I held my chin up.

'Not a bit,' I said. 'The skin's not broken, is it?'

'No; only a round red mark. My God, what was it? What happened?'

'Your turn first,' said I. 'Begin at the beginning.'

'I came upon it quite suddenly,' he said. 'It was lying coiled like a sleeping dog behind a big beech. Before I could fire, it slithered off in the direction where I knew you were. I got a snap shot at it among the trees, but I must have missed, for I heard it rustling away. I shouted to you and ran after it. There was a circle of absolute darkness on the ground, and your voice came from the middle of it. I couldn't see you at all, but I clutched at the blackness and my hands met yours. They met something else, too.'

We got back to the house and had put the guns away before Daisy came home from her shopping. We had also scrubbed and brushed and washed. She came into the smoking-room.

'You lazy folk,' she said. 'It has cleared up, and why are you still indoors? Let's go out at once.'

I got up.

'Hugh has told me you've got a dislike of the wood,' I said, 'and it's a lovely wood. Come and see; he and I will walk on each side of you and hold your hands. The dogs shall protect you as well.'

'But not one of them will go a yard into the wood,' said she.

'Oh yes, they will. At least we'll try them. You must promise to come if they do.'

Hugh whistled them up, and down we went to the gate. They sat panting for it to be opened, and scuttled into the thickets in pursuit of interesting smells.

'And who says there are no birds in it?' said Daisy. 'Look at that robin! Why, there are two of them. Evidently house-hunting.'

The Believer

SYDNEY HORLER

During the first half of this century, Sydney Horler along with a select circle of writers like Edgar Wallace and Sapper provided the reading public with its diet of high adventure, spying and crime fighting. A journalist by profession, Horler left Fleet Street in 1919 to devote himself full time to writing fiction. Between then and his death in 1954 he published over 150 novels and innumerable short stories. This authentic-sounding little tale, which Horler subtitled 'Ten Minutes of Horror', shows all his storytelling ability and no little mastery of the macabre to the very best.

UNTIL his death, quite recently, I used to visit at least once a week a Roman Catholic priest. The fact that I am a Protestant did nothing to shake our friendship. Father R—— was one of the finest characters I have ever known; he was capable of the broadest sympathies, and was, in the best sense of that frequently-abused term, 'a man of the world'. He was good enough to take considerable interest in my work as a novelist, and I often discussed plots and situations with him.

The story I am about to relate occurred about eighteen months ago – ten months before his illness. I was then writing my novel *The Curse of Doone*. In this story I made the villain take advantage of a ghastly legend attached to an old manor-house in Devonshire and use it for his own ends.

Father R—— listened while I outlined the plot I had in mind, and then said, to my great surprise: 'Certain people may scoff because they will not allow themselves to believe that there is any credence in the vampire tradition.'

'Yes, that is so,' I parried; 'but, all the same, Bram Stoker stirred the public imagination with his *Dracula* – one of the most horrible and yet fascinating books ever written – and I am hoping that my public will extend to me the customary "author's licence".'

My friend nodded.

'Quite,' he replied. 'As a matter of fact,' he went on to say, 'I believe in vampires myself.'

'You do?' I felt the hair on the back of my neck commence to irritate. It is one thing to write about a horror, but quite another to begin to see it assume definite shape.

'Yes,' said Father R——. 'I am forced to believe in vampires for the very good but terrible reason that I have met one!'

I half-rose in my chair. There could be no questioning R——'s word, and yet——

'That, no doubt, my dear fellow,' he continued, 'may appear a very extraordinary statement to have made, and yet I assure you it is the truth. It happened many years ago and in another part of the country – exactly where I do not think I had better tell you.'

'But this is amazing – you say you actually met a vampire face to face?'

'And talked to him. Until now I have never mentioned the matter to a living soul apart from a brother priest.'

It was clearly an invitation to listen; I crammed tobacco into my pipe and leaned back in the chair on the opposite side of the crackling fire. I had heard that Truth was said to be stranger than fiction – but here I was about to have, it seemed, the strange experience of listening to my own most sensational imagining being hopelessly out-done by *fact*!

The name of the small town does not matter (Father R—— started); let it suffice it was in the West of England and was inhabited by a good many people of superior means. There was a large city seventy-five miles away and business men, when they retired, often came to —— to wind up their lives. I was young and very happy there in my work until—— But I am a little previous.

I was on very friendly terms with a local doctor; he often used to come in and have a chat when he could spare the time. We used to try to thrash out many problems which later experience has convinced me are insoluble – in this world, at least.

One night, he looked at me rather curiously I thought.

'What do you think of that man, Farington?' he asked.

Now, it was a curious fact that he should have made that enquiry at that exact moment, for by some subconscious means I happened to be thinking of this very person myself.

The man who called himself 'Joseph Farington' was a stranger who had recently come to settle in ——. That circumstance alone would have caused comment, but when I say that he had bought the largest house on the hill overlooking the town on the south side (representing the best residential quarter) and had had it furnished apparently regardless of cost by one of the famous London houses, that he sought to entertain a great deal but that no one seemed anxious to go twice to 'The Gables'. Well, there was 'something funny' about Farington, it was whispered.

I knew this, of course – the smallest fragment of gossip comes to a priest's ears – and so I hesitated before replying to the doctor's direct question.

'Confess now, Father,' said my companion, 'you are like the rest of us – you don't like the man! He has made me his medical attendant, but I wish to goodness he had chosen someone else. There's "something funny" about him.'

'Something funny' – there it was again. As the doctor's words sounded in my ears I remembered Farington as I had seen him walking up the main street with every other eye half-turned in his direction. He was a big-framed man, the essence of masculinity.

He looked so robust that the thought came instinctively: this man will never die. He had a florid complexion; he walked with the elasticity of youth and his hair was jet-black. Yet from remarks he had made the impression in —— was that Farington must be at least sixty years of age.

'Well, there's one thing, Sanders,' I replied; 'if appearances are anything to go by, Farington will not be giving you much trouble. The fellow looks as strong as an ox.'

'You haven't answered my question,' persisted the doctor. 'Forget your cloth, Father, and tell me exactly what you think of Joseph Farington. Don't you agree that he is a man to give you the shudders?'

'You – a doctor – talking about getting the shudders!' I gently scoffed because I did not want to give my real opinion of Joseph Farington.

'I can't help it – I have an instinctive horror of the fellow. This afternoon I was called up to "The Gables". Farington, like ever so many of his ox-like kind, is really a bit of a hypo-chondriac. He thought there was something wrong with his heart, he said.'

'And was there?'

'The man ought to live to a hundred! But, I tell you, Father, I hated having to be near the fellow, there's something uncanny about him. I felt frightened – yes, frightened – all the time I was in the house. I had to talk to someone about it and as you are the safest person in —— I dropped in. . . . You haven't said anything yourself, I notice.'

'I prefer to wait,' I replied. It seemed the safest answer.

Two months after that conversation with Sanders, not only —— but the whole of the country was startled and horrified by a terrible crime. A girl of eighteen, the belle of the district, was found dead in a field. Her face, in life so beautiful, was revolting in death because of the expression of dreadful horror it held.

The poor girl had been murdered – but in a manner which sent shudders of fear racing up and down people's spines. . . . There was a great hole in the throat, as though a beast of the jungle had attacked. . . .

It is not difficult to say how suspicion for this fiendish crime first started to fasten itself on Joseph Farington, preposterous as the statement may seem. Although he had gone out of his way to become sociable, the man had made no real friends. Sanders, although a clever doctor, was not the most tactful of men and there is no doubt that his refusal to visit Farington professionally – he had hinted as much on the night of his visit to me, you will remember – got noised about. In any case, public opinion was strongly roused; without a shred of direct evidence to go upon, people began to talk of Farington as being the actual murderer. There was some talk among the wild young spirits of setting fire to 'The Gables' one night, and burning Farington in his bed.

It was whilst this feeling was at its height that, very unwillingly, as you may imagine, I was brought into the affair. I received a note from Farington asking me to dine with him one night.

'I have something on my mind which I wish to talk over with you; so please do not fail me.'

These were the concluding words of the letter.

Such an appeal could not be ignored by a man of religion and so I replied accepting.

Farington was a good host; the food was excellent; on the surface there was nothing wrong. But – and here is the curious part – from the moment I faced the man I knew there *was* something wrong. I had the same uneasiness as Sanders, the doctor: *I felt afraid.* The man had an aura of evil; he was possessed of some devilish force or quality which chilled me to the marrow.

I did my best to hide my discomfiture, but when, after dinner, Farington began to speak about the murder of that poor, innocent girl, this feeling increased. And at once the terrible truth leaped into my mind: I knew it was Farington who had done this crime: the man was a monster!

Calling upon all my strength, I challenged him.

'You wished to see me tonight for the purpose of easing your soul of a terrible burden,' I said; 'you cannot deny that it was you who killed that unfortunate girl.'

'Yes,' he replied slowly, 'that is the truth. I killed the girl. The demon which possesses me forced me to do it. But you, as a priest, must hold this confession sacred – you must preserve it as a secret. Give me a few more hours; then I will decide myself what to do.'

I left shortly afterwards. The man would not say anything more.

'Give me a few hours,' he repeated.

That night I had a horrible dream. I felt I was suffocating. Scarcely able to breathe, I rushed to the window, pulled it open – and then fell senseless to the floor. The next thing I remember was Dr Sanders – who had been summoned by my faithful housekeeper – bending over me.

'What happened?' he asked. 'You had a look on your face as though you had been staring into hell.'

'So I had,' I replied.

'Had it anything to do with Farington?' he asked bluntly.

'Sanders,' and I clutched him by the arm in the intensity of my feeling, 'does such a monstrosity as a vampire exist nowadays? Tell me, I implore you!'

The good fellow forced me to take another nip of brandy before he would reply.

Then he put a question himself.

'Why do you ask that?' he said.

'It sounds incredible – and I hope I really dreamed it – but I fainted tonight because I saw – or imagined I saw – the man Farington flying past the window that I had just opened.'

'I am not surprised,' he nodded. 'Ever since I examined the mutilated body of that poor girl I came to the conclusion that she had come to her death through some terrible abnormality.

'Although we hear practically nothing about vampirism nowadays,' he continued, 'that is not to say that ghoulish spirits do not still take up their abode in a living man or woman, thus conferring upon them supernatural powers. What form was the shape you thought you saw?'

'It was like a huge bat,' I replied, shuddering.

'Tomorrow,' said Sanders determinedly, 'I'm going to London to see Scotland Yard. They may laugh at me at first but——'

Scotland Yard did not laugh. But criminals with supernatural powers were rather out of their line, and, besides, as they told Sanders, they had to have *proof* before they could convict Farington. Even my testimony – had I dared to break my priestly pledge, which, of course, I couldn't in any circumstances do – would not have been sufficient.

Farington solved the terrible problem by committing suicide. He was found in bed with a bullet wound in his head.

But, according to Sanders, only the body is dead – the vile spirit is roaming free, looking for another human habitation.

God help its luckless victim.

The Drifting Snow

STEPHEN GRENDON

The name Stephen Grendon conceals the identity of a leading writer of macabre stories who uses this 'cloak' for a certain section of his work. Much of it has been widely published – and adapted for television – in America, but only a few selected items have appeared in Britain. I am pleased to change this pattern with The Drifting Snow, *a really outstanding contribution from Grendon's pen. The story is also a subtle and chilling variation on our theme – the setting is a winter storm and the central character: a snow vampire.*

AUNT Mary's advancing footsteps halted suddenly, short of the table, and Clodetta turned to see what was keeping her. She was standing very rigidly, her eyes fixed upon the French windows just opposite the door through which she had entered, her cane held stiffly before her.

Clodetta shot a quick glance across the table towards her husband, whose attention had also been drawn to his aunt; his face vouchsafed her nothing. She turned again to find that the old lady had transferred her gaze to her, regarding her stonily and in silence. Clodetta felt uncomfortable.

'Who withdrew the curtains from the west windows?'

Clodetta flushed, remembering. 'I did, Aunt. I'm sorry. I forgot about your not wanting them drawn away.'

The old lady made an odd grunting sound, shifting her gaze once again to the French windows. She made a barely perceptible movement, and Lisa ran forward from the shadow of the hall, where she had been regarding the two at table with stern disapproval. The servant went directly to the west windows and drew the curtains.

Aunt Mary came slowly to the table and took her place at its head. She put her cane against the side of her chair, pulled at the chain about her neck so that her lorgnette lay in her lap, and looked from Clodetta to her nephew, Ernest.

Then she fixed her gaze on the empty chair at the foot of the table, and spoke without seeming to see the two beside her.

'I told both of you that none of the curtains over the west windows was to be withdrawn after sundown, and you must have noticed that none of those windows has been for one instant uncovered at night. I took especial care to put you in rooms facing east, and the sitting-room is also in the east.'

'I'm sure Clodetta didn't mean to go against your wishes, Aunt Mary,' said Ernest abruptly.

'No, of course not, Aunt.'

The old lady raised her eyebrows, and went on impassively. 'I didn't think it wise to explain why I made such a request. I'm not going to explain. But I do want to say that there is a very definite danger in drawing away the curtains. Ernest has heard that before, but you, Clodetta, have not.'

Clodetta shot a startled glance at her husband.

The old lady caught it, and said, 'It's all very well to believe that my mind's wandering or that I'm getting eccentric, but I shouldn't advise you to be satisfied with that.'

A young man came suddenly into the room and made for the seat at the foot of the table, into which he flung himself with an almost inaudible greeting to the other three.

'Late again, Henry,' said the old lady.

Henry mumbled something and began hurriedly to eat. The old lady sighed, and began presently to eat also, whereupon Clodetta and Ernest did likewise. The old servant, who had continued to linger behind Aunt Mary's chair, now withdrew, not without a scornful glance at Henry.

Clodetta looked up after a while and ventured to speak, 'You aren't as isolated as I thought you might be up here, Aunt Mary.'

'We aren't, my dear, what with telephones and cars and all. But only twenty years ago it was quite a different thing, I can tell you.' She smiled reminiscently and looked at Ernest. 'Your grandfather was living then, and many's the time he was snow-bound with no way to let anybody know.'

'Down in Chicago when they speak of "up north" or the "Wisconsin woods" it seems very far away,' said Clodetta.

'Well, it *is* far away,' put in Henry abruptly. 'And, Aunt, I hope you've made some provision in case we're locked in here for a day or two. It looks like snow outside, and the radio says a blizzard's coming.'

The old lady grunted and looked at him. 'Ha, Henry – you're overly concerned, it seems to me. I'm afraid you've been regretting this trip ever since you set foot in my house. If you're worrying about a snowstorm, I can have Sam drive you down to Wausau, and you can be in Chicago tomorrow.'

'Of course not.'

Silence fell, and presently the old lady called gently, 'Lisa', and the servant came into the room to help her from her chair, though, as Clodetta had previously said to her husband, 'She didn't need help.'

From the doorway, Aunt Mary bade them all goodnight, looking impressively formidable with her cane in one hand and her unopened lorgnette in the other, and vanished into the dusk of the hall, from which her receding footsteps sounded together with those of the servant, who was seldom seen away from her. These two were alone in the house most of the time, and only very brief periods when the old lady had up her nephew Ernest, 'dear John's boy', or Henry, of whose father the old lady never spoke, helped to relieve the pleasant somnolence of their quiet lives. Sam, who usually slept in the garage, did not count.

Clodetta looked nervously at her husband, but it was Henry who said what was uppermost in their thoughts.

'I think she's losing her mind,' he declared matter-of-factly. Cutting off Clodetta's protest on her lips, he got up and went into the sitting-room, from which came presently the strains of music from the radio.

Clodetta fingered her spoon idly and finally said, 'I do think she is a little queer, Ernest.'

Ernest smiled tolerantly. 'No, I don't think so. I've an idea why she keeps the west windows covered. My grandfather died out there – he was overcome by the cold one night, and froze on the slope of the hill. I don't rightly know how it happened – I was away at the time. I suppose she doesn't like to be reminded of it.'

'But where's the danger she spoke of, then?'

He shrugged. 'Perhaps it lies in her – she might be affected and affect us in turn.' He paused for an instant, and finally added, 'I suppose she *does* seem a little strange to you – but she was like that as long as I can remember; next time you come, you'll be used to it.'

Clodetta looked at her husband for a moment before replying. At last she said, 'I don't think I like the house, Ernest.'

'Oh, nonsense, darling.' He started to get up, but Clodetta stopped him.

'Listen, Ernest. I remembered perfectly well Aunt Mary's not wanting those curtains drawn away – but I just felt I had to do it. I didn't want to but – *something made me do it*.' Her voice was unsteady.

'Why, Clodetta,' he said, faintly alarmed. 'Why didn't you tell me before?'

She shrugged. 'Aunt Mary might have thought I'd gone wool-gathering.'

'Well, it's nothing serious, but you've let it bother you a little and that isn't good for you. Forget it; think of something else. Come and listen to the radio.'

They rose and moved towards the sitting-room together. At the door Henry met them. He stepped aside a little, saying, 'I might have known we'd be marooned up here,' and adding, as Clodetta began to protest, 'We're going to be, all right. There's a wind coming up and it's beginning to snow, and I know what that means.' He passed them and went into the deserted dining-room, where he stood a moment looking at the too long table. Then he turned aside and went over to the French windows, from which he drew away the curtains and stood there peering out into the darkness. Ernest saw him standing at the window, and protested from the sitting-room.

'Aunt Mary doesn't like those windows uncovered, Henry.'

Henry half turned and replied, 'Well, *she* may think it's dangerous, but I can risk it.'

Clodetta, who had been staring beyond Henry into the night through the French windows, said suddenly, 'Why, there's someone out there!'

Henry looked quickly through the glass and replied, 'No, that's the snow; it's coming down heavily, and the wind's drifting it this way and that.' He dropped the curtains and came away from the windows.

Clodetta said uncertainly, 'Why, I could have sworn I saw someone out there, walking past the window.'

'I suppose it does look that way from here,' offered Henry, who had come back into the sitting-room. 'But personally, I think you've let Aunt Mary's eccentricities impress you too much.'

Ernest made an impatient gesture at this, and Clodetta did not answer. Henry sat down before the radio and began to move the dial slowly. Ernest had found himself a book, and was becoming interested, but Clodetta continued to sit with her eyes fixed upon the still slowly moving curtains cutting off the French windows. Presently she got up and left the room, going down the long hall into the east wing, where she tapped gently upon Aunt Mary's door.

'Come in,' called the old lady.

Clodetta opened the door and stepped into the room where Aunt Mary sat in her dressing-robe, her dignity, in the shape of her lorgnette and cane, resting respectively on her bureau and in the corner. She looked surprisingly benign, as Clodetta at once confessed.

'Ha, thought I was an ogre in disguise, did you?' said the old lady, smiling in spite of herself. 'I'm really not, you see, but I have a sort of bogy about the west windows, as you have seen.'

'I wanted to tell you something about those windows, Aunt Mary,' said Clodetta. She stopped suddenly. The expression on the old lady's face had given way to a curiously dismaying one. It was not anger, not distaste – it was a lurking suspense. Why, the old lady was afraid!

'What?' she asked Clodetta shortly.

'I was looking out – just for a moment or so – and I thought I saw someone out there.'

'Of course, you didn't, Clodetta. Your imagination, perhaps, or the drifting snow.'

'My imagination? Maybe. But there was no wind to drift the snow, though one has come up since.'

'I've often been fooled that way, my dear. Sometimes I've gone out in the morning to look for footprints – there weren't any, ever. We're pretty far away from civilisation in a snow-storm, despite our telephones and radios. Our nearest neighbour is at the foot of the long, sloping rise – over three miles away – and all wooded land between. There's no highway nearer than that.'

'It was so clear. I could have sworn to it.'

'Do you want to go out in the morning and look?' asked the old lady shortly.

'Of course not.'

'Then you didn't see anything?'

It was half question, half demand. Clodetta said, 'Oh, Aunt Mary, you're making an issue of it now.'

'Did you or didn't you in your own mind see anything, Clodetta?'

'I guess I didn't, Aunt Mary.'

'Very well. And now do you think we might talk about something more pleasant?'

'Why, I'm sure – I'm sorry, Aunt. I didn't know that Ernest's grandfather had died out there.'

'Ha, he's told you that, has he? Well?'

'Yes, he said that was why you didn't like the slope after sunset – that you didn't like to be reminded of his death.'

The old lady looked at Clodetta impassively. 'Perhaps he'll never know how near right he was.'

'What do you mean, Aunt Mary?'

'Nothing for you to know, my dear.' She smiled again, her sternness dropping from her. 'And now I think you'd better go, Clodetta; I'm tired.'

Clodetta rose obediently and made for the door, where the old lady stopped her. 'How's the weather?'

'It's snowing – hard, Henry says – and blowing.'

The old lady's face showed her distaste at the news. 'I don't like to hear that, not at all. Suppose someone should look down that slope tonight?' She was speaking to herself, having forgotten Clodetta at the door. Seeing her again abruptly, she said, 'But you don't know, Clodetta. Goodnight.'

Clodetta stood with her back against the closed door, wondering what the old lady could have meant. *But you don't know, Clodetta.* That was curious. For a moment or two the old lady had completely forgotten her.

She moved away from the door, and came upon Ernest just turning into the east wing.

'Oh, there you are,' he said. 'I wondered where you had gone.'

'I was talking a bit with Aunt Mary.'

'Henry's been at the west windows again – and now *he* thinks there's someone out there.'

Clodetta stopped short. 'Does he really think so?'

Ernest nodded gravely. 'But the snow's drifting frightfully, and I can imagine how that suggestion of yours worked on his mind.'

Clodetta turned and went back along the hall. 'I'm going to tell Aunt Mary.'

He started to protest, but to no avail, for she was already tapping on the old lady's door, was indeed opening the door and entering the room before he could frame an adequate protest.

'Aunt Mary,' she said, 'I didn't want to disturb you again, but Henry's been at the French windows in the dining-room, and he says he's seen someone out there.'

The effect on the old lady was magical. 'He's seen them!' she exclaimed. Then she was on her feet, coming rapidly over to Clodetta. 'How long ago?' she demanded, seizing her almost roughly by the arms. 'Tell me, quickly. How long ago did he see them?'

Clodetta's amazement kept her silent for a moment, but at last she spoke, feeling the old lady's keen eyes staring at her. 'It was some time ago, Aunt Mary, after supper.'

The old lady's hands relaxed, and with it her tension. 'Oh,' she said, and turned and went back slowly to her chair, taking her cane from the corner where she had put it for the night.

'Then there *is* someone out there?' challenged Clodetta, when the old lady had reached her chair.

For a long time, it seemed to Clodetta, there was no answer. Then presently the old lady began to nod gently, and a barely audible 'Yes' escaped her lips.

'Then we had better take them in, Aunt Mary.'

The old lady looked at Clodetta earnestly for a moment; then she replied, her voice firm and low, her eyes fixed upon the wall beyond. 'We can't take them in, Clodetta – because they're not alive.'

At once Henry's words came flashing into Clodetta's memory – 'She's losing her mind' – and her involuntary start betrayed her thought.

'I'm afraid I'm not mad, my dear – I hoped at first I might be, but I wasn't. I'm not, now. There was only one of them out there at first – the girl; Father is the other. Quite long ago, when I was young, my father did something which he regretted all his days. He had a too strong temper, and it maddened him. One night he found out that one of my brothers – Henry's father – had been very familiar with one of the servants, a very pretty girl, older than I was. He thought she was to blame, though she wasn't, and he didn't find out until too late. He drove her from the house, then and there. Winter had not yet set in, but it was quite cold, and she had some five miles to go to her home. We begged Father not to send her away – though we didn't know what was wrong then – but he paid no attention to us. The girl had to go.

'Not long after she had gone, a biting wind came up, and close upon it a fierce storm. Father had already repented his hasty action, and sent some of the men to look for the girl. They didn't find her, but in the morning she was found frozen to death on the long slope of the hill to the west.'

The old lady sighed, paused a moment, and went on. 'Years later – she came back. She came in a snowstorm, as she went; but she had become vampiric. We all saw her. We were at supper table, and Father saw her first. The boys had already gone upstairs, and Father and the two of us girls, my sister and I, did not recognise her. She was just a dim shape floundering about in the snow beyond the French windows. Father ran out to her, calling to us to send the boys after him. We never saw him alive again. In the morning we found him in the same spot where years before the girl had been found. He, too, had died of exposure.

'Then, a few years after – she returned with the snow, and she brought him along; he, too, had become vampiric. They stayed until the last snow, always trying to lure someone out there. After that, I knew, and had the windows covered during the winter nights, from sunset to dawn, because they never went beyond the west slope.

'Now you know, Clodetta.'

Whatever Clodetta was going to say was cut short by running footsteps in the hall, a hasty rap, and Ernest's head appearing suddenly in the open doorway.

'Come on, you two,' he said, almost gaily, 'There *are* people out on the west slope – a girl and an old man – and Henry's gone out to fetch them in!'

Then, triumphant, he was off. Clodetta came to her feet, but the old lady was before her, passing her and almost running down the hall, calling loudly for Lisa, who presently appeared in nightcap and gown from her room.

'Call Sam, Lisa,' said the old lady, 'and send him to me in the dining-room.'

She ran on into the dining-room, Clodetta close on her heels. The French windows were open, and Ernest stood on the snow-covered terrace beyond, calling his cousin. The old lady went directly over to him, even striding into the snow to his side, though the wind drove the snow against her with great force. The wooded western slope was lost in a snow-fog; the nearest trees were barely discernible.

'Where could they have gone?' Ernest said, turning to the old lady, whom he had thought to be Clodetta. Then, seeing that it was the old lady, he said, 'Why, Aunt Mary – and so little on, too! You'll catch your death of cold.'

'Never mind, Ernest,' said the old lady. 'I'm all right. I've had Sam get up to help you look for Henry – but I'm afraid you won't find him.'

'He can't be far; he just went out.'

'He went before you saw where; he's far enough gone.'

Sam came running into the blowing snow from the dining-room, muffled in a greatcoat. He was considerably older than Ernest, almost the old lady's age. He shot a questioning glance at her and asked, 'Have they come again?'

Aunt Mary nodded. 'You'll have to look for Henry. Ernest will help you. And remember, don't separate. And don't go far from the house.'

Clodetta came with Ernest's overcoat, and together the two women stood there, watching them until they were swallowed up in the wall of driven snow. Then they turned slowly and went back into the house.

The old lady sank into a chair facing the windows. She was pale and drawn, and looked, as Clodetta said afterwards, 'as if she'd fallen together'. For a long time she said nothing. Then, with a gentle little sigh, she turned to Clodetta and spoke.

'Now there'll be three of them out there.'

Then, so suddenly that no one knew how it happened, Ernest and Sam appeared beyond the windows, and between them they dragged Henry. The old lady flew to open the windows, and the three of them, cloaked in snow, came into the room.

'We found him – but the cold's hit him pretty hard, I'm afraid,' said Ernest.

The old lady sent Lisa for cold water, and Ernest ran to get himself other clothes. Clodetta went with him, and in their rooms told him what the old lady had related to her.

Ernest laughed. 'I think you believed that, didn't you, Clodetta? Sam and Lisa do, I know, because Sam told me the story long ago. I think the shock of Grandfather's death was too much for all three of them.'

'But the story of the girl, and then——'

'That part's true, I'm afraid. A nasty story, but it did happen.'

'But those people Henry and I saw!' protested Clodetta weakly.

Ernest stood without movement. 'That's so,' he said, 'I saw them, too. Then they're out there yet, and we'll have to find them!' He took up his overcoat again, and went from the room, Clodetta protesting in a shrill unnatural voice. The old lady met him at the door of the dining-room, having overheard Clodetta pleading with him. 'No, Ernest – you can't go out there again,' she said. 'There's no one out there.'

He pushed gently into the room and called to Sam, 'Coming, Sam? There are still two of them out there – we almost forgot them.'

Sam looked at him strangely. 'What do you mean?' he demanded roughly. He looked challengingly at the old lady, who shook her head.

'The girl and the old man, Sam. We've got to get them, too.'

'Oh, *them*,' said Sam. 'They're dead!'

'Then I'll go out alone,' said Ernest.

Henry came to his feet suddenly, looking dazed. He walked forward a few steps, his eyes travelling from one to the other of them yet apparently not seeing them. He began to speak abruptly, in an unnatural child-like voice.

'*The snow,*' he murmured, '*the snow – the beautiful hands, so little, so lovely – her beautiful hands – and the snow, the beautiful lovely snow, drifting and falling about her. . . .*'

He turned slowly and looked towards the French windows, the others following his gaze. Beyond was a wall of white, where the snow was drifting against the house. For a moment Henry stood quietly watching; then suddenly a white figure came forward from the snow – a young girl, cloaked in long snow-whips, her glistening eyes strangely fascinating.

The old lady flung herself forward, her arms outstretched to cling to Henry, but she was too late. Henry had run towards the windows, had opened them, and even as Clodetta cried out, had vanished into the wall of snow beyond.

Then Ernest ran forward, but the old lady threw her arms around him and held him tightly, murmuring, 'You shall not go! Henry is gone beyond our help!'

Clodetta came to help her, and Sam stood menacingly at the French windows, now closed against the wind and the sinister snow. So they held him, and would not let him go.

'And tomorrow,' said the old lady in a harsh whisper, 'we must go to their graves and stake them down. We should have gone before.'

In the morning they found Henry's body crouched against the bole of an ancient oak, where two others had been found years before. There were almost obliterated marks of where something had dragged him, a long, uneven swath in the snow, and yet no footprints, only strange, hollowed places along the way as if the wind had whirled the snow away, and only the wind.

But on his skin were signs of the snow vampire – the delicate small prints of a young girl's hands.

When it was Moonlight

MANLY WADE WELLMAN

The work of Edgar Allan Poe – particularly his one vampire story Berenice *– is so well-known to the reading public that, as I explained in the Introduction, it is not my intention to reprint any item in this collection. However, it would be a great pity if the Master of the Macabre could not find a place somewhere in the book. To this end, I was delighted when I came across the following story* When it was Moonlight. *For not only does it feature Edgar Allan Poe and a vampire, but it also puts a completely different interpretation on one of Poe's finest stories. Manly Wade Wellman is among the ranks of America's cleverest writers of horror stories and will doubtless please a whole circle of new readers on this side of the Atlantic with his story.*

Let my heart be still a moment, and this mystery explore.
                                                    The Raven

His hand, as slim as a white claw, dipped a quillful of ink and wrote in one corner of the page the date – 3rd March 1842. Then:

THE PREMATURE BURIAL
by Edgar A. Poe

He hated his middle name, the name of his miserly and spiteful stepfather. For a moment he considered crossing out even the initial; then he told himself that he was only wool-gathering, putting off the drudgery of writing. And write he must, or starve – the Philadelphia *Dollar Newspaper* was clamouring for the story he had promised. Well, today he had heard a tag of gossip – his mother-in-law had it from a neighbour – that revived in his mind a subject always fascinating.

He began rapidly, to write, in a fine copperplate hand:

There are certain themes of which the interest is all-absorbing, but which are entirely too horrible for the purposes of legitimate fiction . . .

This would really be an essay, not a tale, and he could do it justice. Often he thought of the whole world as a vast fat cemetery, close set with tombs in which not all the occupants were at rest – too many struggled unavailingly against their smothering shrouds, their locked and weighted coffin lids. What were his own literary labours, he mused, but a struggle against being shut down and throttled by a society as heavy and grim and senseless as clods heaped by a sexton's spade?

He paused, and went to the slate mantelshelf for a candle. His kerosene lamp had long ago been pawned, and it was dark for mid afternoon, even in March. Elsewhere in the house his mother-in-law swept busily, and in the room next to his sounded the quiet breathing of his invalid wife. Poor Virginia slept, and for the moment knew no pain. Returning with his light, he dipped more ink and continued down the sheet:

To be buried while alive is, beyond question, the most terrific of these extremes which has ever fallen to the lot of mere mortality. That it has frequently, very frequently, fallen will scarcely be denied . . .

Again his dark imagination savoured the tale he had heard that day. It had happened here in Philadelphia, in this very quarter, less than a month ago. A widower had gone, after weeks of mourning, to his wife's tomb, with flowers. Stooping to place them on the marble slab, he had heard noise beneath. At once joyful and aghast, he fetched men and crowbars, and recovered the body, all untouched by decay. At home that night, the woman returned to consciousness.

So said the gossip, perhaps exaggerated, perhaps not. And the house was only six blocks away from Spring Garden Street, where he sat.

Poe fetched out his notebooks and began to marshal bits of narrative for his composition – a gloomy tale of resurrection in Baltimore, another from France, a genuinely creepy citation from the *Chirurgical Journal* of Leipzig; a sworn case of revival, by electrical impulses, of a dead man in London. Then he added an experience of his own, romantically embellished, a dream adventure of his boyhood in Virginia. Just as he thought to make an end, he had a new inspiration.

Why not learn more about that reputed Philadelphia burial and the one who rose from seeming death? It would point up his piece, give it a timely local climax, ensure acceptance – he could hardly risk a rejection. Too, it would satisfy his own curiosity. Laying down the pen, Poe got up. From a peg he took his wide black hat, his old military cloak that he had worn since his ill-fated cadet days at West Point. Huddling it round his slim little body, he opened the front door and went out.

March had come in like a lion and, lion-like, roared and rampaged over Philadelphia. Dry, cold dust blew up into Poe's full grey eyes, and he hardened his mouth under the gay dark moustache. His shins felt goosefleshy; his striped trousers were unseasonably thin and his shoes badly needed mending. Which way lay his journey?

He remembered the name of the street, and something about a ruined garden. Eventually he came to the place, or what must be the place – the garden was certainly ruined, full of dry, hardy weeds that still stood in great ragged clumps after

131

the hard winter. Poe forced open the creaky gate, went up the rough-flagged path to the stoop. He saw a bronzed nameplate – 'Gauber', it said. Yes, that was the name he had heard. He swung the knocker loudly, and thought he caught a whisper of movement inside. But the door did not open.

'Nobody lives there, Mr Poe,' said someone from the street. It was a grocery boy, with a heavy basket on his arm. Poe left the doorstep. He knew the lad; indeed he owed the grocer eleven dollars.

'Are you sure?' Poe prompted.

'Well' – and the boy shifted the weight of his burden – 'if anybody lived here, they'd buy from our shop, wouldn't they? And I'd deliver, wouldn't I? But I've had this job for six months, and never set foot inside that door.'

Poe thanked him and walked down the street, but did not take the turn that would lead home. Instead he sought the shop of one Pemberton, a printer and a friend, to pass the time of day and ask for a loan.

Pemberton could not lend even one dollar – times were hard – but he offered a drink of Monogahela whiskey, which Poe forced himself to refuse; then a supper of crackers, cheese and garlic sausage, which Poe thankfully shared. At home, unless his mother-in-law had begged or borrowed from the neighbours, would be only bread and molasses. It was past sundown when the writer shook hands with Pemberton, thanked him with warm courtesy for his hospitality, and ventured into the evening.

Thank Heaven, it did not rain. Poe was saddened by storms. The wind had abated and the March sky was clear save for a tiny fluff of scudding cloud and a banked dark line at the horizon, while up rose a full moon the colour of frozen cream. Poe squinted from under his hat brim at the shadow-pattern on the disc. Might he not write another story of a lunar voyage – like the one about Hans Pfaal, but dead serious this time? Musing thus, he walked along the dusk-filling street until he came again opposite the ruined garden, the creaky gate, and the house with the doorplate marked: 'Gauber'.

Hello, the grocery boy had been wrong. There was light inside the front window, water-blue light – or was there? Anyway, motion – yes, a figure stooped there, as if to peer out at him.

Poe turned in at the gate, and knocked at the door once again.

Four or five moments of silence; then he heard the old lock grating. The door moved inwards, slowly and noisily. Poe fancied that he had been wrong about the blue light, for he saw only darkness inside. A voice spoke:

'Well, sir.'

The two words came huskily but softly, as though the door-opener scarcely breathed. Poe swept off his broad black hat and made one of his graceful bows.

'If you will pardon me . . .' He paused, not knowing whether he addressed man or woman. 'This is the Gauber residence?'

'It is,' was the reply, soft, hoarse and sexless. 'Your business, sir?'

Poe spoke with official crispness; he had been a sergeant-major of artillery before he was twenty-one, and knew how to inject the proper note. 'I am here on public duty,' he announced. 'I am a journalist, tracing a strange report.'

'Journalist?' repeated his interrogator. 'Strange report? Come in, sir.'

Poe complied, and the door closed abruptly behind him, with a rusty snick of the lock. He remembered being in jail once, and how the door of his cell had slammed just so. It was not a pleasant memory. But he saw more clearly, now he was inside – his eyes got used to the tiny trickle of moonlight.

He stood in a dark hallway, all panelled in wood, with no furniture, drapes or pictures. With him was a woman, in full skirt and down-drawn lace cap, a woman as tall as he and with

133

intent eyes that glowed as from within. She neither moved nor spoke, but waited for him to tell her more of his errand.

Poe did so, giving his name and, stretching a point, claiming to be a sub-editor of the *Dollar Newspaper*, definitely assigned to the interview. 'And now, madam, concerning this story that is rife concerning a premature burial. . . .'

She had moved very close, but as his face turned towards her she drew back. Poe fancied that his breath had blown her away like a feather; then, remembering Pemberton's garlic sausage, he was chagrined. To confirm his new thought, the woman was offering him wine – to sweeten his breath.

'Would you take a glass of canary, Mr Poe?' she invited, and opened a side door. He followed her into a room papered in pale blue. Moonglow, drenching it, reflected from that paper and seemed an artificial light. That was what he had seen from outside. From an undraped table his hostess lifted a bottle, poured wine into a metal goblet and offered it.

Poe wanted that wine, but he had recently promised his sick wife, solemnly and honestly, to abstain from even a sip of the drink that so easily upset him. Through thirsty lips he said: 'I thank you kindly, but I am a temperance man.'

'Oh,' and she smiled. Poe saw white teeth. Then: 'I am Elva Gauber – Mrs John Gauber. The matter of which you ask I cannot explain clearly, but it is true. My husband was buried, in the Eastman Lutheran Churchyard . . .'

'I had heard, Mrs Gauber, that the burial concerned a woman.'

'No, my husband. He had been ill He felt cold and quiet. A physician, a Dr Mechem, pronounced him dead, and he was interred beneath a marble slab in his family vault.' She sounded weary, but her voice was calm. 'This happened shortly after the New Year. On Valentine's Day, I brought flowers. Beneath his slab he stirred and struggled. I had him brought forth. And he lives – after a fashion – today.'

'Lives today?' repeated Poe. 'In this house?'

'Would you care to see him? Interview him?'

Poe's heart raced, his spine chilled. It was his peculiarity that such sensations gave him pleasure. 'I would like nothing better,' he assured her, and she went to another door, an inner one.

Opening it, she paused on the threshold, as though summoning her resolution for a plunge into cold, swift water. Then she started down a flight of steps.

Poe followed, unconsciously drawing the door shut behind him.

The gloom of midnight, of prison – yes, of the tomb – fell at once upon those stairs. He heard Elva Gauber gasp:

'No – the moonlight – let it in. . . .' And then she fell, heavily and limply, rolling downstairs.

Aghast, Poe quickly groped his way after her. She lay against a door at the foot of the flight, wedged against the panel. He touched her – she was cold and rigid, without motion or elasticity of life. His thin hand groped for and found the knob of the lower door, flung it open. More dim reflected moonlight, and he made shift to drag the woman into it.

Almost at once she sighed heavily, lifted her head, and rose. 'How stupid of me,' she apologised hoarsely.

'The fault was mine,' protested Poe. 'Your nerves, your health, have naturally suffered. The sudden dark – the closeness – overcame you.' He fumbled in his pocket for a tinderbox. 'Suffer me to strike a light.'

But she held out a hand to stop him. 'No, no. The moon is sufficient.' She walked to a small, oblong pane set in the wall. Her hands, thin as Poe's own, with long grubby nails, hooked on the sill. Her face, bathed in the full light of the moon, strengthened and grew calm. She breathed deeply, almost voluptuously. 'I am quite recovered,' she said. 'Do not fear for me. You need not stand so near, sir.'

He had forgotten that garlic odour, and drew back contritely. She must be as sensitive to the smell as . . . as . . . what was it that was sickened and driven by garlic? Poe could not remember, and he took time to note that they were in a basement, stone-walled and with a floor of dirt. In one corner water seemed to drip, forming a dank pool of mud. Close to this set into the wall, showed a latched trap-door of planks, thick and wide, cleated cross-wise, as though to cover a window. But no window would be set so low. Everything smelt earthy and close, as though fresh air had been shut out for decades.

'Your husband is here?' he enquired.

'Yes.' She walked to the shutter-like trap, unlatched it and drew it open.

The recess beyond was as black as ink, and from it came a feeble mutter. Poe followed Elva Gauber, and strained his eyes. In a little stone-flagged nook a bed had been made up. Upon it lay a man, stripped almost naked. His skin was as white as dead bone, and only his eyes, now opening, had life. He gazed at Elva Gauber and past her at Poe.

'Go away,' he mumbled.

'Sir,' ventured Poe formally, 'I have come to hear of how you came to life in the grave . . .'

'It's a lie,' broke in the man on the pallet. He writhed halfway to a sitting posture, labouring upwards as against a crushing weight. The wash of moonlight showed how wasted and fragile he was. His face stared and snarled bare-toothed, like a skull. 'A lie, I say!' he cried, with a sudden strength that might well have been his last. 'Told by this monster who is not – my wife . . .'

The shutter-trap slammed upon his cries. Elva Gauber faced Poe, withdrawing a pace to avoid his garlic breath.

'You have seen my husband,' she said. 'Was it a pretty sight, sir?'

He did not answer, and she moved across the dirt to the stair doorway. 'Will you go up first?' she asked. 'At the top, hold the door open, that I may have' – she said 'life', or, perhaps, 'light'. Poe could not be sure which.

Plainly she, who had almost welcomed his intrusion at first, now sought to lead him away. Her eyes, compelling as shouted commands, were fixed upon him. He felt their power, and bowed to it.

Obediently he mounted the stairs, and stood with the upper door wide. Elva Gauber came up after him. At the top her eyes again seized his. Suddenly Poe knew more than ever before about the mesmeric impulses he loved to write about. 'I hope,' she said measuredly, 'that you have not found your visit fruitless. I live here alone – seeing nobody, caring for the poor thing that was once my husband, John Gauber. My mind is not clear. Perhaps my manners are not good. Forgive me, and good night.'

Poe found himself ushered from the house and outside the wind was howling once again. The front door closed behind him, and the lock grated.

The fresh air, the whip of gale in his face, and the absence of Elva Gauber's impelling gaze suddenly brought him back, as though from sleep, to a realisation of what had happened – or what had not happened.

He had come out, on this uncomfortable March evening to investigate the report of a premature burial. He had seen a ghastly sick thing, that had called the gossip a lie. Somehow, then, he had been drawn abruptly away – stopped from full study of what might be one of the strangest adventures it was ever a writer's good fortune to know. Why was he letting things drop at this stage?

He decided not to let them drop. That would be worse than staying away altogether.

He made up his mind, formed quickly a plan. Leaving the doorstep, he turned from the gate, slipped quickly around the house. He knelt by the foundation at the side, just where a small oblong pane was set flush with the ground.

Bending his head, he found that he could see plainly inside, by reason of the flood of moonlight – a phenomenon, he realised, for generally an apartment was disclosed only by light within. The open doorway to the stairs, the swamp mess of mud in the corner, the out-flung trapdoor, were discernible. And something stood or huddled at the exposed niche – something that bent itself upon and above the frail white body of John Gauber.

Full skirt, white cap – it was Elva Gauber. She bent herself down, her face was touching the face or shoulder of her husband.

Poe's heart, never the healthiest of organs, began to drum and race. He pressed closer to the pane, for a better glimpse of what went on in the cellar. His shadow cut away some of the light. Elva Gauber turned to look.

Her face was as pale as the moon itself. Like the moon, it was shadowed in irregular patches. She came quickly, almost running, towards the pane where Poe crouched. He saw her, plainly and at close hand.

Dark, wet, sticky stains lay upon her mouth and cheeks. Her tongue roved out, licking at the stains——

Blood!

Poe sprang up and ran to the front of the house. He forced his thin, trembling fingers to seize the knocker, to swing it heavily again and again. When there was no answer, he pushed heavily against the door itself – it did not give. He moved to a window, rapped on it, pried at the sill, lifted his fist to smash the glass.

A silhouette moved beyond the pane, and threw it up. Something shot out at him like a pale snake striking – before he could move back, fingers had twisted in the front of his coat. Elva Gauber's eyes glared into his.

138

Her cap was off, her dark hair fallen in disorder. Blood still smeared and dewed her mouth and jowls.

'You have pried too far,' she said, in a voice as measured and cold as the drip from icicles. 'I was going to spare you, because of the odour about you that repelled me – the garlic. I showed you a little, enough to warn any wise person, and let you go. Now . . .'

Poe struggled to free himself. Her grip was immovable, like the clutch of a steel trap. She grimaced in triumph, yet she could not quite face him – the garlic still clung to his breath.

'Look in my eyes,' she bade him. 'Look – you cannot refuse, you cannot escape. You will die, with John – and the two of you, dying, shall rise again like me. I'll have two fountains of life while you remain – two companions after you die.'

'Woman,' said Poe, fighting against her stabbing gaze, 'you are mad.'

She snickered gustily. 'I am sane, and so are you. We both know that I speak the truth. We both know the futility of your struggle.' Her voice rose a little. 'Through a chink in the tomb, as I lay dead, a ray of moonlight streamed and struck my eyes. I woke. I struggled. I was set free. Now at night, when the moon shines – Ugh! Don't breathe that herb in my face!'

She turned her head away. At that instant it seemed to Poe that a curtain of utter darkness fell and with it sank down the form of Elva Gauber.

He peered in the sudden gloom. She was collapsed across the window sill, like a discarded puppet in its booth. Her hand still twisted in the bosom of his coat, and he pried himself loose from it, finger by steely, cold finger. Then he turned to flee from this place of shadowed peril to body and soul.

As he turned, he saw whence had come the dark. A cloud had come up from its place on the horizon – the fat, sooty bank he had noted there at sundown – and now it obscured the moon. Poe paused, in mid-retreat, gazing.

His thoughtful eye gauged the speed and size of the cloud. It curtained the moon, would continue to curtain it for – well, ten minutes. And for that ten minutes Elva Gauber would lie motionless, lifeless. She had told the truth about the moon giving her life. Hadn't she fallen like one slain on the stairs when they were darkened? Poe began grimly to string the evidence together.

It was Elva Gauber, not her husband, who had died and gone to the family vault. She had come back to life, or a mockery of life, by touch of the moon's rays. Such light was an unpredictable force – it made dogs howl, it flogged mad-men to violence, it brought fear, or black sorrow, or ecstasy. Old legends said that it was the birth of fairies, the transformation of werewolves, the motive power of broom-riding witches. It was surely the source of the strength and evil animating what had been the corpse of Elva Gauber – and he, Poe, must not stand there dreaming.

He summoned all the courage that was his, and scrambled in at the window through which clumped the woman's form. He groped across the room to the cellar door, opened it and went down the stairs, through the door at the bottom, and into the stone-walled basement.

It was dark, moonless still. Poe paused only to bring forth his tinder box, strike a light and kindle the end of a tightly twisted linen rag. It gave a feeble steady light, and he found his way to the shutter, opened it and touched the naked, wasted shoulder of John Gauber.

'Get up,' he said. 'I've come to save you.'

The skull-face feebly shifted its position to meet his gaze. The man managed to speak, moaningly:

'Useless. I can't move – unless she lets me. Her eyes keep me here – half-alive. I'd have died long ago, but somehow . . .'

Poe thought of a wretched spider, paralysed by the sting of a mud-wasp, lying helpless in its captive's close den until the hour of feeding comes. He bent down, holding his blazing tinder close. He could see Gauber's neck, and it was a mass of tiny puncture wounds, some of them still beaded with blood drops fresh or dried. He winced, but bode firm in his purpose.

'Let me guess the truth,' he said quickly. 'Your wife was brought home from the grave, came back to a seeming of life. She put a spell on you, or played a trick – made you a helpless prisoner. That isn't contrary to nature, that last. I've studied mesmerism.'

'It's true,' John Gauber mumbled.

'And nightly she comes to drink your blood?'

Gauber weakly nodded. 'Yes. She was beginning just now, but ran upstairs. She will be coming back.'

'Good,' said Poe bleakly. 'Perhaps she will come back to more than she expects. Have you ever heard of vampires? Probably not, but I have studied them, too. I began to guess, I think, when first she was so repelled by the odour of garlic. Vampires lie motionless by day and walk and feed at night. They are creatures of the moon – their food is blood. Come.'

Poe broke off, put out his light, and lifted the man in his arms. Gauber was as light as a child. The writer carried him to the slanting shelter of the closed-in staircase, and there set him against the wall. Over him Poe spread his old cadet cloak. In the gloom, the grey of the cloak harmonised with the grey of the wall stones. The poor fellow would be well hidden.

Next Poe flung off his coat, waist-coat and shirt. Heaping his clothing in a deeper shadow of the stairway, he stood up, stripped to the waist. His skin was almost as bloodlessly pale as Gauber's, his chest and arms almost as gaunt. He dared believe that he might pass momentarily for the unfortunate man.

The cellar sprang full of light again. The cloud must be passing from the moon. Poe listened. There was a dragging sound above, then footsteps.

Elva Gauber, the blood drinker by night, had revived.

Now for it. Poe hurried to the niche, thrust himself in and pulled the trapdoor shut after him.

He grinned, sharing a horrid paradox with the blackness around him. He had heard all the fabled ways of destroying vampires – transfixing stakes, holy water, prayer, fire. But he, Edgar Allan Poe, had evolved a new way. Myriads of tales whispered frighteningly of fiends lying in wait for normal men, but who ever heard of a normal man lying in wait for a fiend? Well, he had never considered himself normal, in spirit, or brain, or taste.

He stretched out, feet together, hands crossed on his bare midriff. Thus it would be in the tomb, he found himself thinking. To his mind came a snatch of poetry by a man named Bryant, published long ago in a New England review – 'Breathless darkness, and the narrow house'. It was breathless and dark enough in this hole, Heaven knew, and narrow as well. He rejected, almost hysterically, the implication of being buried. To break the ugly spell, that daunted him where thought of Elva Gauber failed, he turned sideways to face the wall, his naked arm lying across his cheek and temple.

As his ear touched the musty bedding, it brought to him once again the echo of footsteps, footsteps descending stairs. They were rhythmic, confident. They were eager.

Elva Gauber was coming to seek again her interrupted repast.

Now she was crossing the floor. She did not pause or turn aside – she had not noticed her husband, lying under the cadet cloak in the shadow of the stairs. The noise came straight to the trapdoor, and he heard her fumbling for the latch.

Light, blue as skimmed milk, poured into his nook. A shadow fell in the midst of it, full upon him. His imagination, ever outstripping reality, whispered that the shadow had weight, like lead – oppressive, baleful.

'John,' said the voice of Elva Gauber in his ear, 'I've come back. You know why – you know what for.' Her voice sounded greedy, as though it came through loose, trembling lips. 'You're my only source of strength now. I thought tonight, that a stranger – but he got away. He had a cursed odour about him, anyway.'

Her hand touched the skin of his neck. She was prodding him, like a butcher fingering a doomed beast.

'Don't hold yourself away from me, John,' she was commanding, in a voice of harsh mockery. 'You know it won't do any good. This is the night of the full moon, and I have power for anything, anything!' She was trying to drag his arm away from his face. 'You won't gain by——' She broke off, aghast. Then, in a wild-dry-throated scream:

'You're not John!'

Poe whipped over on his back, and his bird-claw hands shot out and seized her – one hand clinching upon her snaky disorder of dark hair, the other digging its fingertips into the chill flesh of her arm.

The scream quivered away into a horrible breathless rattle. Poe dragged his captive violently inwards, throwing all his collected strength into the effort. Her feet were jerked from the floor and she flew into the recess, hurtling above and beyond Poe's recumbent body. She struck the inner stones with a crashing force that might break bones, and would have collapsed upon Poe; but, at the same moment, he had released her and slid swiftly out upon the floor of the cellar.

With frantic haste he seized the edge of the back-flung trap-door. Elva Gauber struggled up on hands and knees, among the tumbled bedclothes in the niche; then Poe had slammed the panel shut.

She threw herself against it from within, yammering and wailing like an animal in a trap. She was almost as strong as he, and for a moment he thought that she would win out of the niche. But, sweating and wheezing, he bore against the planks with his shoulder, bracing his feet against the earth. His fingers found the latch, lifted it, forced it into place.

'Dark,' moaned Elva Gauber from inside. 'Dark – no moon ——' Her voice trailed off.

Poe went to the muddy pool in the corner, thrust in his hands. The mud was slimy but workable. He pushed a double handful of it against the trapdoor, sealing cracks and edges. Another handful, another. Using his palms like trowels, he coated the boards with thick mud.

'Gauber,' he said breathlessly, 'how are you?'

'All right – I think.' The voice was strangely strong and clear. Looking over his shoulder, Poe saw that Gauber had come upright of himself, still pale but apparently steady. 'What are you doing?' Gauber asked.

'Walling her up,' jerked out Poe, scooping still more mud. 'Walling her up forever, with her evil.'

He had a momentary flash of inspiration, a symbolic germ of a story; in it a man sealed a woman into such a nook of the wall, and with her an embodiment of active evil – perhaps in the form of a black cat.

Pausing at last to breathe deeply, he smiled to himself. Even in the direst of danger, the most heart-breaking moment of toil and fear, he must ever be coining new plots for stories.

'I cannot thank you enough,' Gauber was saying to him. 'I feel that all will be well – if only she stays there.'

Poe put his ear to the wall. 'Not a whisper of motion, sir. She's shut off from moonlight – from life and power. Can you help me with my clothes? I feel terribly chilled.'

His mother-in-law met him on the threshold when he returned to the house in Spring Garden Street. Under the white widow's cap, her strong-boned face was drawn with worry.

'Eddie, are you ill?' She was really asking if he had been

144

drinking. A look reassured her. 'No,' she answered herself, 'but you've been away from home so long. And you're dirty, Eddie – filthy. You must wash.'

He let her lead him in, pour hot water into a basin. As he scrubbed himself, he formed excuses, a banal lie about a long walk for inspiration, a moment of dizzy weariness, a stumble into a mud puddle.

'I'll make you some nice hot coffee, Eddie,' his mother-in-law offered.

'Please,' he responded, and went back to his own room with the slate mantlepiece. Again he lighted the candle, sat down and took up his pen.

His mind was embellishing the story inspiration that had come to him at such a black moment, in the cellar of the Gauber house. He'd work on that tomorrow. The *United States Saturday Post* would take it, he hoped. Title? He would call it simply 'The Black Cat'.

But to finish the present task! He dipped his pen in ink. How to begin? How to end? How, after writing and publishing such an account, to defend himself against the growing whisper of his insanity?

He decided to forget it, if he could – at least to seek healthy company, comfort, quiet – perhaps even to write some light verse, some humorous articles and stories. For the first time in his life, he had had enough of the macabre.

Quickly he wrote a final paragraph:

There are moments when, even to the sober eye of Reason, the world of our sad Humanity may assume the semblance of a Hell – but the imagination of man is no Carathis, to explore with impunity its every cavern. Alas! The grim legion of sepulchral terrors cannot be regarded as altogether fanciful – but, like the Demons in whose company Afrasiab made his voyage down the Oxus, they must sleep, or they will devour us – they must be suffered to slumber, or we will perish.

That would do for the public, decided Edgar Allan Poe. In any case, it would do for the Philadelphia *Dollar Newspaper*. His mother-in-law brought in the coffee.

Over the River

P. SCHUYLER MILLER

Of all the stories you will read in this collection, Over the
River *is probably the most extraordinary, the most gruesome
and the most unusual. It is, of course, a vampire story – but
told from the point of view of a vampire! In the pages that
follow you can put yourself in the position of a living dead
man; feel his need for blood, join him in the desperate search
for a victim, and live his terror of sunlight and the sign of the
cross.* Over the River *is certainly one of my all-time favourite
horror stories and it is a great pity that its skilled and imagina-
tive author has written so few other tales. I challenge anyone to
remain unmoved by this brilliant tale.*

THE shape of his body showed in the frozen mud, where he had
lain face down under the fallen tree. His footprints were sharp
in the melting snow, and his feet had left dark, wet blotches
where he had climbed the rock. He had lain there for a long
time. Long enough it was for time to have lost its meaning.

The moon was coming up over the nearer mountain, full and
white, etched across with the pattern of naked branches. Its
light fell on his upturned face, on his sunken, brilliant eyes and
the puffy blue of jowls on which the beard had started to grow,
then stopped. It shone down on the world of trees and rocks of
which he was a part, and gave it life.

The night was warm. In the valley the snow had long been
gone. Flowers were pushing up through the moist earth; frogs
were Pan-piping in every low spot; great trout stirred in the
deep pools of the river. It was May, but on the mountain, under
the north-facing ledges where the sun never came, the snow

was still banked deep with an edge of blue ice, and needles of frost glistened in the black mud of the forest floor.

It was May. All through the warm night, squadrons of birds were passing across the face of the moon. All night long their voices drifted down out of the dark like gossip from another world. But to a listener in the night another voice was clearer, louder, more insistent – now like the striking of crystal cymbals, now like an elfin chuckling, always a breathless, never-ending whisper – the voice of running water.

He heard none of these things. He stood where he had first come into the full moonlight, his face turned up to receive it, drinking in its brightness. It tingled in him like a draught from the things he had forgotten, in another world. It dissolved the dull ache of cold that was in his body and mind, that stiffened his swollen limbs, and lay like an icy nugget behind his eyes. It soaked into him, and into the world about him, so that every corner shone with its own pale light, white and vaporous, as far as he could see.

It was a strange world. What that other world had been like, before, he did not remember, but this was different. The moonlight flooded it with a pearly mist through which the columns of the trees rose like shadowy stalagmites. The light-mist was not from the moon alone; it was a part of this new world and of the things that were in it. The grey lichens under his feet were outlined with widening ripples of light. Light pulsed through the rough bark of the tree trunks and burned like tiny corpse-candles at the tip of every growing twig. The spruces and balsams were furred with silvery needles of light. A swirling mist of light hung ankle-deep over the forest floor, broken by black islands of rock. Light was in everything in this new world he was in, save only for the rock, and for himself.

He drank in the moonlight through every pore, and it burned gloriously in him and flowed down through every vein and bone of his body, driving out the dank cold that was in his flesh. But the light that soaked into him did not shine out again as it did from the budding trees, and the moss, and the lichens. He looked down at his swollen hands and flexed their puffed blue fingers; he moved his toes in their sodden boots, and felt the clammy touch of the wet rags that clung to his body. Under them, out of the moonlight, he was still cold with that pervading chill that was like the frozen breath of winter in him. He squatted in the pool of light that lay over the ledge and stripped them from him, clumsily and painfully, then lay back on the stone and stared up into the smiling visage of the moon.

Time passed, but whether it was minutes or hours, or whether there were still such things as minutes and hours, he could not have said. Time had no meaning for him in this new, strange world. Time passed, because the moon was higher and its light stronger and warmer on his naked flesh, but he did not sense its passage. Every part of the forest pulsed with its own inner light in response. As the feeling of warmth grew in him it brought another feeling, a dull hunger gnawing at his vitals, making him restless. He moved close to a great beech whose limbs reached high above the tops of the other trees around it, and felt the quick chill as its shadow fell across him. Then he had clasped it in both arms, his whole body pressing eagerly against its glowing trunk, and the light that welled out of it was thrilling through him like a flame, stirring every atom of him. He tweaked a long, pointed bud from a twig. It lay in his palm like a jewel of pale fire before he raised it to his mouth and felt its warmth spread into him.

He ate buds as long as he could find them, stripping them from the twigs with clumsy fingers, grubbing hungrily in the moss for the ones that fell. He crushed them between his teeth and swallowed them, and the fire that glowed in them spread into his chilled flesh and warmed it a little. He tore patches of lichen from the rock, but they were tough and woody and he could not swallow them. He broke off spruce twigs, needled with the life-light, but the resin in them burned his lips and tongue and choked him.

He sat, hunched against a rock, staring blindly into the growing depths of the forest. The things he had swallowed had helped a little to alleviate the cold that was in his bones, but they did not dull the gnawing hunger or the thirst that was torturing him. They had life, and the warmth that was life, but not the thing he needed – the thing he must somehow have.

At the edge of his field of vision something moved. It drifted noiselessly through the burning treetops, like a puff of luminous cloud. It settled on a branch above his head, and he twisted his neck back and stared up at it with hollow, burning eyes. The white light-mist was very bright about it. He could feel its warmth, even at this distance. And there was something more. The hunger gripped him, fiercer than ever, and thirst shrivelled his gullet.

The owl had seen him and decided that he was another rotting stump. It sat hunched against the trunk of the great spruce, looking and listening for its prey. Presently it was rewarded by some small sound or a wafted scent, and spread its silent wings to float like a phantom into the night. It did not see the mis-shapen thing, it had thought a stump, struggle to its feet and follow.

A porcupine, high in a birch, saw the owl pass and ignored it, as it well could. A roosting crow woke suddenly and froze on its perch, petrified with terror. But the great bird swept past, intent on other prey.

There were clearings in the forest, even this high, where trees had been cut off and brambles had followed. All manner of small creatures followed the brambles, and here was rich hunting for the owl and its kind.

He came to the edge of the clearing in time to see the owl strike and hear the scream of the hurt rabbit. To his eyes it was as though a bolt of shining fire had plunged through the night to strike a second ball of fire on the ground. Shambling forward, careless of the briars, he hurled himself on the two animals before the owl could free itself or take the air again.

The huge bird slashed at him savagely with beak and talons, laying open the puffy flesh of his face in great, curving gashes, but he bit deep into its breast, through feathers and skin, tearing at its flesh with his teeth and letting the hot, burning blood gush into his parched throat and spill over his cracked lips. His fingers kneaded and tore at its body, breaking it into bits that he could stuff into his mouth. Feathers and bone he spat out, and the rabbit's fur when the owl was gone, but the hollow in his belly was filled, and the thirst gone, and the aching cold in his numbed bones had been washed away. It seemed to him that his fingers were shining a little with the same wan light that emanated from the other things of the forest.

He hunted all that night, through the clearing and the nearby forest, and found and ate two wood mice and a handful of grubs and other insects. He found that the tightly coiled fiddleheads of growing ferns were full of life and more palatable than buds or lichens. As the deadening cold left him he could move more freely, think more keenly, but the thirst was growing on him again.

Out of the lost memories of that world he had left, the murmur of running water came to him. Water should quench thirst. He could hear it below him on the mountainside, through the mist, splashing over bare stones, gurgling through tunnels in the roots and moss. He heard it in the distance, far below in the valley, roaring against the boulders and leaping over ledges in foaming abandon. As he listened, a chill crept over him, as though a shadow were passing, but the feeling left him. Slowly and painfully he began to pick his way down the mountainside.

The water burst out at the base of a rock wall, lay for a little in a deep, clear pool under the cliff and then slipped away through the moss, twisting and turning, sliding over flat stones and diving into crevices, welling up in tiny, sparkling fountains and vanishing again under tangles of matted roots and fallen tree trunks, growing and running ever faster until it leaped over the last cliff and fell in a spatter of flashing drops into the valley. He saw it, and stopped.

Black vapour lay close over it like a carpet. It made a pathway of black, winding through the luminous mist that hung over the forest floor. Where the rill lay quiet in a pool it was thin, and the moonlight struck through and sparkled on the clear water, but where the little stream hurried over roots and stones, the black fog lay dense and impenetrable, dull and lifeless.

He licked his lips uneasily with his swollen tongue and moved cautiously forward. The chill had come on him again, numbing his nerves, dulling his labouring brain. Water quenched thirst; he still remembered that somehow, and this singing, shining stuff was water. At the base of the cliff, where the water welled up under the rock, the black fog was thinnest. He knelt and dipped his cupped hands into the water.

As the black mist closed over them, all feeling went out of his hands. Cold – terrible, numbing cold – ate its way like acid into his flesh and bones. The mist was draining the warmth – the life – out of him, through his hands and arms – sucking him dry of the life-stuff he had drunk with the owl's blood and soaked in from the moon's white rays. He swayed to his feet, then collapsed in a heap beside the stream.

He lay there helpless for a long time. Little by little the moonlight revived him. Little by little the numbness went out of his muscles, and he could move his legs and grip things with his fingers. He pulled his legs under him and got to his feet, leaning against the cliff for support. He stared with burning eyes at the water, and felt the first clutching at his gullet and the hunger gnawing in his vitals. Water was death to him. The black fog that lay close over running water was deadly, draining the life-force out of whatever touched it. It was death! But blood – fresh, burning, glowing blood was life!

Something rattled in the shadow of the cliff. His eyes found it – a lolloping bundle of fiery spines, humping along a worn path that led over the rocks to the little pool, a porcupine come to drink. He sensed the life in it, and hunger twisted his belly, but the black barrier of running water was between him and it.

It shambled down to the pool's edge and drank, the glow of its bristling body shining through the black fog over the water. It crossed the little rill where it was narrowest, below the pool, and came rattling up the path towards him, unafraid.

He killed it. His face and body were studded with quills before it was dead, but he tore open its body with his two numb hands and let its hot blood swill down his throat and give him back the warmth and life that the black mist had drained out of him. Blood was all he needed – he had learned that – and he left the porcupine's limp carcass by the path and turned back into the forest.

Water was everywhere, here on the lower slopes of the mountain. Its black runways ribbed the glowing floor of the forest on every side. It made a wall of cold about the place where he was, so that he had to climb back to the summit of the ridge and go around its sources.

The sun rose, bringing a scathing golden light that shrivelled his pallid flesh, and brought the thirst up unbearably in his throat, driving him to the shelter of a cave. Blood would quench that awful, growing thirst, and drive out the cold that crept relentlessly over him, but it was hard to find blood. Other things would kill the cold – buds and growing things – but they could not quench the thirst or appease the savage hunger in him.

There was another night, at last, and he stood in the bright light of the shrinking moon high on a bare spur overlooking the valley. All the world lay before him, washed in silver and lined with black. He could see mountain after mountain, furred with the light of growing trees, blanketed in the glowing mist, their bald black crowns outlined against the moonlit clouds. He could see the mountain torrents streaking down their flanks, like inky ribbons, joining, broadening, flowing down to join the river that roared sullenly under its black shroud in the valley at his feet.

The valley was full of life. It was alive with growing things, and the white mist that rose from them and clothed them filled it in the brim with a broth of light through which the river and its tributaries cut sharp black lines of cold. There were other lights – yellow constellations of lamplight scattered over the silver meadows. Many of them clustered at the mouth of the valley, where the mountains drew apart, but they grew fewer and fewer as they followed the black barrier of the river, and at the head of the valley below him one glowing spark burned alone.

He stood with the moonlight washing his naked, dead-white body, staring at that speck of golden light. There was something he should know about it – something that was hidden in that other world he had been in. There was something that drew him to it – an invisible thread, stretched across space through the white night, binding him to it.

The next day he lay buried under a rotting log, halfway down the mountain. The following night, soon after moon-up, he came on a doe, its back broken, pinned under a fallen tree. He tore its throat out and drank the fuming blood that poured heat and life through his body, waking him, filling him with vigour. The cold was gone, and he was sure now that his fingers were glowing with a light of their own. Now he was really alive!

He followed a ridge, and before sunrise he came to the river's edge. The blackness was an impenetrable wall, hiding the other shore. Through it he could hear the rush of running water over gravel, the gurgle of eddies and the mutter of rapids. The sound tormented him and brought the thirst back into his throat, but he drew back into the forest, for the sky was already brightening in the east.

When the moon rose on the fourth night he had found nothing to eat. Its light brought him down out of the forest again, to the river's edge, where it broaded into a quiet mill-pond. The black fog was thin over the glassy surface of the water, and through it he saw the yellow lamplight of the house that had drawn him down from the mountain.

He stood waist-deep in the weeds that bordered the pond, watching those two yellow rectangles. Back in the icy blankness of his mind a memory was struggling to be known. But it belonged to the other world, the world he had left behind, and it faded.

The reflection of the lights lay in the still water of the pond. So still was it that the mist was but a black gauze drawn across the lamplight, dulling it. The water lay like a sheet of black glass, hard and polished, with the phantoms of the pines on its other bank growing upside-down in its quiet depths. The stars were reflected there in little winking spots, and the dwindling circle of the moon.

He did not hear the door slam, there among the pines. A new feeling was growing in him. It was strange. It was not thirst – not hunger. It submerged them in its all-powerful compulsion. It gripped his muscles and took them out of his control, forcing him step by step through the cat-tails to the river's edge. There was something he must do. Something——

She came out of the shadows and stood in the moonlight on the other bank, looking up at the moon. The lamplight was behind her and the silver torrent of the moon, poured over her slim, white body, over her shining black hair, caressing every line and curve of her long, slim figure. Her own light clung to her like a silver aura, soft and warm, welling out of her white skin and clinging lovingly about her, cloaking her beauty with light. That beauty drew him – out of the shadows, out of the forest, into the moonlight.

She did not see him at first. The night was warm and there was the first perfume of spring in the air. She stood on a rock at the water's edge, her arms lifted, her hands clasping her flood of night-black hair behind her head. All her young body was taut, stretching, welcoming the moonlight and the touch of the night breeze that sent little cat-paws shivering over the glassy water. The moon seemed to be floating in the water, there just beyond her reach. She knotted her hair in a bun behind her head and stepped down quickly into the water. She stood with it just above her knees, watching the ripples widen and break the mirror surface of the pond. She followed their spread across that glassy disc.

She saw him.

He stood there, his face half in shadow, hunched and naked. His arms were skeleton's arms and his ribs showed under skin that hung in flabby white folds from his shoulders. His eyes were black pits and a stubble of black beard was smeared across his sagging cheeks. The mark of the owl's claws was across his face and it was pocked with purple blotches where he had pulled out the porcupine quills. Some of them were still in his side, where the beast's tail had lashed him. His flesh was livid white in the moonlight, blotched and smeared with the dark stain of death.

She saw him and knew him. Her hand went to the little cross that glowed like a coal of hidden fire in the hollow of her throat. Her voice rose and choked back:

'Joe! *Joe!*'

He saw her and remembered her. The thread he had felt on the mountain had been her presence, pulling him to her, stronger than thirst or hunger, stronger than death, stronger even than the black fog over the river. It was between them now, tightening, dragging him step by step into the silent water.

Ripples broke against his legs and he felt the black mist rising from them, felt the numbness creeping into his feet, into his legs, up into his body. It was a day since he had killed the deer and had blood to warm him. He could not go on. He stood knee-deep, staring at her across the little space that separated them. He tried to speak, to call her name, but he had forgotten words.

Then she screamed and ran, a stream of white fire through the shadows, and he heard the house door slam after her and saw the shades come down, one after the other, over the yellow lamplight. He stood there, staring after her, until the cold crept up and began to choke him, and he turned and stumbled painfully ashore.

The moon found him high on the mountain, climbing from ledge to ledge, above the sources of the rushing torrents that walled him in, making his way towards the saddle that closed the valley's end. He could not cross running water, but he could go around it. He killed a rabbit and its blood helped him to go on, with the cold seeping up through his bones and hunger and thirst tearing at him like wild things. The new hunger, the yearning that drew him to the girl in the valley, was stronger than they. It was all that mattered now.

The moon was still in the sky when he stood under the pines before the closed door of the house. Half the night was gone, and clouds were gathering, filling up the sky and strewing long streamers across the moon's shrunken face. In the east thunder muttered, rolling among the mountains until it died away beneath the sound of the river.

The tie that was between them was like a rope of iron, pulling him across the narrow clearing to the doorstep of the house. The door was closed and the shades drawn over the windows on either side of it, but yellow lamplight streamed out through cracks in its weathered panels. He raised a hand to touch it and drew back as he saw the pattern of crossed planks that barred him and his kind.

He whimpered low in his throat, like the doe he had killed. The cross wove a steel net across the doorway that he could not break. He stepped back, off the doorstep. Then the door opened. She stood there.

Her back was to the light and he could see only the slim silhouette of her body, with the cross of golden fire at her throat and the aura of silvery mist clinging about her, so warm and bright that he was sure it must drown out the moonlight. Even through the dress she wore the fire of her young vitality shone out. He stood bathing in it, yearning for it, as the hunger and thirst and aching longing welled up in him through the bitter cold.

It was a minute perhaps, or five minutes, or only seconds until she spoke. Her voice was faint.

'Joe,' she said. 'Joe dear. You're hurt. Come inside.'

The pattern of the cross on the door could not bar him after her welcome. He felt the barrier dissolve as he stepped through. The clouds had drawn away and the moon made a bright spot through the open door. He stood in it, watching her, seeing the familiar room with its scrubbed board floor, its plastered walls, its neat, black stove – seeing them as if for the first time. They stirred no memory in him. But the girl drew him.

He saw her dark eyes blacken with horror and the blood drain out of her cheeks and lips as she saw him for the first time in the lamplight. He looked down at his hands – the flesh cheese-white and sloughing – at his naked, discoloured body, smeared with mud and stained with spilled blood. He whimpered, down in his throat, and took a stumbling step towards her, but her hand went up to the little crucifix at her throat and she slipped quickly around the table, placing it between them.

He stared at the cross. The golden fire that burned in it separated them as surely as the cold black fog of running water had done. Across the table he could feel its pure radiance, hot as sunlight. It would shrivel him to a cinder. He whined again, in agony, like a whipped dog. The longing for her was sheer torment now, drowning out all else, but it could not force him nearer.

The girl followed his gaze. The crucifix had been his gift – before – in that other world. She knew that, though he did not. Slowly she unfastened the ribbon that held it and dropped it into his outstretched hand.

The cross burned into his flesh like a hot coal. He snatched back his hand but the burning metal clung. He felt the heat of it coursing up his arm, and hurled it savagely across the room. He seized the table with both hands and flung it out of his way. Then she was before him, her back against the wall, her face a mask of horror. He heard her scream.

In him the terrible yearning that had drawn him down from the mountain had submerged the hunger and thirst and cold that had been his only driving forces before he knew her. Now, as they stood face to face, the older, stronger forces surged up in him and took possession of his numbed mind. With her scream a dam in him seemed to burst. He felt her warm, slim body twisting and jerking under his tightening fingers. He sensed the fragrance that rose from her. He saw her eyes, mad with fear, staring into his.

When it was over the hunger was gone, and the thirst. The cold had gone out of his bones. His muscles were no longer cramped and leaden. The yearning was gone, too. He looked down incuriously at the heap of shredded rags on the floor and turned to go.

At that moment the storm broke. The door was still open, and as he turned it seemed to be closed by a curtain of falling water. The black fog swirled among the raindrops, blotting out the world. He thrust out an exploring hand, marked with the charred brand of the cross, and snatched it back as he felt the chill of the mist.

He heard their voices only a moment before they stood there

– three men, dripping, crowded together in the doorway, staring at the thing on the floor – and at him. For a flicker he remembered: Louis – her brother – and Jean and old Paul. The dogs were with them, but they slunk back, whining, afraid.

Louis knew him, as his sister had – as the others did. His whisper had hate in it as much as fear. It was on all their faces. They knew the curse that was on the unshriven of Joe Labatie's blood. They had known what it meant when he did not come down from the mountain on the night of the first storm. But only Louis, of them all, had seen the tree topple and pin him down. Louis it was who had made the mark of the cross in the snow that drifted over him and left him there. Louis Larue, who would not see the Labatie curse fall on his sister or her children after her.

It was old Paul whose gun bellowed. They saw the buckshot tear through that death-white body – saw the dark fluid that dripped from the awful wound – saw the dead thing that was Joe Labatie, his skull's eyes burning, as he surged towards them. They ran.

Louis held his ground, but the thing that rushed upon him was like a charging bear. It struck him and hurled him to the floor. Its slippery fingers bit into his shoulders; its hideous face hung close to his. But the crucifix at his throat saved him, as it might have saved her, and the thing recoiled and plunged out into the storm.

The rain was like ice on his naked body as he fled, rinsing the strength out of him as it might dissolve salt. The black mist filled the forest, blotting out the silver light of its living things. It closed over his body and sank into it, sucking out the unnatural life he had drunk in blood, draining it of warmth. He felt the great cold growing in him again. The moon was gone, and he was blind – cold and numb and blind. He crashed into a tree, and then another, and then his weakening legs buckled under him and he fell face down at the river's edge.

He lay in the running water, shrouded in the black fog, feeling them approach. He heard their footsteps on the gravel, and felt their hands on him, dragging him out of the water, turning him over. He saw them – three pillars of white light, the yellow fire of their crucifixes at their throats, the black mist billowing around their bodies as they stood staring down at him. He felt Louis' boot as it swung brutally into his side and felt the bones snap and the flesh tear, but there was no pain – only the cold, the bitter, freezing cold that was always in him.

He knew that they were busy at something, but the cold was creeping up into his brain, behind his eyes, as the rain wrapped him in its deadly mist. Perhaps when the moon rose again its light would revive him. Perhaps he would kill again and feel the hot blood in his throat, and be free of the cold. He could barely see now, though his eyes were open and staring. He could see that old Paul had a long stake of wood in his hands, sharpened to a point. He saw Louis take it and raise it in both hands above his head. He saw Louis' teeth shine white in a savage grin.

He saw the stake sweep down——

Drink My Blood

RICHARD MATHESON

Probably the most famous – and certainly the most brilliant – vampire novel of recent years is Richard Matheson's I Am Legend. This fiendishly convincing tale is set in the year 1976 and describes the experiences of the one man still untouched in a world overrun by vampires. Since its publication in 1954, I Am Legend has achieved almost classic stature and assured its author a permanent place in the front rank of horror writers. This story which I have selected for my anthology predates Legend by some three years, but clearly illustrates Mr Matheson's fascination with the vampire. It may well make every parent take a second look at their children for similar signs to those which make Jules such a strange boy....

THE people on the block decided definitely that Jules was crazy when they heard about his composition.

There had been suspicions for a long time.

He made people shiver with his blank stare. His coarse guttural tongue sounded unnatural in his frail body. The paleness of his skin upset many children. It seemed to hang loose around his flesh. He hated sunlight.

And his ideas were a little out of place for the people who lived on the block.

Jules wanted to be a vampire.

People declared it common knowledge that he was born on a night when winds uprooted trees. They said he was born with three teeth. They said he'd used them to fasten himself on his mother's breast drawing blood with the milk.

They said he used to cackle and bark in his crib after dark.

They said he walked at two months and sat staring at the moon whenever it shone.

Those were things that people said.

His parents were always worried about him. An only child, they noticed his flaws quickly.

They thought he was blind until the doctor told them it was just a vacuous stare. He told them that Jules, with his largehead might be a genius or an idiot. It turned out he was an idiot.

He never spoke a word until he was five. Then one night coming up to supper, he sat down at the table and said, 'Death.'

His parents were torn between delight and disgust. They finally settled for a place in between the two feelings. They decided that Jules couldn't have realised what the word meant.

But Jules did.

From that night on, he built up such a large vocabulary that everyone who knew him was astonished. He not only acquired every word spoken to him, words from signs, magazines, books; he made up his own words.

Like nighttouch. Or killove. They were really several words that melted into each other. They said things Jules felt but couldn't explain with other words.

He used to sit on the porch while the other children played hop-scotch, stickball and other games. He sat there and stared at the sidewalk and made up words.

Until he was twelve Jules kept pretty much out of trouble. Of course there was the time they found him undressing Olive Jones in an alley. And another time he was discovered dissecting a kitten on his bed.

But there were many years in between. Those scandals were forgotten.

In general he went through childhood merely disgusting people.

He went to school but never studied. He spent about two or three terms in each grade. The teachers all knew him by his first name. In some subjects like reading and writing he was almost brilliant.

In others he was hopeless.

One Saturday when he was twelve, Jules went to the movies. He saw *Dracula*.

When the show was over he walked, a throbbing nerve mass, through the little girl and boy ranks.

He went home and locked himself in the bathroom for two hours.

His parents pounded on the door and threatened but he wouldn't come out.

Finally he unlocked the door and sat down at the supper table. He had a bandage on his thumb and a satisfied look on his face.

The morning after he went to the library. It was Sunday. He sat on the steps all day waiting for it to open. Finally he went home.

The next morning he came back instead of going to school.

He found *Dracula* on the shelves. He couldn't borrow it because he wasn't a member and to be a member he had to bring in one of his parents.

So he stuck the book down his pants and left the library and never brought it back.

He went to the park and sat down and read the book through. It was late evening before he finished.

He started at the beginning again, reading as he ran from street light to street light, all the way home.

He didn't hear a word of the scolding he got for missing lunch and supper. He ate, went in his room and read the book to the finish. They asked him where he got the book. He said he found it.

As the days passed Jules read the story over and over. He never went to school.

Late at night, when he had fallen into an exhausted slumber, his mother used to take the book into the living-room and show it to her husband.

One night they noticed that Jules had underlined certain sentences with dark shaky pencil lines.

Like: 'The lips were crimson with fresh blood and the stream had trickled over her chin and stained the purity of her lawn death robe.'

Or: 'When the blood began to spurt out, he took my hands in one of his, holding them tight and, with the other seized my neck and pressed my mouth to the wound. . . .'

When his mother saw this, she threw the book down the garbage chute.

The next morning when Jules found the book missing he screamed and twisted his mother's arm until she told him where the book was.

Then he ran down to the cellar and dug in the piles of garbage until he found the book.

Coffee grounds and egg yolk on his hands and wrists, he went to the park and read it again.

For a month he read the book avidly. Then he knew it so well he threw it away and just thought about it.

Absence notes were coming from school. His mother yelled. Jules decided to go back for a while.

He wanted to write a composition.

One day he wrote it in class. When everyone was finished writing, the teacher asked if anyone wanted to read their compositions to the class.

Jules raised his hand.

The teacher was surprised. But she felt charity. She wanted to encourage him. She drew in her tiny jab of a chin and smiled.

'All right,' she said, 'pay attention, children. Jules is going to read us his composition.'

Jules stood up. He was excited. The paper shook in his hands.

'My Ambition by . . .'

'Come to the front of the class, Jules, dear.'

Jules went to the front of the class. The teacher smiled lovingly. Jules started again.

'My Ambition by Jules Dracula.'

The smile sagged.

'When I grow up I want to be a vampire.'

The teacher's smiling lips jerked down and out. Her eyes popped wide.

'I want to live forever and get even with everybody and make all the girls vampires. I want to smell of death.'

'Jules!'

'I want to have a foul breath that stinks of dead earth and crypts and sweet coffins.'

The teacher shuddered. Her hands twitched on her green blotter. She couldn't believe her ears. She looked at the children. They were gaping. Some of them were giggling. But not the girls.

'I want to be all cold and have rotten flesh with stolen blood in the veins.'

'That will . . . hrrumph!'

The teacher cleared her throat mightily.

'That will be all, Jules,' she said.

Jules talked louder and desperately.

'I want to sink my terrible white teeth in my victims' necks. I want them to . . .'

'Jules! Go to your seat this instant!'

'I want them to slide like razors in the flesh and into the veins,' read Jules ferociously.

The teacher jolted to her feet. Children were shivering. None of them were giggling.

'Then I want to draw my teeth out and let the blood flow easy in my mouth and run hot in my throat and . . .'

The teacher grabbed his arm. Jules tore away and ran to a corner. Barricaded behind a stool he yelled:

166

'And drip off my tongue and run out of my lips down my victim's throats! I want to drink girls' blood!'

The teacher lunged for him. She dragged him out of the corner. He clawed at her and screamed all the way to the door and the principal's office.

'That is my ambition! That is my ambition! That is my ambition!'

It was grim.

Jules was locked in his room. The teacher and the principal sat with Jules' parents. They were talking in sepulchral voices.

They were recounting the scene.

All along the block parents were discussing it. Most of them didn't believe it at first. They thought their children made it up.

Then they thought what horrible children they'd raised if the children could make up such things.

So they believed it.

After that everyone watched Jules like a hawk. People avoided his touch and look. Parents pulled their children off the street when he approached. Everyone whispered tales of him.

There were more absence notes.

Jules told his mother he wasn't going to school any more. Nothing would change his mind. He never went again.

When a truant officer came to the apartment Jules would run over the roofs until he was far away from there.

A year wasted by.

Jules wandered the streets searching for something; he didn't know what. He looked in alleys. He looked in garbage cans. He looked in lots. He looked on the east side and the west side and in the middle.

He couldn't find what he wanted.

He rarely slept. He never spoke. He stared down all the time. He forgot his special words.

Then.

One day in the park, Jules strolled through the zoo.

An electric shock passed through him when he saw the vampire bat.

His eyes grew wide and his discoloured teeth shone dully in a wide smile.

From that day on, Jules went daily to the zoo and looked at the bat. He spoke to it and called it the Count. He felt in his heart it was really a man who had changed.

A rebirth of culture struck him.

He stole another book from the library. It told all about wild life.

He found the page on the vampire bat. He tore it out and threw the book away.

He learned the section by heart.

He knew how the bat made its wound. How it lapped up the blood like a kitten drinking cream. How it walked on folded wing stalks and hind legs like a black furry spider. Why it took no nourishment but blood.

Month after month Jules stared at the bat and talked to it. It became the one comfort in his life. The one symbol of dreams come true.

One day Jules noticed that the bottom of the wire covering the cage had come loose.

He looked around, his black eyes shifting. He didn't see anyone looking. It was a cloudy day. Not many people were there.

Jules tugged at the wire.

It moved a little.

Then he saw a man come out of the monkey house. So he pulled back his hand and strolled away whistling a song he had just made up.

Late at night, when he was supposed to be asleep he would walk barefoot past his parents' room. He would hear his father and mother snoring. He would hurry out, put on his shoes and run to the zoo.

Every time the watchman was not around, Jules would tug at the wiring.

He kept on pulling it loose.

When he had finished and had to run home, he pushed the wire in again. Then no one could tell.

All day Jules would stand in front of the cage and look at the Count and chuckle and tell him he'd soon be free again.

He told the Count all the things he knew. He told the Count he was going to practise climbing down walls head first.

He told the Count not to worry. He'd soon be out. Then, together, they could go all around and drink girls' blood.

One night Jules pulled the wire out and crawled under it into the cage.

It was very dark.

He crept on his knees to the little wooden house. He listened to see if he could hear the Count squeaking.

He stuck his arm in the black doorway. He kept whispering.

He jumped when he felt a needle jab in his finger.

With a look of great pleasure on his thin face, Jules drew the fluttering hairy bat to him.

He climbed down from the cage with it and ran out of the zoo; out of the park. He ran down the silent streets.

It was getting late in the morning. Light touched the dark skies with grey. He couldn't go home. He had to have a place.

He went down an alley and climbed over a fence. He held tight to the bat. It lapped at the dribble of blood from his finger.

He went across a yard and into a little deserted shack.

It was dark inside and damp. It was full of rubble and tin cans and soggy cardboard and excrement.

Jules made sure there was no way the bat could escape.

Then he pulled the door tight and put a stick through the metal loop.

He felt his heart beating hard and his limbs trembling.

He let go of the bat. It flew to a dark corner and hung on the wood.

Jules feverishly tore off his shirt. His lips shook. He smiled a crazy smile.

He reached down into his pants pocket and took out a little penknife he had stolen from his mother.

He opened it and ran a finger over the blade. It sliced through the flesh.

With shaking fingers he jabbed at his throat. He hacked. The blood ran through his fingers.

'Count! Count!' he cried in frenzied joy. 'Drink my red blood! Drink me! Drink me!'

He stumbled over the tin cans and slipped and felt for the bat. It sprang from the wood and soared across the shack and fastened itself on the other side.

Tears ran down Jules' cheeks.

He gritted his teeth. The blood ran across his shoulders and across his thin hairless chest.

His body shook in fever. He staggered back towards the other side. He tripped and felt his side torn open on the sharp edge of a tin can.

His hands went out. They clutched the bat. He placed it against his throat. He sank on his back on the cool wet earth. He sighed.

He started to moan and clutch at his chest. His stomach heaved. The black bat on his neck silently lapped his blood.

Jules felt his life seeping away.

He thought of all the years past. The waiting. His parents. School. Dracula. Dreams. For this. This sudden glory.

Jules's eyes flickered open.

The side of the reeking shack swam about him.

It was hard to breathe. He opened his mouth to gasp in the air. He sucked it in. It was foul. It made him cough. His skinny body lurched on the cold ground.

Mists crept away in his brain.

One by one like drawn veils.

Suddenly his mind was filled with terrible clarity.

He knew he was lying half-naked on garbage and letting a flying bat drink his blood.

With a strangled cry, he reached up and tore away the furry throbbing bat. He flung it away from him. It came back fanning his face with its vibrating wings.

Jules staggered to his feet.

He felt for the door. He could hardly see. He tried to stop his throat from bleeding so.

He managed to get the door open.

Then, lurching into the dark yard, he fell on his face in the long grass blades.

He tried to call out for help.

But no sounds save a bubbling mockery of words came from his lips.

He heard the fluttering wings.

Then, suddenly they were gone.

Strong fingers lifted him gently. Through dying eyes Jules saw the tall dark man whose eyes shone like rubies.

'My son,' the man said.

Pillar of Fire

RAY BRADBURY

Ray Bradbury has become to the horror story fan of today something of a latter-day Edgar Allan Poe. He unquestionably leads the field and displays an inventiveness that even the great Poe could hardly have failed to admire. It is not surprising, therefore, to discover how very difficult it is to obtain a story by Bradbury which has not already been anthologised. Busy as he always is on a new film, play or novel, Ray took time off to send me the following tale which has never been published in England before. He calls it a 'special – in-a-way-vampire-but-not-vampire story'. To even hint at its flavour would be to rob you of some of the totally unique ingredients which make this a highpoint not only of this book but also of the entire vampire story genre.

HE came out of the earth, hating. Hate was his father; hate was his mother.

It was good to walk again. It was good to leap up out of the earth, off of your back, and stretch your cramped arms violently and try to take a deep breath!

He *tried*. He cried out.

He couldn't breathe. He flung his arms over his face and tried to breathe. It was impossible. He walked on the earth, he came out of the earth. But he was dead. He couldn't breathe. He could take air into his mouth and force it half down his throat, with withered moves of long-dormant muscles, wildly, wildly! And with this little air he could shout and cry! He wanted to have tears, but he couldn't make them come, either. All he knew was that he was standing upright, he was dead, he shouldn't be walking! He couldn't breathe and yet he stood.

The smells of the world were all about him. Frustratedly, he tried to smell the smells of autumn. Autumn was burning the land down into ruin. All across the country the ruins of summer lay; vast forests bloomed with flame, tumbled down timber on empty, unleafed timber. The smoke of the burning was rich, blue, and invisible.

He stood in the graveyard, hating. He walked through the world and yet could not taste nor smell of it. He heard, yes. The wind roared on his newly opened ears. But he was dead. Even though he walked he knew he was dead and should expect not too much of himself or this hateful living world.

He touched the tombstone over his own empty grave. He knew his own name again. It was a good job of carving.

WILLIAM LANTRY

That's what the gravestone said.
His fingers trembled on the cool stone surface.

BORN 1898 – DIED 1933

Born *again* . . .?

What year? He glared at the sky and the midnight autumnal stars moving in slow illuminations across the windy black. He read the tiltings of centuries in those stars. Orion thus and so, Aurega here! and where Taurus? *There!*

His eyes narrowed. His lips spelled out the year:

'2349.'

An odd number. Like a school sum. They used to say a man couldn't encompass any number over a hundred. After that it was all so damned abstract there was no use counting. This was the year 2349! A numeral, a sum. And here he was, a man who had lain in his hateful dark coffin, hating to be buried, hating the living people above who lived and lived and lived, hating them for all the centuries, until today, now, born out of hatred, he stood by his own freshly excavated grave, the smell of raw earth in the air, perhaps, but he could not smell it!

'I,' he said, addressing a poplar tree that was shaken by the wind, 'am an anachronism.' He smiled faintly.

He looked at the graveyard. It was cold and empty. All of the stones had been ripped up and piled like so many flat bricks, one atop another, in the far corner by the wrought iron fence. This had been going on for two endless weeks. In his deep secret coffin he had heard the heartless, wild stirring as the men jabbed the earth with cold spades and tore out the coffins and carried away the withered ancient bodies to be burned. Twisting with fear in his coffin, he had waited for them to come to him.

Today they had arrived at his coffin. But – late. They had dug down to within an inch of the lid. Five o'clock bell, time for quitting. Home to supper. The workers had gone off. Tomorrow they would finish the job, they said, shrugging into their coats.

Silence had come to the emptied tomb-yard.

Carefully, quietly, with a soft rattling of sod, the coffin lid had lifted.

William Lantry stood trembling now, in the last cemetery on Earth.

'Remember?' he asked himself, looking at the raw earth. 'Remember those stories of the last man on earth? Those stories of men wandering in ruins, alone? Well you, William Lantry, are a switch on the old story. Do you *know* that? You are the last *dead* man in the whole damned world!'

There were no more dead people. Nowhere in any land was there a dead person. Impossible? Lantry did not smile at this. No, not impossible at all in this foolish, sterile, unimaginative, antiseptic age of cleansings and scientific methods! People died, oh my god, yes. But – *dead* people? Corpses? They didn't exist!

What *happened* to dead people?

The graveyard was on a hill. William Lantry walked through the dark burning night until he reached the edge of the graveyard and looked down upon the new town of Salem. It was all illumination, all colour. Rocket ships cut fire above it, crossing the sky to all far ports of earth.

In his grave the new violence of this future world had driven down and seeped into William Lantry. He had been bathed in it for years. He knew all about it, with a hating dead man's knowledge of such things.

Most important of all, he knew what these fools did with dead men.

He lifted his eyes. In the centre of the town a massive stone finger pointed at the stars. It was three hundred feet high and fifty feet across. There was a wide entrance and a drive in front of it.

In the town, theoretically, thought William Lantry, say you have a dying man. In a moment he will be dead. What happens? No sooner is his pulse cold than a certificate is flourished, made out, his relatives pack him into a car-beetle and drive him swiftly to——

The Incinerator!

That functional finger, that Pillar of Fire pointing at the stars. Incinerator. A functional, terrible name. But truth is truth in this future world.

Like a stick of kindling your Mr Dead Man is shot into the furnace.

Flume!

William Lantry looked at the top of the gigantic pistol shoving at the stars. A small pennant of smoke issued from the top.

There's where your dead people go.

'Take care of yourself, William Lantry,' he murmured. 'You're the last one, the rare item, the last dead man. All the other graveyards of earth have been blasted up. This is the last graveyard and you're the last dead man from the centuries. These people don't believe in having dead people about, much less walking dead people. Everything that can't be used goes up like a matchstick. Superstitions right along with it!'

He looked at the town. All right, he thought, quietly. I hate you. You hate me, or you *would* if you knew I existed. You don't believe in such things as vampires or ghosts. Labels without referents, you cry! You snort. All right, snort! Frankly, I don't believe in *you*, either! I don't *like* you! You and your Incinerators.

He trembled. How very close it had been. Day after day they had hauled out the other dead ones, burned them like so much kindling. An edict had been broadcast around the world. He had heard the digging men talk as they worked!

'I guess it's a good idea, this cleaning up the graveyards,' said one of the men.

'Guess so,' said another. 'Grisly custom. Can you imagine? Being buried, I mean! Unhealthy! All them germs!'

'Sort of a shame. Romantic, kind of. I mean, leaving just this one graveyard untouched all these centuries. The other graveyards were cleaned out, what year was it, Jim?'

'About 2260, I think. Yeah, that was it, 2260, almost a hundred years ago. But some Salem Committee they got on their high horse and they said, "Look here, let's have just *one* graveyard left, to remind us of the customs of the barbarians." And the gover'ment scratched its head, thunk it over, and said, "Okay. Salem it is. But all other graveyards go, you understand, all!"'

'And away they went,' said Jim.

'Sure, they sucked out 'em with fire and steam shovels and rocket-cleaners. If they knew a man was buried in a cow-

176

pasture, they fixed him! Evacuated them, they did. Sort of cruel, I say.'

'I hate to sound old-fashioned, but still there were a lot of tourists came here every year, just to see what a real graveyard was like.'

'Right. We had nearly a million people in the last three years visiting. A good revenue. But – a government order is an order. The government says no more morbidity, so flush her out we do! Here we go. Hand me that spade, Bill.'

William Lantry stood in the autumn wind, on the hill. It was good to walk again, to feel the wind and to hear the leaves scuttling like mice on the road ahead of him. It was good to see the bitter cold stars almost blown away by the wind.

It was even good to know fear again.

For fear rose in him now, and he could not put it away. The very fact that he was walking made him an enemy. And there was not another friend, another dead man, in all of the world, to whom one could turn for help or consolation. It was the whole melodramatic living world against one William Lantry. It was the whole vampire-disbelieving, body-burning, graveyard-annihilating world against a man in a dark suit on a dark autumn hill. He put out his pale cold hands into the city illumination. You have pulled the tombstones, like teeth, from the yard, he thought. Now I will find some way to push your damnable Incinerators down into rubble. I will make dead people again, and I will make friends in so doing. I cannot be alone and lonely. I must start manufacturing friends very soon. Tonight.

'War is declared,' he said, and laughed. It was pretty silly, one man declaring war on an entire world.

The world did not answer back. A rocket crossed the sky on a rush of flame, like an Incinerator taking wing.

Footsteps. Lantry hastened to the edge of the cemetery. The diggers, coming back to finish up their work? No. Just someone, a man, walking by.

As the man came abreast the cemetery gate, Lantry stepped swiftly out. 'Good evening,' said the man, smiling.

Lantry struck the man in the face. The man fell. Lantry bent quietly down and hit the man a killing blow across the neck with the side of his hand.

Dragging the body back into shadow, he stripped it, changed clothes with it. It wouldn't do for a fellow to go wandering about this future world with ancient clothing on. He found a small pocket knife in the man's coat; not much of a knife, but enough if you knew how to handle it properly. He knew how.

He rolled the body down into one of the already opened and exhumed graves. In a minute he had shovelled dirt down upon it, just enough to hide it. There was little chance of it being found. They wouldn't dig the same grave twice.

He adjusted himself in his new loose-fitting metallic suit. Fine, fine.

Hating, William Lantry walked down into town, to do battle with the Earth.

II

The Incinerator was open. It never closed. There was a wide entrance, all lighted up with hidden illumination, there was a helicopter landing table and a beetle drive. The town itself was dying down after another day of the dynamo. The lights were going dim, and the only quiet, lighted spot in the town now was the Incinerator. God, what a practical name, what an unromantic name.

William Lantry entered the wide, well-lighted door. It was an entrance, really; there were no doors to open or shut. People could go in and out, summer or winter, the inside was always warm. Warm from the fire that rushed whispering up the high round flue to where the whirlers, the propellers, the air-jets pushed the leafy grey ashes on away for a ten mile ride down the sky.

There was the warmth of the bakery here. The halls were floored with rubber parquet. You couldn't make a noise if you wanted to. Music played in hidden throats somewhere. Not music of death at all, but music of life and the way the sun lived inside the Incinerator; or the sun's brother, anyway. You could hear the flame floating inside the heavy brick wall.

William Lantry descended a ramp. Behind him he heard a whisper and turned in time to see a beetle stop before the entrance way. A bell rang. The music, as if at a signal, rose to ecstatic heights. There was joy in it.

From the beetle, which opened from the rear, some attendants stepped carrying a golden box. It was six feet long and there were sun symbols on it. From another beetle the relatives of the man in the box stepped and followed as the attendants took the golden box down a ramp to a kind of altar. On the side of the altar were the words, 'WE THAT WERE BORN OF THE SUN RETURN TO THE SUN'. The golden box was deposited upon the altar, the music leaped upward, the Guardian of this place spoke only a few words, then the attendants picked up the golden box, walked to a transparent wall, a safety lock also transparent, and opened it. The box was shoved into the glass slot. A moment later an inner lock opened, the box was injected into the interior of the flue and vanished instantly in quick flame.

The attendants walked away. The relatives without a word turned and walked out. The music played.

William Lantry approached the glass fire lock. He peered through the wall at the vast, glowing, never-ceasing heart of the Incinerator. It burned steadily without a flicker, singing to itself peacefully. It was so solid it was like a golden river flowing up out of the earth towards the sky. Anything you put into the river was borne upwards, vanished.

Lantry felt again his unreasoning hatred of this thing, this monster, cleansing fire.

A man stood at his elbow. 'May I help you, sir?'

'What?' Lantry turned abruptly. 'What did you say?'

'May I be of service?'

'I – that is——' Lantry looked quickly at the ramp and the door. His hands trembled at his sides. 'I've never been in here before.'

'Never?' The Attendant was surprised.

That had been the wrong thing to say, Lantry realised. But it was said, nevertheless. 'I mean,' he said. 'Not really. I mean, when you're a child, somehow, you don't pay attention. I suddenly realised tonight that I didn't really *know* the Incinerator.'

The Attendant smiled. 'We never know anything, do we, really? I'll be glad to show you around.'

'Oh, no. Never mind. It – it's a wonderful place.'

'Yes, it is.' The Attendant took pride in it. 'One of the finest in the world, I think.'

'I——' Lantry felt he must explain further. 'I haven't had many relatives die on me since I was a child. In fact, none. So, you see I haven't been here for many years.'

'I see.' The Attendant's face seemed to darken somewhat.

What've I said now, thought Lantry. What in God's name is wrong? What've I done? If I'm not careful I'll get myself shoved right into that damnable fire trap. What's wrong with this fellow's face? He seems to be giving me more than the usual going over.

'You wouldn't be one of the men who've just returned from Mars, would you?' asked the Attendant.

'No. Why do you ask?'

'No matter.' The Attendant began to walk off. 'If you want to know anything, just ask me.'

'Just one thing,' said Lantry.

'What's that?'

'This.'

Lantry dealt him a stunning blow across the neck.

He had watched the fire-trap operator with expert eyes. Now, with the sagging body in his arms, he touched the button that opened the warm outer lock, placed the body in, heard the music rise, and saw the inner lock open. The body shot out into the river of fire. The music softened.

'Well done, Lantry, well done.'

Barely an instant later another attendant entered the room. Lantry was caught with an expression of pleased excitement on his face. The Attendant looked around as if expecting to find someone, then he walked towards Lantry. 'May I help you?'

'Just looking,' said Lantry.

'Rather late at night,' said the Attendant.

'I couldn't sleep.'

That was the wrong answer, too. Everybody slept in this world. Nobody had insomnia. If you did you simply turned on a hypno-ray, and, sixty seconds later, you were snoring. Oh, he was just *full* of wrong answers. First he had made the fatal error of saying he had never been in the Incinerator before, when he knew damned well that all children were brought here on tours, every year, from the time they were four, to instil the idea of the clean fire death and the Incinerator in their minds. Death was a bright fire, death was warmth and the sun. It was not a dark, shadowed thing. That was important in their education. And he, pale thoughtless fool, had immediately gabbled out his ignorance.

And another thing, this paleness of his. He looked at his

hands and realised with growing terror that a pale man also was non-existent in this world. They would suspect his paleness. That was why the first Attendant had asked, 'Are you one of those men newly returned from Mars?' Here, now, this new Attendant was clean and bright as a copper penny, his cheeks red with health and energy. Lantry hid his pale hands in his pockets. But he was fully aware of the searching the Attendant did on his face.

'I mean to say,' said Lantry, 'I didn't *want* to sleep. I wanted to think.'

'Was there a service held here a moment ago?' asked the Attendant, looking about.

'I don't know, I just came in.'

'I thought I heard the fire lock open and shut.'

'I don't know,' said Lantry.

The man pressed a wall button. 'Anderson?'

A voice replied. 'Yes.'

'Locate Saul for me, will you?'

'I'll ring the corridors.' A pause. 'Can't find him.'

'Thanks.' The Attendant was puzzled. He was beginning to make little sniffing motions with his nose. 'Do you – *smell* anything?'

Lantry sniffed. 'No. Why?'

'I *smell* something.'

Lantry took hold of the knife in his pocket. He waited.

'I remember once when I was a kid,' said the man. 'And we found a cow lying dead in the field. It had been there two days in the hot sun. That's what this smell is. I wonder what it's from?'

'Oh, I know what it is,' said Lantry quietly. He held out his hand. 'Here.'

'What?'

'Me, of course.'

'You?'

'Dead several hundred years.'

'You're an odd joker.' The Attendant was puzzled!

'Very.' Lantry took out the knife. 'Do you know what this is?'

'A knife.'

'Do you ever use knives on people any more?'

'How do you mean?'

'I mean – killing them, with knives or guns or poison?'

'You *are* an odd joker!' The man giggled awkwardly.

'I'm going to kill you,' said Lantry.

'Nobody kills anybody,' said the man.

'Not any more they don't. But they used to, in the old days.'

'I know they did.'

'This will be the first murder in three hundred years. I just killed your friend. I just shoved him into the fire lock.'

That remark had the desired effect. It numbed the man so completely, it shocked him so thoroughly with its illogical aspects that Lantry had time to walk forward. He put the knife against the man's chest. 'I'm going to kill you.'

'That's silly,' said the man, numbly. 'People don't do that.'

'Like this,' said Lantry. 'You see?'

The knife slid into the chest. The man stared at it for a moment. Lantry caught the falling body.

III

The Salem flue exploded at six that morning. The great fire chimney shattered into ten thousand parts and flung itself into the earth and into the sky and into the houses of the sleeping people. There was fire and sound, more fire than autumn made burning in the hills.

William Lantry was five miles away at the time of the explosion. He saw the town ignited by the great spreading cremation of it. And he shook his head and laughed a little bit, and clapped his hands smartly together.

Relatively simple. You walked around killing people who didn't believe in murder, had only heard of it indirectly as some dim gone custom of the old barbarian races. You walked into the control-room of the Incinerator and said, 'How do you work this Incinerator?' and the control man told you, because everybody told the truth in this world of the future, nobody lied, there was no reason to lie, there was no danger to lie *against*. There was only one criminal in the world, and nobody knew *he* existed yet.

Oh, it was an incredibly beautiful set-up. The Control Man had told him just how the Incinerator worked, what pressure gauges controlled the flood of fire gases going up the flue, what levers were adjusted or readjusted. He and Lantry had had quite a talk. It was an easy free world. People trusted people. A moment later Lantry had shoved a knife in the Control Man also and set the pressure gauges for an overload to occur half an hour later, and walked out of the Incinerator halls, whistling.

Now even the sky was palled with the vast black cloud of the explosion.

'This is only the first,' said Lantry, looking at the sky. 'I'll tear all the others down before they even suspect there's an unethical man loose in their society. They can't account for a variable like me. I'm beyond their understanding. I'm incomprehensible, impossible, therefore I do not exist. My God, I can kill hundreds of thousands of them before they even realise murder is out in the world again. I can make it look like an accident each time. Why, the idea is so huge, it's unbelievable!'

The fire burned the town. He sat under a tree for a long time, until morning. Then, he found a cave in the hills, and went in, to sleep.

He awoke at sunset with a sudden dream of fire. He saw himself pushed into the flue, cut into sections by flame, burned away to nothing. He sat up on the cave floor, laughing at himself. He had an idea.

He walked down into the town and stepped into an audio booth. He dialled *Operator*. 'Give me the Police Department,' he said.

'I beg your pardon?' said the operator.

He tried again. 'The Law Force,' he said.

'I will connect you with the Peace Control,' she said, at last.

A little fear began ticking inside him like a tiny watch. Suppose the operator recognised the term Police Department as an anachronism, took his audio number, and sent someone out to investigate? No, she wouldn't do that. Why should she suspect? Paranoids were non-existent in this civilisation.

'Yes, the Peace Control,' he said.

A buzz. A man's voice answered. 'Peace Control. Stephens speaking.'

'Give me the Homicide Detail,' said Lantry, smiling.

'The *what*?'

'Who investigates murders?'

'I beg your pardon, what are you talking about?'

'Wrong number.' Lantry hung up, chuckling. Ye gods, there was no such thing as a Homicide Detail. There were no murders, therefore they needed no detectives. Perfect, perfect!

The audio rang back. Lantry hesitated, then answered.

'Say,' said the voice on the phone. 'Who *are* you?'

'The man just left who called,' said Lantry, and hung up again.

He ran. They would recognise his voice and perhaps send someone out to check. People didn't lie. *He* had just lied. They knew his voice. Anybody who lied needed a psychiatrist. They would come to pick him up to see why he was lying. For no *other* reason. They suspected him of nothing else. Therefore – he must run.

Oh, how very carefully he must act from now on. He knew nothing of this world, this odd straight truthful ethical world. Simply by looking pale you were suspect. Simply by not sleeping nights you were suspect. Simply by not bathing, by smelling like a – dead cow? – you were suspect. Anything.

He must go to a library. But that was dangerous, too. What were libraries like today? Did they have books or did they have film spools which projected books on a screen? Or did people have libraries at home, thus eliminating the necessity of keeping large main libraries?

He decided to chance it. His use of archaic terms might well make him suspect again, but now it was very important he learn all that could be learned of this foul world into which he had come again. He stopped a man on the street. 'Which way to the library?'

The man was not surprised. 'Two blocks east, one block north.'

'Thank you.'

Simple as that.

He walked into the library a few minutes later.

'May I help you?'

He looked at the librarian. May I help you, may I help you. What a world of helpful people! 'I'd like to "have" Edgar Allan Poe.' His verb was carefully chosen. He didn't say 'read'. He was too afraid that books were passé, that printing itself was a lost art. Maybe all 'books' today were in the form of fully de-lineated three-dimensional motion pictures. How in hell could you make a motion picture out of Socrates, Schopenhauer, Nietzsche and Freud?

'What was that name again?'

'Edgar Allan Poe.'

'There is no such author listed in our files.'

'Will you please check?'

She checked. 'Oh, yes. There's a red mark on the file card. He was one of the authors in the Great Burning of 2265.'

'How ignorant of me.'

'That's all right,' she said. 'Have you heard much of him?'

'He had some interesting barbarian ideas on death,' said Lantry.

'Horrible ones,' she said, wrinkling her nose. 'Ghastly.'

'Yes. Ghastly. Abominable, in fact. Good thing he was burned. Unclean. By the way, do you have any of Lovecraft?'

'Is that a sex book?'

Lantry exploded with laughter. 'No, no. It's a man.'

She riffled the file. 'He was burned, too. Along with Poe.'

'I suppose that applies to Machen and a man named Derleth and one named Ambrose Bierce, also?'

'Yes.' She shut the file cabinet. 'All burned. And good riddance.' She gave him an odd warm look of interest. 'I bet you've just come back from Mars.'

'Why do you say that?'

'There was another explorer in here yesterday. He'd just made the Mars hop and return. He was interested in supernatural literature, also. It seems there are actually "tombs" on Mars.'

'What are "tombs"?' Lantry was learning to keep his mouth closed.

'You know, those things they once buried people in.'

'Barbarian custom. Ghastly!'

'*Isn't* it? Well, seeing the Martian tombs made this young explorer curious. He came and asked if we had any of those authors you mentioned. Of course we haven't even a smitch of their stuff.' She looked at his pale face. 'You *are* one of the Martian rocket men, aren't you?'

'Yes,' he said. 'Got back on the ship the other day.'

'The other young man's name was Burke.'

'Of course. Burke! Good friend of mine!'

'Sorry I can't help you. You'd best get yourself some vitamin shots and some sun-lamp. You look terrible, Mr ——?'

'Lantry. I'll be good. Thanks ever so much. See you next Hallows' Eve!'

'Aren't you the clever one.' She laughed. 'If there *were* a Hallows' Eve, I'd make it a date.'

'But they burned *that*, too,' he said.

'Oh, they burned everything,' she said. 'Good night.'

'Good night.' And he went out.

Oh, how carefully he was balanced in this world! Like some kind of dark gyroscope, whirling with never a murmur, a very silent man. As he walked along the eight o'clock evening street he noticed with particular interest that there was not an unusual amount of lights about. There were the usual street lights at each corner, but the blocks themselves were only faintly illuminated. Could it be that these remarkable people were not *afraid of the dark?* Incredible nonsense! *Everyone* was afraid of the dark. *Even he* himself had been afraid, as a child. It was as natural as eating.

A little boy ran by on pelting feet, followed by six others. They yelled and shouted and rolled on the dark cool October lawn, in the leaves. Lantry looked on for several minutes before addressing himself to one of the small boys who was for a moment taking a respite, gathering his breath into his small lungs, as a boy might blow to refill a punctured paper bag.

'Here, now,' said Lantry. 'You'll wear yourself out.'

'Sure,' said the boy.

'Could you tell me,' said the man, 'why there are no street lights in the middle of the blocks?'

'Why?' asked the boy.

'I'm a teacher, I thought I'd test your knowledge,' said Lantry.

'Well,' said the boy, 'you don't need lights in the middle of the block, that's why.'

'But it gets rather dark,' said Lantry.

'So?' said the boy.

'Aren't you afraid?' asked Lantry.

'Of what?' asked the boy.

'The dark,' said Lantry.

'Ho, ho,' said the boy. 'Why should I be?'

'Well,' said Lantry. 'It's black, it's dark. And after all, street lights were invented to take away the dark and take away fear.'

'That's silly. Street lights were made so you could see where you were walking. Outside of that there's nothing.'

'You miss the whole point——' said Lantry. 'Do you mean to say you would sit in the middle of an empty lot all night and not be afraid?'

'Of what?'

'Of what, of what, of what, you little ninny! Of the dark!'

'Ho ho.'

'Would you go out in the hills and stay all night in the dark?'

'Sure.'

'Would you stay in a deserted house alone?'

'Sure.'

'And not be afraid?'

'Sure.'

'You're a liar!'

'Don't you call me nasty names!' shouted the boy. Liar was the improper noun, indeed. It seemed to be the worst thing you could call a person.

Lantry was completely furious with the little monster. 'Look,' he insisted. 'Look into my eyes . . .'

The boy looked.

Lantry bared his teeth slightly. He put out his hands, making a clawlike gesture. He leered and gesticulated and wrinkled his face into a terrible mask of horror.

'Ho ho,' said the boy. 'You're funny.'

'*What* did you say?'

'You're funny. Do it again. Hey, gang, c'mere! This man does funny things!'

'Never mind.'

'Do it again, sir.'

'Never mind, never mind. Good night!' Lantry ran off.

'Good night, sir. And mind the dark, sir!' called the little boy.

Of all the stupidity, of all the rank, gross, crawling, jelly-mouthed stupidity! He had never seen the like of it in his life! Bringing the children up without so much as an *ounce* of imagination! Where was the fun in being children if you didn't imagine things?

He stopped running. He slowed and for the first time began to appraise himself. He ran his hand over his face and bit his finger and found that he himself was standing midway in the block and he felt uncomfortable. He moved up to the street corner where there was a glowing lantern. 'That's better,' he said, holding his hands out like a man to an open warm fire.

He listened. There was not a sound except the night breathing of the crickets. Faintly there was a fire-hush as a rocket swept the sky. It was the sound a torch might make brandished gently on the dark air.

He listened to himself and for the first time he realised what there was so peculiar to himself. There was not a sound in him. The little nostril and lung noises were absent. His lungs did not take nor give oxygen or carbon-dioxide; they did not move. The hairs in his nostrils did not quiver with warm combing air. That faint purrling whisper of breathing did not sound in his nose. Strange. Funny. A noise you never heard when you were alive, the breath that fed your body, and yet, once dead, oh how you missed it!

The only other time you ever heard it was on deep dreamless awake nights when you wakened and listened and heard first your nose taking and gently poking out the air, and then the dull deep dim red thunder of the blood in your temples, in your eardrums, in your throat, in your aching wrists, in your warm loins, in your chest. All of those little rhythms, gone. The wrist beat gone, the throat pulse gone, the chest vibration gone. The sound of the blood coming up down around and through, up down around and through. Now it was like listening to a statue.

And yet he *lived*. Or, rather, moved about. And how was this done, over and above scientific explanations, theories, doubts?

By one thing, and one thing alone.

Hatred.

Hatred was a blood in him, it went up down around and through, up down around and through. It was a heart in him, not beating, true, but warm. He was – what? Resentment. Envy. They said he could not lie any longer in his coffin in the cemetery. He had *wanted* to. He had never had any particular desire to get up and walk around. It had been enough, all these centuries, to lie in the deep box and feel but *not feel* the ticking of the million insect watches in the earth around, the moves of worms like so many deep thoughts in the soil.

But then they had come and said, 'Out you go and into the furnace!' And that is the worst thing you can say to any man. You cannot tell him what to do. If you say you are dead, he will want not to be dead. If you say there are no such things as vampires, by God, that man will try to *be* one just for spite. If you say a dead man cannot walk he will test his limbs. If you say murder is no longer occurring, he will make it occur. He was, *in toto*, all the impossible things. They had given birth to him with their damnable practices and ignorances. Oh, how wrong they were. They needed to be shown. He would *show* them! Sun is *good*, so is *night*, there is nothing wrong with dark, *they* said.

Dark is horror, he shouted, silently, facing the little houses. It is *meant* for contrast. You must fear, you hear! That has always been the way of this world. You destroyers of Edgar Allan Poe and fine big-worded Lovecraft, you burner of Hallowe'en masks and destroyer of pumpkin jack-o-lanterns! I will make night what it *once* was, the thing against which man built all his lanterned cities and his many children!

As if in answer to this, a rocket, flying low, trailed a long rakish feather of flame. It made Lantry flinch and draw back.

IV

It was but ten miles to the little town of Science Port. He made it by dawn, walking. But even this was not good. At four in the morning a silver beetle pulled up on the road beside him.

'Hello,' called the man inside.

'Hello,' said Lantry wearily.

'Why are you walking?' asked the man.

'I'm going to Science Port.'

'Why don't you ride?'

'I *like* to walk.'

'*Nobody* likes to walk. Are you sick? May I give you a ride?'

'Thanks, but I like to walk.'

The man hesitated, then closed the beetle door. 'Good night.'

When the beetle was gone over the hill, Lantry retreated into a nearby forest. A world full of bungling helping people. By God, you couldn't even *walk* without being accused of sickness. That meant only one thing. He must not walk any longer, he had to ride. He should have accepted that fellow's offer.

The rest of the night he walked far enough off the highway so that if a beetle rushed by he had time to vanish in the underbrush. At dawn he crept into an empty dry water-drain and closed his eyes.

The dream was as perfect as a rimed snowflake.

He saw the graveyard where he had lain deep and ripe over the centuries. He heard the early morning footsteps of the labourers returning to finish their work.

'Would you mind passing me the shovel, Jim?'

'Here you go.'

'Wait a minute, wait a minute!'

'What's up?'

'Look here. We didn't finish last night, did we?'

'No.'

'There was one more coffin, wasn't there?'

'Yes.'

'Well, here it is, and open!'

'You've got the wrong hole.'

'What's the name say on the gravestone?'

'Lantry. William Lantry.'

'That's him, that's the one! Gone!'

'What could have happened to it?'

'How do I know. The body was here last night.'

'We can't be sure, we didn't look.'

'God, man, people don't bury empty coffins. He was in his box. Now he isn't.'

'Maybe this box was empty.'

'Nonsense. Smell that smell? He was here all right.'

A pause.

'Nobody would have taken the body, would they?'

'What for?'

'A curiosity, perhaps.'

'*Don't be ridiculous. People just don't steal. Nobody steals.*'

'*Well, then, there's only one solution.*'

'*And?*'

'*He got up and walked away.*'

A pause. In the dark dream, Lantry expected to hear laughter. There was none. Instead, the voice of the gravedigger, after a thoughtful pause, said, 'Yes. That's it, indeed. He got up and walked away.'

'*That's interesting to think about,*' *said the other.*

'*Is'nt it, though?*'

Silence.

Lantry awoke. It had all been a dream, but God, how realistic. How strangely the two men had carried on. But not un-naturally, oh, no. That was exactly how you expected men of the future to talk. Men of the future. Lantry grinned wryly. That was an anachronism for you. This *was* the future. This was happening *now*. It wasn't 300 years from now, it was now, not then, or any other time. This wasn't the Twentieth Century. Oh, how calmly those two men in the dream had said, 'He got up and walked away.' '– interesting to think about.' '*Isn't* it, though?' With never a quaver in their voices. With not so much as a glance over their shoulders or a tremble of spade in hand. But, of course, with their perfectly honest, logical minds, there was but one explanation; certainly nobody had *stolen* the corpse. '*Nobody* steals.' The corpse had simply got up and walked off. The corpse was the only one who could have *possibly* moved the corpse. By the few casual slow words of the grave-diggers Lantry knew what they were thinking. Here was a man that had lain in suspended animation, not really dead, for hundreds of years. The jarring about, the activity, had brought him back.

Everyone had heard of those little green toads that are sealed for centuries inside mud rocks or in ice patties, alive, alive oh! And how when scientists chipped them out and warmed them like marbles in their hands the little toads leapt about and frisked and blinked. Then it was only logical that the grave-diggers think of William Lantry in like fashion.

But what if the various parts were fitted together in the next day or so? If the vanished body and the shattered, exploded incinerator were connected? What if this fellow named Burke, who had returned pale from Mars, went to the library again and said to the young woman he wanted some books and she said, 'Oh, your friend Lantry was in the other day.' And he'd say, 'Lantry who? Don't know anyone by that name.' And she'd say, 'Oh, he *lied*.' And people in this time didn't lie. So it would all form and coalesce, item by item, bit by bit. A pale man who was pale and shouldn't be pale had lied and people don't lie, and a walking man on a lonely country road had walked and people don't walk anymore, and a body was missing from a cemetery, and the Incinerator had blown up and and—

They would come after him. They would find him. He would be easy to find. He walked. He lied. He was pale. They would find him and take him and stick him through the open fire lock of the nearest burner and that would be your Mr William Lantry, like a Fourth of July set-piece!

There was only one thing to be done efficiently and completely. He arose in violent moves. His lips were wide and his dark eyes were flared and there was a trembling and burning all through him. He must kill and kill and kill and kill and kill. He must make his enemies into friends, into people like himself who walked but shouldn't walk, who were pale in a land of pinks. He must kill and then kill and then kill again. He must make bodies and dead people and corpses. He must destroy Incinerator after flue after burner after Incinerator. Explosion on explosion. Death on death. Then, when the Incinerators were all thrown in ruin, and the hastily established morgues were jammed with the bodies of people shattered by the explosion, then he would begin to make friends, his enrolment of the dead in his own cause.

Before they traced and found and killed him, they must be killed themselves. So far he was safe. He could kill and they would not kill back. People simply do not go around killing. That was his safety margin. He climbed out of the abandoned drain, stood in the road.

He took the knife from his pocket and hailed the next beetle.

It was like the Fourth of July! The biggest damned firecracker of them all. The Science Port Incinerator split down the middle and flew apart. It made a thousand small explosions that ended with a greater one. It fell upon the town and crushed houses and burned trees. It woke people from sleep and then put them to sleep again, forever, an instant later.

William Lantry, sitting in a beetle that was not his own, tuned idly to a station on the audio dial. The collapse of the Incinerator had killed some four hundred people. Many had been caught in flattened houses, others struck by flying metal. A temporary morgue was being set up at——

An address was given.

Lantry noted it with a pad and pencil.

He could go on this way, he thought, from town to town, from country to country, destroying the burners, the Pillars of Fire, until the whole clean magnificent framework of flame and cauterisation was tumbled. He made a fair estimate – each explosion averaged five hundred dead. You could work up to a hundred thousand in no time.

He pressed the floor stud of the beetle. Smiling, he drove off through the dark streets of the city.

The city coroner had requisitioned an old warehouse. From midnight until four in the morning the grey beetles hissed down the rain-shiny streets, turned in, and the bodies were laid out on the cold concrete floors, with white sheets over them. It was a continuous flow until about four-thirty; then it stopped. There were about two hundred bodies there, white and cold.

The bodies were left alone; nobody stayed behind to tend them. There was no use tending the dead; it was a useless procedure; the dead could take care of themselves.

About five o'clock, with a touch of dawn in the east, the first trickle of relatives arrived to identify their sons or their fathers or their mothers or their uncles. The people moved quickly into the warehouse, made the identification, moved quickly out again. By six o'clock, with the sky still lighter in the east, this trickle had passed on, also.

William Lantry walked across the wide wet street and entered the warehouse.

He held a piece of blue chalk in one hand.

He walked by the coroner who stood in the entranceway talking to two others. '. . . drive the bodies to the Incinerator in Mellin Town, tomorrow . . .' The voices faded.

Lantry moved, his feet echoing faintly on the cool concrete. A wave of sourceless relief came to him as he walked among the shrouded figures. He was among his own. And – better than that, by God! he had *created* these! He had made them dead! He had procured for himself a vast number of recumbent friends!

Was the coroner watching? Lantry turned his head. No. The warehouse was calm and quiet and shadowed in the dark morning. The coroner was walking away now, across the street, with his two attendants, a beetle had drawn up on the other side of the street, and the coroner was going over to talk with whoever was in the beetle.

William Lantry stood and made a blue chalk pentagram on the floor by each of the bodies. He moved swiftly, swiftly, without a sound, without blinking. In a few minutes, glancing up now and then to see if the coroner was still busy, he had chalked the floor by a hundred bodies. He straightened up and put the chalk in his pocket.

Now is the time for all good men to come to the aid of their party, now is the time for all good men to come to the aid of their party, now is the time for all good men to come to the aid of their party, now is the time. . . .

Lying in the earth, over the centuries, the processes and thoughts of passing peoples and passing times had seeped down to him, slowly, as into a deep-buried sponge. From some death-memory in him now, ironically, repeatedly, a black typewriter clacked out black even lines of pertinent words:

Now is the time for all good men, for all good men, to come to the aid of——

William Lantry.

Other words——

Arise my love, and come away——

The quick brown fox jumped over . . . *Paraphrase it.* The quick risen body jumped over the tumbled Incinerator. . . .

Lazarus, come forth from the tomb. . . .

He knew the right words. He need only speak them as they had been spoken over the centuries. He need only gesture with his hands and speak the words, the dark words that would cause these bodies to quiver, rise and walk!

And when they had risen he would take them through the town, they would kill others and the others would rise and walk. By the end of the day there would be thousands of good friends walking with him. And what of the naive, living people of this year, this day, this hour? They would be completely unprepared for it. They would go down to defeat because they would not be expecting war of any sort. They wouldn't believe it possible, it would all be over before they could convince themselves that such an illogical thing could happen.

He lifted his hands. His lips moved. He said the words. He began in a chanting whisper and then raised his voice, louder. He said the words again and again and again. His eyes were closed tightly. His body swayed. He spoke faster and faster. He began to move forward among the bodies. The dark words flowed from his mouth. He was enchanted with his own formulae. He stooped and made further blue symbols on the concrete, in the fashion of long-dead sorcerers, smiling, confident. Any moment now the first tremor of the still bodies, any moment now the rising, the leaping up of the cold ones!

His hands lifted in the air. His head nodded. He spoke, he spoke, he spoke. He gestured. He talked loudly over the bodies, his eyes flaring, his body tensed. 'Now!' he cried violently. 'Rise, *all* of you!'

Nothing happened.

'Rise!' he screamed, with a terrible torment in his voice.

The sheets lay in white blue-shadow folds over the silent bodies.

'Hear me, and act!' he shouted.

Far away, on the street, a beetle hissed along.

Again, again, again he shouted, pleaded. He got down by each body and asked of it his particular violent favour. No reply. He strode wildly between the even white rows, flinging his arms up, stooping again and again to make blue symbols!

Lantry was very pale. He licked his lips. 'Come on, get up,' he said. 'They have, they always have, for a thousand years. When you make a mark – so! and speak a word – so! they always rise! Why not you now, why not you! Come on, come *on*, before *they* come back!'

The warehouse went up into shadow. There were steel beams across and down. In it, under the roof, there was not a sound, except the raving of a lonely man.

Lantry stopped.

Through the wide doors of the warehouse he caught a glimpse of the last cold stars of morning.

This was the year 2349.

His eyes grew cold and his hands fell to his sides. He did not move.

Once upon a time people shuddered when they heard the wind about the house, once people raised crucifixes and wolf-bane, and believed in walking dead and bats and loping white wolves. And as long as they believed, then so long did the dead, the bats, the loping wolves exist. The mind gave birth and reality to them.

But . . .

He looked at the white-sheeted bodies.

These people did not believe.

They had never believed. They would never believe. They had never imagined that the dead might walk. The dead went up flues in flame. They had never heard superstition, never trembled or shuddered or doubted in the dark. Walking dead people could not exist, they were illogical. This was the year 2349, man, after all!

Therefore, these people could not rise, could not walk again. They were dead and flat and cold. Nothing, chalk, imprecation, superstition, could wind them up and set them walking. They were dead and *knew* they were dead!

He was alone.

There were live people in the world who moved and drove beetles and drank quiet drinks in little dimly illumined bars by country roads, and kissed women and talked much good talk all day and every day.

But he was not alive.

Friction gave him what little warmth he possessed.

There were two hundred dead people here in this warehouse now, cold upon the floor. The first dead people in a hundred years who were allowed to be corpses for an extra hour or more. The first not to be immediately trundled to the Incinerator and lit like so much phosphorus.

He should be happy with them, among them.

He was not.

They were completely dead. They did not know nor believe in walking once the heart had paused and stilled itself. They were deader than dead ever was.

He was indeed alone, more alone than any man had ever been. He felt the chill of his aloneness moving up into his chest, strangling him quietly.

William Lantry turned suddenly and gasped.

While he had stood there, someone had entered the warehouse. A tall man with white hair, wearing a light-weight tan overcoat and no hat. How long the man had been nearby there was no telling.

There was no reason to stay here. Lantry turned and started to walk slowly out. He looked hastily at the man as he passed and the man with the white hair looked back at him, curiously. Had he heard? The imprecations, the pleadings, the shoutings? Did he suspect? Lantry slowed his walk. Had this man seen him make the blue chalk marks? But then, would he interpret them as symbols of an ancient superstition? Probably not.

Reaching the door, Lantry paused. For a moment he did not want to do anything but lie down and be coldly, really dead again and be carried silently down the street to some distant burning flue and there dispatched in ash and whispering fire. If he was indeed alone and there was no chance to collect an army to his cause, what, then, existed as a reason for going on? Killing? Yes, he'd kill a few thousand more. But that wasn't enough. You can only do so much of that before they drag you down.

He looked at the cold sky.

A rocket went across the black heaven, trailing fire.

Mars burned red among a million stars.

Mars. The library. The librarian. Talk. Returning rocket men. Tombs.

Lantry almost gave a shout. He restrained his hand, which wanted so much to reach up into the sky and touch Mars. Lovely red star on the sky. Good star that gave him sudden new hope. If he had a living heart now it would be thrashing wildly, and sweat would be breaking out of him and his pulses would be stammering, and tears would be in his eyes!

He would go down to wherever the rockets sprang up into space. He would go to Mars, one way or another. He would go to the Martian tombs. There, there, by God, were bodies, he would bet his last hatred on it, that would rise and walk and work with him! Theirs was an ancient culture, much different from that of Earth, patterned on the Egyptian, if what the librarian had said was true. And the Egyptian – what a crucible of dark superstition and midnight terror that culture had been! Mars it *was*, then. Beautiful Mars!

But he must not attract attention to himself. He must move carefully. He wanted to run, yes, to get away, but that would be the worst possible move he could make. The man with the white hair was glancing at Lantry from time to time, in the entranceway. There were too many people about. If anything happened he would be outnumbered. So far he had taken on only *one* man at a time.

Lantry forced himself to stop and stand on the steps before the warehouse. The man with the white hair came on on to the steps also and stood, looking at the sky. He looked as if he was going to speak at any moment. He fumbled in his pockets, took out a packet of cigarettes.

V

They stood outside the morgue together, the tall pink, white-haired man, and Lantry, hands in their pockets. It was a cool night with a white shell of a moon that washed a house here, a road there and, further on, parts of a river.

'Cigarette?' The man offered Lantry one.

'Thanks.'

They lit up together. The man glanced at Lantry's mouth. 'Cool night.'

'Cool.'

They shifted their feet. 'Terrible accident.'

'Terrible.'

'So many dead.'

'So many.'

Lantry felt himself some sort of delicate weight upon a scale. The other man did not seem to be looking at him, but rather listening and feeling towards him. There was a feathery balance here that made for vast discomfort. He wanted to move away and get out from under this balancing, weighing. The tall white-haired man said, 'My name's McClure.'

'Did you have any friends inside?' asked Lantry.

'No. A casual acquaintance. Awful accident.'

'Awful.'

They balanced each other. A beetle hissed by on the road with its seventeen tyres whirling quietly. The moon showed a little town further over in the black hills.

'I say,' said the man McClure.

'Yes.'

'Could you answer me a question?'

'Be glad to.' He loosened the knife in his coat pocket, ready.

'Is your name Lantry?' asked the man at last.

'Yes.'

'*William* Lantry?'

'Yes.'

'Then you're the man who came out of the Salem graveyard day before yesterday, aren't you?'

'Yes.'

'Good Lord, I'm glad to meet you, Lantry! We've been trying to find you for the past twenty-four hours!'

The man seized his hand, pumped it, slapped him on the back.

'What, what?' said Lantry.

'Good Lord, man, why did you run off? Do you realise what an instance this is? We want to talk to you!'

McClure was smiling, glowing. Another handshake, another slap. 'I *thought* it was you!'

The man is mad, thought Lantry. Absolutely mad. Here I've toppled his incinerators, killed people, and he's shaking my hand. Mad, mad!

'Will you come along to the Hall?' said the man, taking his elbow.

'Wh-what hall?' Lantry stepped back.

'The Science Hall, of course. It isn't every year we get a real case of suspended animation. In small animals, yes, but in a man, hardly! Will you come?'

'What's the act!' demanded Lantry, glaring. 'What's all this talk.'

'My dear fellow, what do you mean?' the man was stunned.

'Never mind. Is that the only reason you want to see me?'

'What other reason would there be, Mr Lantry? You don't know how glad I am to see you!' He almost did a little dance. 'I suspected. When we were in there together. You being so pale and all. And then the way you smoked your cigarette, something about it, and a lot of other things, all subliminal. But it is you, isn't it, it *is* you!'

'It is I. William Lantry.' Dryly.

'Good fellow! Come along!'

The beetle moved swiftly through the dawn streets. McClure talked rapidly.

Lantry sat, listening, astounded. Here was this fool, McClure, playing his cards for him! Here was this stupid scientist, or whatever, accepting him not as a suspicious baggage, a murderous item. Oh no! Quite the contrary! Only as a suspended animation case was he considered! Not as a dangerous man at all. Far from it!

'Of course,' cried McClure, grinning, 'you didn't know where to go, whom to turn to. It was all quite incredible to you.'

'Yes.'

'I had a feeling you'd be there at the morgue tonight,' said McClure, happily.

'Oh?' Lantry stiffened.

'Yes. Can't explain it. But you, how shall I put it? Ancient Americans? You had funny ideas on death. And you were among the dead so long, I felt you'd be drawn back by the accident, by the morgue and all. It's not very logical. Silly, in fact. It's just a feeling. I hate feelings but there it was. I came on a, I guess you'd call it a hunch, wouldn't you?'

'You might call it that.'

'And there you were!'

'There I was,' said Lantry.

'Are you hungry?'

'I've eaten.'

'How did you get around?'

'I hitch-hiked.'

'You *what?*'

'People gave me rides on the road.'

'Remarkable.'

'I imagine it sounds that way.' He looked at the passing houses. 'So this is the era of space travel, is it?'

'Oh, we've been travelling to Mars for some forty years now.'

'Amazing. And those big funnels, those towers in the middle of every town?'

'Those. Haven't you heard? The Incinerators. Oh, of course, they hadn't anything of that sort in your time. Had some bad luck with them. An explosion in Salem and one here, all in a forty-eight hour period. You looked as if you were going to speak; what is it?'

'I was thinking,' said Lantry. 'How fortunate I got out of my coffin when I did. I might well have been thrown into one of your Incinerators and burned up.'

'That would have been terrible, wouldn't it have?'

'Quite.'

Lantry toyed with the dials on the beetle dash. He wouldn't go to Mars. His plans were changed. If this fool simply refused to recognise an act of violence when he stumbled upon it, then let him be a fool. If they didn't connect the two explosions with a man from the tomb, all well and good. Let them go on deluding themselves. If they couldn't imagine someone being mean and nasty and murderous, heaven help them. He rubbed his hands with satisfaction. No, no Martian trip for you, as yet, Lantry lad. First we'll see what can be done boring from the inside. Plenty of time. The Incinerators can wait an extra week or so. One has to be subtle, you know. Any more immediate explosions might cause quite a ripple of thought.

McClure was gabbling wildly on.

'Of course, you don't have to be examined immediately. You'll want a rest. I'll put you up at my place.'

'Thanks. I don't feel up to being probed and pulled. Plenty of time in a week or so.'

They drew up before a house and climbed out.

'You'll want sleep, naturally.'

'I've been asleep for centuries. Be glad to stay awake. I'm not a bit tired.'

'Good.' McClure let them into the house. He headed for the drink bar. 'A drink will fix us up.'

'You have one,' said Lantry. 'Later for me. I just want to sit down.'

'By all means sit.' McClure mixed himself a drink. He looked around the room, looked at Lantry, paused for a moment with the drink in his hand, tilted his head to one side, and put his tongue in his cheek. Then he shrugged and stirred the drink. He walked slowly to a chair and sat, sipping the drink quietly. He seemed to be listening for something. 'There are cigarettes on the table,' he said.

'Thanks.' Lantry took one and lit it and smoked it. He did not speak for some time.

Lantry thought, I'm taking this all too easily. Maybe I should kill and run. He's the only one that has found me, yet. Perhaps this is all a trap. Perhaps we're simply sitting here waiting for the police. Or whatever in hell they use for police these days. He looked at McClure. No. They weren't waiting for police. They were waiting for something else.

McClure didn't speak. He looked at Lantry's face and he looked at Lantry's hands. He looked at Lantry's chest a long time, with easy quietness. He sipped his drink. He looked at Lantry's feet.

Finally he said, 'Where'd you get the clothing?'

'I asked someone for clothes and they gave these things to me. Darned nice of them.'

'You'll find that's how we are in this world. All you have to do is ask.'

McClure shut up again. His eyes moved. Only his eyes and nothing else. Once or twice he lifted his drink.

A little clock ticked somewhere in the distance.

'Tell me about yourself, Mr Lantry.'

207

'Nothing much to tell.'

'You're modest.'

'Hardly. You know about the past. I know nothing of the future, or I should say "today" and day before yesterday. You don't learn much in a coffin.'

McClure did not speak. He suddenly sat forward in his chair and then leaned back and shook his head.

They'll never suspect me, thought Lantry. They aren't superstitious, they simply *can't* believe in a dead man walking. Therefore, I'll be safe. I'll keep putting off the physical check-up. They're polite. They won't force me. Then, I'll work it so I can get to Mars. After that, the tombs, in my own good time, and the plan. God, how simple. How naive these people are.

McClure sat across the room for five minutes. A coldness had come over him. The colour was very slowly going from his face, as one sees the colour of medicine vanishing as one presses the bulb at the top of a dropper. He leaned forward, saying nothing, and offered another cigarette to Lantry.

'Thanks.' Lantry took it. McClure sat deeply back into his easy chair, his knees folded one over the other. He did not look at Lantry, and yet somehow did. The feeling of weighing and balancing returned. McClure was like a tall thin master of hounds listening for something that nobody else could hear. There are little silver whistles you can blow that only dogs can hear. McClure seemed to be listening acutely, sensitively for such an invisible whistle, listening with his eyes and with his half-opened, dry mouth, and with his aching, breathing nostrils.

Lantry sucked the cigarette, sucked the cigarette, sucked the cigarette, and, as many times, blew out, blew out, blew out. McClure was like some lean red-shagged hound listening and listening with a slick slide of eyes to one side, with an apprehension in that hand that was so precisely microscopic that one only sensed it, as one sensed the invisible whistle, with some part of the brain deeper than eyes or nostril or ear. McClure was all chemist's scale, all antennae.

The room was so quiet the cigarette smoke made some kind of invisible noise rising to the ceiling. McClure was a thermometer, a chemist's scales, a listening hound, a litmus paper, an antenna; all these. Lantry did not move. Perhaps the feeling would pass. It had passed before. McClure did not move for a long while and then, without a word, he nodded at the sherry decanter, and Lantry refused as silently. They sat looking but not looking at each other, again and away, again and away.

McClure stiffened slowly. Lantry saw the colour getting paler in those lean cheeks, and the hand tightening on the sherry glass, and a knowledge come at last to stay, never to go away, into the eyes.

Lantry did not move. He could not. All of this was of such a fascination that he wanted only to see, to hear, what would happen next. It was McClure's show from here on in.

McClure said, 'At first I thought it was the finest psychosis I have ever seen. You, I mean. I thought, he's convinced himself, Lantry's convinced himself, he's quite insane, he's told himself to do all these little things.' McClure talked as if in a dream, and continued talking and didn't stop.

'I said to myself, he purposely doesn't breathe through his nose. I watched your nostrils, Lantry. The little nostril hairs never once quivered in the last hour. That wasn't enough. It was a fact I filed. It wasn't enough. He breathes through his mouth, I said, on purpose. And then I gave you a cigarette and you sucked and blew, sucked and blew. None of it ever came out your nose. I told myself, well, that's all right. He doesn't inhale. Is that terrible, is that suspect? All in the mouth, all in the mouth. And then, I looked at your chest. I watched. It never moved up or down, it did nothing. He's convinced himself, I said to myself. He's convinced himself about all this. He doesn't move his chest, except slowly, when he thinks you're not looking. That's what I told myself.'

The words went on in the silent room, not pausing, still in a dream. 'And then I offered you a drink but you don't drink and I thought, he doesn't drink, I thought. Is *that* terrible? And I watched and watched you all this time. Lantry holds his breath, he's fooling himself. But now, yes, now, I understand it quite well. Now I know everything the way it is. Do you know how I know? I do not hear breathing in the room. I wait and I hear nothing. There is no beat of heart or intake of lung. The room is so silent. Nonsense, one might say, but I know. At the Incinerator I knew. There is a difference. You enter a room where a man is on a bed and you know immediately whether he will look up and speak to you or whether he will not speak to you ever again. Laugh if you will, but one can tell. It is a subliminal thing. It is the whistle the dog hears when no human hears. It is the tick of a clock that has ticked so long one no longer notices. Something is in a room when a man lives in it. Something is not in the room when a man is dead in it.'

McClure shut his eyes a moment. He put down his sherry glass. He waited a moment. He took up his cigarette and puffed it and then put it down in a black tray.

'I am alone in this room,' he said.

Lantry did not move.

'You are dead,' said McClure. 'My mind does not know this. It is not a thinking thing. It is a thing of the senses and the sub-conscious. At first I thought, this man *thinks* he is dead, risen from the dead, a vampire. Is that not logical? Would not any man, buried as many centuries, raised in a superstitious, ignorant culture, think likewise of himself once risen from the tomb? Yes, that is logical. This man has hypnotised himself and fitted his bodily functions so that they would in no way interfere

210

with his self-delusion, his great paranoia. He governs his breathing. He tells himself, I cannot hear my breathing, therefore I am dead. His inner mind censors the sound of breathing. He does not allow himself to eat or drink. These things he probably does in his sleep, with part of his mind, hiding the evidences of this humanity from his deluded mind at other times.'

McClure finished it. 'I was wrong. You are not insane. You are not deluding yourself. Nor me. This is all very illogical and – I must admit – almost frightening. Does that make you feel good, to think you frighten me? I have no label for you. You're a very odd man, Lantry. I'm glad to have met you. This will make an interesting report indeed.'

'Is there anything wrong with me being dead?' said Lantry. 'Is it a crime?'

'You must admit it's highly unusual.'

'But, still now, is it a crime?' asked Lantry.

'We have no crime, no criminal court. We want to examine you, naturally, to find out how you have happened. It is like that chemical which, one minute is inert, the next is living cell. Who can say where what happened to what. You are that impossibility. It is enough to drive a man quite insane.'

'Will I be released when you are done fingering me?'

'You will not be held. If you don't wish to be examined, you will not be. But I am hoping you will help by offering us your services.'

'I might,' said Lantry.

'But tell me,' said McClure. 'What were you doing at the morgue?'

'Nothing.'

'I heard you talking when I came in.'

'I was merely curious.'

'You're lying. That is very bad, Mr Lantry. The truth is far better. The truth, is, is it not, that you are dead and, being the only one of your sort, were lonely. Therefore you killed people to have company.'

'How does that follow?'

McClure laughed. 'Logic, my dear fellow. Once I *knew* you were really dead, a moment ago, really a – what do you call it – a vampire (silly word!), I tied you immediately to the Incinerator blasts. Before that there was no reason to connect you. But once the piece fell into place, the fact that you were dead, then it was simple to guess your loneliness, your hate, your envy, all of the tawdry motivations of a walking corpse. It took only an instant then to see the Incinerators blown to blazes, and then to think of you, among the bodies at the morgue, seeking help, seeking friends and people like yourself to work with——'

'You're too damned smart!' Lantry was out of the chair. He was halfway to the other man when McClure rolled over and scuttled away, flinging the sherry decanter. With a great despair Lantry realised that, like a damned idiot, he had thrown away his one chance to kill McClure. He should have done it earlier. It had been Lantry's one weapon, his safety margin. If people in a society never *killed* each other, they never *suspected* one another. You could walk up to any one of them and kill him.

'Come back here!' Lantry threw the knife.

McClure got behind a chair. The idea of flight, of protection, of fighting, was still new to him. He had part of the idea, but there was still a bit of luck on Lantry's side if Lantry wanted to use it.

'Oh, no,' said McClure, holding the chair between himself and the advancing man. 'You want to kill me. It's odd, but true. I can't understand it. You want to cut me with that knife or something like that, and it's up to me to prevent you from doing such an odd thing.'

'I *will* kill you!' Lantry let it slip out. He cursed himself. That was the worst possible thing to say.

Lantry lunged across the chair, clutching at McClure.

212

McClure was very logical. 'It won't do you any good to kill me. You *know* that.' They wrestled and held each other in a wild, toppling shuffle. Tables fell over, scattering articles. 'You remember what happened in the morgue?'

'I don't care!' screamed Lantry.

'You didn't raise *those* dead, did you?'

'I don't care!' cried Lantry.

'Look here,' said McClure, reasonably. 'There will never be any more like you, ever, there's no use.'

'Then I'll destroy all of you, all of you!' screamed Lantry.

'And then what? You'll still be alone, with no more like you about.'

'I'll go to Mars. They have tombs there. I'll find more like myself!'

'No,' said McClure. 'The executive order went through yesterday. All of the tombs are being deprived of their bodies. They'll be burned in the next week.'

They fell together to the floor. Lantry got his hands on McClure's throat.

'Please,' said McClure. 'Do you see, you'll *die*.'

'What do you mean?' cried Lantry.

'Once you kill all of us, and you're alone, you'll die! The hate will die. That hate is what moves you, *nothing else!* That envy moves you. Nothing else! You'll die, inevitably. You're not immortal. You're not even alive, you're nothing but a moving hate.'

'I don't care!' screamed Lantry, and began choking the man, beating his head with his fists, crouched on the defenceless body. McClure looked up at him with dying eyes.

The front door opened. Two men came in.

'I say,' said one of them. 'What's going on? A new game?'

Lantry jumped back and began to run.

'Yes, a new game!' said McClure, struggling up. 'Catch him and you win!'

The two men caught Lantry. 'We win,' they said.

'Let me go!' Lantry thrashed, hitting them across their faces, bringing blood.

'Hold him tight!' cried McClure.

They held him.

'A rough game, what?' one of them said. 'What do we do *now*?'

The beetle hissed along the shining road. Rain fell out of the sky and a wind ripped at the dark green wet trees. In the beetle, his hands on the half-wheel, McClure was talking. His voice was a susurrant, a whispering, a hypnotic thing. The two other men sat in the back seat. Lantry sat, or rather lay, in the front seat, his head back, his eyes faintly open, the glowing green light of the dash dials showing on his cheeks. His mouth was relaxed. He did not speak.

McClure talked quietly and logically, about life and moving, about death and not moving, about the sun and the great sun Incinerator, about the emptied tombyard, about hatred and how hate lived and made a clay man live and move, and how illogical it all was, it all was, it all was. One was dead, was dead, was dead, that was all, all, all. One did not try to be otherwise. The car whispered on the moving road. The rain spatted gently on the windshield. The men in the back seat conversed quietly. Where were they going, going? To the Incinerator, of course. Cigarette smoke moved slowly up on the air, curling and tying into itself in grey loops and spirals. One was dead and must accept it.

Lantry did not move. He was a marionette, the strings cut. There was only a tiny hatred in his heart, in his eyes, like twin coals, feeble, glowing, fading.

I am Poe, he thought. I am all that is left of Edgar Allan Poe, and I am all that is left of Ambrose Bierce and all that is left of a man named Lovecraft. I am a grey night bat with sharp teeth, and I am a square black monolith monster. I am Osiris and Bal and Set. I am the Necronomicon, the Book of the Dead. I am the house of Usher, falling into flame. I am the Red Death. I am the man mortared into the catacomb with a cask of Amontillado . . . I am a dancing skeleton. I am a coffin, a shroud, a lightning bolt reflected in an old house window. I am an autumn-empty tree, I am a rapping, flinging shutter. I am a yellowed volume turned by a claw hand. I am an organ played in an attic at midnight. I am a mask, a skull mask behind an oak tree on the last day of October. I am a poison apple bobbing in a water tub for child noses to bump at, for child teeth to snap . . . I am a black candle lighted before an inverted cross. I am a coffin lid, a sheet with eyes, a foot-step on a black stairwell. I am Dunsany and Machen and I am The Legend of Sleepy Hollow. I am The Monkey's Paw and I am The Phantom Rickshaw. I am The Cat and the Canary, The Gorilla, The Bat. I am the ghost of Hamlet's father on the castle wall.

All of these things am I. And now these last things will be burned. While I lived *they* still lived. While I moved and hated and existed, *they* still existed. I am *all* that remembers them. I am all of them that *still* goes on, and will *not* go on after tonight. Tonight, all of us, Poe and Bierce and Hamlet's father, we burn together. They will make a big heap of us and burn us like a bonfire, like things of Guy Fawkes' day, gasoline, torchlight, cries and all!

And what a wailing will we put up. The world will be clean of us, but in our going we shall say, oh what is the world like, clean of fear, where is the dark imagination from the dark time, the thrill and the anticipation, the suspense of old October, gone, never more to come again, flattened and smashed and burned by the rocket people, by the Incinerator people, destroyed and obliterated, to be replaced by doors that open and close and lights that go on or off without fear. If only you could remember how once *we* lived, what Hallowe'en was to us, and what Poe was, and how we gloried in the dark morbidities. One more drink, dear friends, of Amontillado, before the burning. All of this, all, exists, but in one last brain on earth. A whole world dying tonight. One more drink, pray.

'Here we are,' said McClure.

The Incinerator was brightly lighted. There was quiet music nearby. McClure got out of the beetle, came around to the other side. He opened the door. Lantry simply lay there. The talking and the logical talking had slowly drained him of life. He was no more than wax now, with a small glow in his eyes. This future world, how the men *talked* to you, how logically they reasoned away your life. They wouldn't believe in him. The force of their disbelief froze him. He could not move his arms or his legs. He could only mumble senselessly, coldly, eyes flickering.

McClure and the two others helped him out of the car, put him in a golden box and rolled him on a roller table into the warm glowing interior of the building.

I am Edgar Allan Poe, I am Ambrose Bierce, I am Hallowe'en, I am a coffin, a shroud, a Monkey's Paw, a Phantom, a Vampire. . . .

'Yes, yes,' said McClure, quietly, over him. 'I know. I know.'

The table glided. The walls swung over him and by him, the music played. You are dead, you are logically dead.

I am Usher, I am the Maelstrom, I am the MS Found In A Bottle, I am the Pit and I am the Pendulum, I am the Telltale Heart, I am the Raven nevermore, nevermore.

'Yes,' said McClure, as they walked softly. 'I know.'

'I am in the catacomb,' cried Lantry.

'Yes, the catacomb,' said the walking man over him.

'I am being chained to a wall, and there is no bottle of Amontillado here!' cried Lantry weakly, eyes closed.

'Yes,' someone said.

There was movement. The flame door opened.

'Now someone is mortaring up the cell, closing me in!'

'Yes, I *know*.' A whisper.

The golden box slid into the flame lock.

'I'm being walled in! A very good joke indeed! Let us be gone!' A wild scream and much laughter.

'We know, we understand. . . .'

The inner flame lock opened. The golden coffin shot forth into flame.

'For the love of God, Montresor! For the love of God!'

Dr Porthos

BASIL COPPER

Modern writers tackling the vampire theme are, of course, faced with the difficulty of not repeating themes, situations and plots which have been used before. In fact when I was putting this collection together, I was forced to exclude a number of extremely well-written stories simply because they followed similar lines to items which I had already determined to use. No such problem, however, arose over Basil Copper's contribution Dr Porthos, *which he wrote especially for this collection. In it he has cleverly combined a Gothic style of writing and a modern 'twist' ending. With this tale, Mr Copper again affirms that he is one of the most promising and inventive horror story writers to emerge in Britain in recent years.*

I

NERVOUS debility, the doctor says. And yet Angelina has never been ill in her life. Nervous debility! Something far more powerful is involved here; I am left wondering if I should not call in specialist advice. Yet we are so remote and Dr Porthos is well spoken of by the local people. Why on earth did we ever come to this house? Angelina was perfectly well until then. It is extraordinary to think that two months can have wrought such a change in my wife.

In the town she was lively and vivacious; yet now I can hardly bear to look at her without profound emotion. Her cheeks are sunken and pale, her eyes dark and tired, her bloom quite gone at twenty-five. Could it be something in the air of this place? Some fever engendered by the unhealthy position of the house?

It seems barely possible. But in that case Dr Porthos' ministrations should have proved effective. But so far all his skills have been powerless to produce any change for the better. If it had not been for the terms of my uncle's will we would never have come at all.

Friends may call it cupidity, the world may think what it chooses, but the plain truth is that I needed the money. My own health is far from robust and long hours in the family business – ours is an honoured and well-established counting house – had made it perfectly clear to me that I must seek some other mode of life. And yet I could not afford to retire. The terms of my uncle's will, as retailed to me by the family solicitors, afforded the perfect solution.

An annuity – a handsome annuity to put it bluntly – but with the proviso that my wife and I should reside in the old man's house for a period of not less than five years from the date the terms of the will become effective. I hesitated long; both my wife and I were fond of town life and my uncle's estate was in a remote area, where living for the country people was primitive and amenities few. As I had understood it from the solicitor, the house itself had not even the benefit of gas-lighting; in summer it was not so bad but the long months of winter would be melancholy indeed with only the glimmer of candles and the pale sheen of oil lamps to relieve the gloom of the lonely old place.

I debated with Angelina and then set off one weekend alone for a tour of the estate. I had cabled ahead and after a long, cold railway journey which itself occupied most of the day, I was met at my destination by a horse and chaise. The next part of my pilgrimage occupied nearly four hours and I was dismayed on seeing into what a wild and remote region my uncle had chosen to penetrate in order to select a dwelling.

The night was dark but the moon occasionally burst its veiling of cloud to reveal in feeble detail the contours of rock and hill and tree; the chaise jolted and lurched over an unmade road, which was deeply rutted by the wheels of the few vehicles which had torn up the surface in their passing over many months. My solicitor had wired to an old friend, Dr Porthos, to whose good offices I owed my mode of transport, and he had promised to greet me on arrival at the village nearest the estate.

Sure enough, he came out from under the great porch of the timbered hostelry as our carriage grated into the inn-yard. He was a tall, spare man, with square pince-nez which sat firmly on his thin nose; he wore a many-pleated cape like an ostler and the green top hat, worn rakishly over one eye, gave him a somewhat dissipated look. He greeted me effusively but there was something about the man which did not endear him to me.

There was nothing that one could isolate. It was just his general manner; perhaps the coldness of his hand, which struck my palm with the clamminess of a fish. Then too, his eyes had a most disconcerting way of looking over the tops of his glasses; they were a filmy grey and their piercing glance seemed to root one to the spot. To my dismay I learned I was not yet at my destination. The estate was still some way off, said the doctor, and we would have to stay the night at the inn. My ill-temper at his remarks was soon dissipated by the roaring fire and the good food with which he plied me; there were few travellers at this time of year and we were the only ones taking dinner in the vast oak-panelled dining-room.

The doctor had been my uncle's medical attendant and though it was many years since I had seen my relative I was curious to know what sort of person he had been.

'The Baron was a great man in these parts,' said Porthos. His genial manner emboldened me to ask a question to which I had long been awaiting an answer.

'Of what did my uncle die?' I asked.

Firelight flickered through the gleaming redness of Dr

Porthos' wineglass and tinged his face with amber as he replied simply, 'Of a lacking of richness in the blood. A fatal quality in his immediate line, I might say.'

I pondered for a moment. 'Why do you think he chose me as his heir?' I added.

Dr Porthos' answer was straight and clear and given without hesitation.

'You were a different branch of the family,' he said. 'New blood, my dear sir. The Baron was most particular on that account. He wanted to carry on the great tradition.'

He cut off any further questions by rising abruptly. 'Those were the Baron's own words as he lay dying. And now we must retire as we still have a fair journey before us in the morning.'

II

Dr Porthos' words come back to me in my present trouble. 'Blood, new blood. . . .' What if this be concerned with those dark legends the local people tell about the house? One hardly knows what to think in this atmosphere. My inspection of the house with Dr Porthos confirmed my worst fears; sagging lintels, mouldering cornices, worm-eaten panelling. The only servitors a middle-aged couple, husband and wife who have been caretakers here since the Baron's death; the local people sullen and unco-operative, so Porthos says. Certainly, the small hamlet a mile or so from the mansion had every door and window shut as we clattered past and not a soul was stirring.

The house has a Gothic beauty, I suppose, viewed from a distance; it is of no great age, being largely re-built on the remains of an older pile destroyed by fire. The restorer – whether he be my uncle or some older resident I have not bothered to discover – had the fancy of adding turrets, a draw-bridge with castellated towers and a moated surround. Our footsteps echoed mournfully over this as we turned to inspect the grounds.

I was surprised to see marble statuary and worn obelisks, all tumbled and awry, as though the uneasy dead were bursting from the soil, protruding over an ancient moss-grown wall adjoining the courtyard of the house.

Dr Porthos smiled sardonically. 'The old family burial ground,' he explained. 'Your uncle is interred here. He said he likes to be near the house.'

III

Well, it is done; we came not two months since and then began the profound and melancholy change of which I have already spoken. Not just the atmosphere – though the very stones of the house seem steeped in evil whispers – but the surroundings, the dark, unmoving trees, even the furniture, seem to exude something inimical to life as we knew it; as it is still known to those fortunate enough to dwell in towns.

A poisonous mist rises from the moat at dusk; it seems to doubly emphasise our isolation. The presence of Angelina's own maid and a handyman who was in my father's employ before me, do little to dispel the ambience of this place. Even their sturdy matter of factness seems affected by a miasma that wells from the pores of the building. It has become so manifest of late that I even welcome the daily visits of Dr Porthos, despite the fact that I suspect him to be the author of our troubles.

They began a week after our arrival when Angelina failed to awake by my side as usual; I shook her to arouse her and my screams must have awakened the maid. I think I fainted then and came to myself in the great morning-room; the bed had been awash with blood, which stained the sheets and pillows around my dear wife's head; Porthos' curious grey eyes had a steely look in them which I had never seen before. He administered a powerful medicine and had then turned to attend to me.

Whatever attacked Angelina had teeth like the sharpest canine, Porthos said; he had found two distinct punctures in Angelina's throat, sufficient to account for the quantities of blood. Indeed, there had been so much of it that my own hands and linen were stained with it where I had touched her; I think it was this which had made me cry out so violently. Porthos had announced that he would sit up by the patient that night.

Angelina was still asleep, as I discovered when I tiptoed in later; Porthos had administered a sleeping draught and had advised me to take the same to settle my nerves, but I declined. I said I would wait up with him. The doctor had some theory about rats or other nocturnal creatures and sat long in the library looking through some of the Baron's old books on natural history. The man's attitude puzzles me; what sort of creature would attack Angelina in her own bedroom? Looking at Porthos' strange eyes, my old fears are beginning to return, bringing with them new ones.

IV

There have been three more attacks, extending over a fortnight. My darling grows visibly weaker, though Porthos has been to the nearest town for more powerful drugs and other remedies. I am in purgatory; I have not known such dark hours in my life until now. Yet Angelina herself insists that we should stay to see this grotesque nightmare through. The first evening of our vigil both Porthos and I slept; and in the morning the result was as the night before. Considerable emissions of blood and the bandage covering the wound had been removed to allow the creature access to the punctures. I hardly dare conjecture what manner of beast could have done this.

I was quite worn out and on the evening of the next day I agreed to Porthos' suggestion that I should take a sleeping draught. Nothing happened for several nights and Angelina began to recover; then the terror struck again. And so it will go on, my reeling senses tell me. I daren't trust Porthos and on the other hand I cannot accuse him before the members of my household. We are isolated here and any mistake I make might be fatal.

On the last occasion I almost had him. I woke at dawn and found Porthos stretched on the bed, his long, dark form quivering, his hands at Angelina's throat. I struck at him, for I did not know who it was, being half asleep, and he turned, his grey eyes glowing in the dim room. He had a hypodermic syringe half full of blood in his hand. I am afraid I dashed it to the floor and shattered it beneath my heel.

In my own heart I am convinced I have caught this creature which has been plaguing us, but how to prove it? Dr Porthos is staying in the house now; I dare not sleep and continually refuse the potions he urgently presses upon me. How long before he destroys me as well as Angelina? Was man ever in such an appalling situation since the world began?

I sit and watch Porthos, who stares at me sideways with those curious eyes, his inexpressive face seeming to hint that he can afford to watch and wait and that his time is coming; my pale wife, in her few intervals of consciousness, sits and fearfully watches both of us. Yet I cannot even confide in her for she would think me mad. I try to calm my racing brain. Sometimes. I think I shall go insane altogether, the nights are so long. God help me.

V

It is over. The crisis has come and gone. I have laid the mad demon which has us in thrall. I caught him at it. Porthos writhed as I got my hands at his throat. I would have killed him at his foul work; the syringe glinted in his hand. Now he has slipped aside, eluded me for the moment. My cries brought in the servants who have my express instructions to hunt him down. He shall not escape me this time. I pace the corridors of this worm-eaten mansion and when I have cornered him I shall destroy him. Angelina shall live! And my hands will perform the healing work of destruction. . . . But for now I must rest. Already it is dawn again. I will sit in this chair by the pillar, where I can watch the hall. I sleep.

VI

Later. I awake to pain and cold. I am lying on earth. Something slippery trickles over my hand. I open my eyes. I draw my hand across my mouth. It comes away scarlet. I can see more clearly now. Angelina is here too. She looks terrified but somehow sad and composed. She is holding the arm of Dr Porthos. He is poised above me, his face looking satanic in the dim light of the crypt beneath the house. He whirls a mallet while shriek after shriek disturbs the silence of this place. Dear Lord, the stake is against *my breast*!

The Living Dead

ROBERT BLOCH

Robert Bloch's name has constantly been before the public's eye in recent months as the screenwriter of a number of highly successful new horror and thriller films. In fact, ever since his great triumph with Psycho, *produced by Alfred Hitchcock, Bloch has devoted far more time to the screen than his many thousands of avid readers really like. It was therefore quite a red letter day when I was compiling this collection to learn that he had taken a little time off from scripts and written a new horror story. And that it was a vampire story with a difference! This, then, marks the first book publication anywhere of* The Living Dead – *a story containing all the elements of shock, terror and compulsive readability which make Robert Bloch stories unique.*

ALL day long he rested, while the guns thundered in the village below. Then, in the slanting shadows of the late afternoon, the rumbling echoes faded into the distance and he knew it was over. The American advance had crossed the river. They were gone at last, and it was safe once more.

Above the village, in the crumbling ruins of the great château atop the wooded hillside, Count Barsac emerged from the crypt.

The Count was tall and thin – cadaverously thin, in a manner most hideously appropriate. His face and hands had a waxen pallor; his hair was dark, but not as dark as his eyes and the hollows beneath them. His cloak was black, and the sole touch of colour about his person was the vivid redness of his lips when they curled in a smile.

He was smiling now, in the twilight, for it was time to play the game.

The name of the game was Death, and the Count had played it many times.

He had played it in Paris on the stage of the Grand Guignol; his name had been plain Eric Karon then, but still he'd won a certain renown for his interpretation of bizarre roles. Then the war had come and, with it, his opportunity.

Long before the Germans took Paris, he'd joined their Underground, working long and well. As an actor he'd been invaluable.

And this, of course, was his ultimate reward – to play the supreme role, not on the stage, but in real life. To play without the artifice of spotlights, in true darkness; this was the actor's dream come true. He had even helped to fashion the plot.

'Simplicity itself,' he told his German superiors. 'Château Barsac has been deserted since the Revolution. None of the peasants from the village dare to venture near it, even in daylight because of the legend. It is said, you see, that the last Count Barsac was a vampire.'

And so it was arranged. The short-wave transmitter had been set up in the large crypt beneath the château, with three skilled operators in attendance, working in shifts. And he, 'Count Barsac', in charge of the entire operation, as guardian angel. Rather, as guardian demon.

'There is a graveyard on the hillside below,' he informed them. 'A humble resting place for poor and ignorant people. It contains a single imposing crypt – the ancestral tomb of the Barsacs. We shall open that crypt, remove the remains of the last Count, and allow the villagers to discover that the coffin is empty. They will never dare come near the spot or the château again, because this will prove that the legend is true – Count Barsac is a vampire, and walks once more.'

The question came then. 'What if there are sceptics? What if someone does not believe?'

And he had his answer ready. 'They will believe. For at night I shall walk – I, Count Barsac.'

After they saw him in the make-up, wearing the black cloak there were no more questions. The role was his.

The role was his, and he'd played it well. The Count nodded to himself as he climbed the stairs and entered the roofless foyer of the château, where only a configuration of cobwebs veiled the radiance of the rising moon.

Now, of course, the curtain must come down. If the American advance had swept past the village below, it was time to make one's bow and exit. And that too had been well arranged.

During the German withdrawal another advantageous use had been made of the tomb in the graveyard. A cache of Air Marshal Goering's art treasures now rested safely and undisturbed within the crypt. A truck had been placed in the château. Even now the three wireless operators would be playing new parts – driving the truck down the hillside to the tomb, placing the *objets d'art* in it.

By the time the Count arrived there, everything would be packed. They would then don the stolen American Army uniforms, carry the forged identifications and permits, drive through the lines across the river, and rejoin the German forces at a predesignated spot. Nothing had been left to chance. Some day, when he wrote his memoirs . . .

But there was not time to consider that now. The Count glanced up through the gaping aperture in the ruined roof. The moon was high. It was time to leave.

In a way he hated to go. Where others saw only dust and cobwebs he saw a stage – the setting of his finest performance. Playing a vampire's role had not addicted him to the taste of blood – but as an actor he enjoyed the taste of triumph. And he had triumphed here.

'Parting is such sweet sorrow.' Shakespeare's line. Shakespeare, who had written of ghosts and witches, of bloody apparitions. Because Shakespeare knew that his audiences, the stupid masses, believed in such things – just as they still believed today. A great actor could always make them believe.

The Count moved into the shadowy darkness outside the entrance of the château. He started down the pathway towards the beckoning trees.

It was here, amid the trees, that he had come upon Raymond, one evening weeks ago. Raymond had been his most appreciative audience – a stern, dignified, white-haired elderly man, mayor of the village of Barsac. But there had been nothing dignified about the old fool when he'd caught sight of the Count looming up before him out of the night. He'd screamed like a woman and run.

Probably Raymond had been prowling around, intent on poaching, but all that had been forgotten after his encounter in the woods. The mayor was the one to thank for spreading the rumours that the Count was again abroad. He and Clodez, the oafish miller, had then led an armed band to the graveyard and entered the Barsac tomb. What a fright they got when they discovered the Count's coffin open and empty!

The coffin had contained only dust that had been scattered to the winds, but they could not know that. Nor could they know about what had happened to Suzanne.

The Count was passing the banks of the small stream now. Here, on another evening, he'd found the girl – Raymond's daughter, as luck would have it – in an embrace with young Antoine LeFevre, her lover. Antoine's shattered leg had invalided him out of the army, but he ran like a deer when he glimpsed the cloaked and grinning Count. Suzanne had been left behind and that was unfortunate, because it was necessary to dispose of her. Her body had been buried in the woods, beneath great stones, and there was no question of discovery; still, it was a regrettable incident.

In the end, however, everything was for the best. Now silly superstitious Raymond was doubly convinced that the vampire walked. He had seen the creature himself, had seen the empty tomb and the open coffin; his own daughter had disappeared. At his command none dared venture near the graveyard, the woods, or the château beyond.

Poor Raymond! He was not even a mayor any more – his village had been destroyed in the bombardment. Just an ignorant, broken old man, mumbling his idiotic nonsense about the 'living dead'.

The Count smiled and walked on, his cloak fluttering in the breeze, casting a bat-like shadow on the pathway before him. He could see the graveyard now, the tilted tombstones rising from the earth like leprous fingers rotting in the moonlight. His smile faded; he did not like such thoughts. Perhaps the greatest tribute to his talent as an actor lay in his actual aversion to death, to darkness and what lurked in the night. He hated the sight of blood, had developed within himself an almost claustro-phobic dread of the confinement of the crypt.

Yes, it had been a great role, but he was thankful it was ending. It would be good to play the man once more, and cast off the creature he had created.

As he approached the crypt he saw the truck waiting in the shadows. The entrance to the tomb was open, but no sounds issued from it. That meant his colleagues had completed their task of loading and were ready to go. All that remained now was to change his clothing, remove the make-up and depart.

The Count moved to the darkened truck. And then . . .

Then they were upon him, and he felt the tines of the pitch-fork bite into his back, and as the flash of lanterns dazzled his eyes he heard the stern command. 'Don't move!'

He didn't move. He could only stare as they surrounded him – Antoine, Clodez, Raymond, and the others, a dozen peasants from the village. A dozen armed peasants, glaring at him in mingled rage and fear, holding him at bay.

But how could they dare?

The American Corporal stepped forward. That was the answer, of course – the American Corporal and another man in uniform, armed with a sniper's rifle. They were responsible. He didn't even have to see the riddled corpses of the three short-wave operators piled in the back of the truck to understand what had happened. They'd stumbled on his men while they worked, shot them down, then summoned the villagers.

Now they were jabbering questions at him, in English, of course. He understood English, but he knew better than to reply. 'Who are you? Were these men working under your orders? Where were you going with this truck?'

The Count smiled and shook his head. After a while they stopped, as he knew they would.

The Corporal turned to his companion. 'Okay,' he said. 'Let's go.' The other man nodded and climbed into the cab of the truck as the motor coughed into life. The Corporal moved to join him, then turned to Raymond.

'We're taking this across the river,' he said. 'Hang on to our friend here – they'll be sending a guard detail for him within an hour.'

Raymond nodded.

The truck drove off into the darkness.

And as it was dark now – the moon had vanished behind a cloud. The Count's smile vanished, too, as he glanced around at his captors. A rabble of stupid clods, surly and ignorant. But armed. No chance of escaping. And they kept staring at him, and mumbling.

'Take him into the tomb.'

It was Raymond who spoke, and they obeyed, prodding their captive forward with pitchforks. That was when the Count recognised the first faint ray of hope. For they prodded him most gingerly, no man coming close, and when he glared at them their eyes dropped.

They were putting him in the crypt because they were

afraid of him. Now the Americans were gone, they feared him once more – feared his presence and his power. After all, in their eyes he was a vampire – he might turn into a bat and vanish entirely. So they wanted him in the tomb for safe-keeping.

The Count shrugged, smiled his most sinister smile, and bared his teeth. They shrank back as he entered the doorway. He turned and, on impulse, furled his cape. It was an instinctive final gesture, in keeping with his role – and it provoked the appropriate response. They moaned, and old Raymond crossed himself. It was better, in a way, than any applause.

In the darkness of the crypt the Count permitted himself to relax a trifle. He was off stage now. A pity he'd not been able to make his exit the way he'd planned, but such were the fortunes of war. Soon he'd be taken to the American head-quarters and interrogated. Undoubtedly there would be some unpleasant moments, but the worst that could befall him was a few months in a prison camp. And even the Americans must bow to him in appreciation when they heard the story of his masterful deception.

It was dark in the crypt, and musty. The Count moved about restlessly. His knee grazed the edge of the empty coffin set on a trestle in the tomb. He shuddered involuntarily, loosening his cape at the throat. It would be good to remove it, good to be out of here, good to shed the role of vampire forever. He'd played it well, but now he was anxious to be gone.

There was a mumbling audible from outside, mingled with another and less identifiable noise – a scraping sound. The Count moved to the closed door of the crypt and listened intently; but now there was only silence.

What were the fools doing out there? He wished the Americans would hurry back. It was too hot in here. And why the sudden silence?

Perhaps they'd gone.

Yes. That was it. The Americans had told them to wait and guard him, but they were afraid. They really believed he was a vampire – old Raymond had convinced them of that. So they'd run off. They'd run off, and he was free, he could escape now . . .

So the Count opened the door.

And he saw them then, saw them standing and waiting, old Raymond staring sternly for a moment before he moved forward. He was holding something in his hand, and the Count recognised it, remembering the scraping sound that he'd heard.

It was a long wooden stake with a sharp point.

Then he opened his mouth to scream, telling them it was only a trick, he was no vampire, they were a pack of superstitious fools . . .

But all the while they bore him back into the crypt, lifting him up and thrusting him into the open coffin, holding him there as the grim-faced Raymond raised the pointed stake above his heart.

It was only when the stake came down that he realised there's such a thing as playing a role too well.

The Girl with the Hungry Eyes

FRITZ LEIBER

This final item is perhaps not a vampire story in the true tradition – for The Girl with the Hungry Eyes *is not after blood to feed her living-dead body, but something far more sinister. Nevertheless don't be taken off guard, for the girl's need of a life force obtained from others is very apparent. You enter this tale – which is in many ways a comment on our modern society – very much at your own risk. Author Fritz Leiber is best known as a Science Fiction writer, but with this tale demonstrates a talent of much wider dimensions. The Girl with the Hungry Eyes* will leave you thinking *– perhaps the best accolade anyone can give a short story.*

ALL right, I'll tell you why the Girl gives me the creeps. Why I can't stand to go down town and see the mob slavering up at her on the tower, with that pop bottle or pack of cigarettes or whatever it is beside her. Why I hate to look at magazines any more because I know she'll turn up somewhere in a brassière or a bubble bath. Why I don't like to think of millions of Americans drinking in that poisonous half-smile. It's quite a story – more story than you're expecting.

No, I haven't suddenly developed any long-haired indignation at the evils of advertising and the national glamour-girl complex. That'd be a laugh for a man in my racket, wouldn't it? Though I think you'll agree there's something a little perverted about trying to capitalise on sex that way. But it's okay with me. And I know we've had the Face and the Body and the Look and what not else, so why shouldn't someone come along who sums it all up so completely, that we have to call her the Girl and blazon her on all the billboards from Times Square to Telegraph Hill?

But the Girl isn't like any of the others. She's unnatural. She's morbid. She's unholy.

Oh, these are modern times, you say, and the sort of thing I'm hinting at went out with witchcraft. But you see I'm not altogether sure myself what I'm hinting at, beyond a certain point. There are vampires and vampires, and not all of them suck blood.

And there were the murders, if they were murders. Besides, let me ask you this. Why, when America is obsessed with the Girl, don't we find out more about her? Why doesn't she rate a *Time* cover with a droll biography inside? Why hasn't there been a feature in *Life* or *The Post*? A profile in the *New Yorker*? Why hasn't *Charm* or *Mademoiselle* done her career saga? Not ready for it? Nuts!

Why haven't the movies snapped her up? Why hasn't she been on 'Information, Please'? Why don't we see her kissing candidates at political rallies? Why isn't she chosen queen of some sort of junk or other at a convention?

Why don't we read about her tastes and hobbies, her views of the Russian situation? Why haven't the columnists interviewed her in a kimono on the top floor of the tallest hotel in Manhattan and told us who her boy friends are?

Finally – and this is the real killer – why hasn't she ever been drawn or painted?

Oh, no she hasn't. If you knew anything about commercial art you'd know that. Every blessed one of those pictures was worked up from a photograph. Expertly? Of course. They've got the top artists on it. But that's how it's done.

And now I'll tell you the why of all that. It's because from the top to the bottom of the whole world of advertising, news, and business, there isn't a solitary soul who knows where the Girl came from, where she lives, what she does, who she is, even what her name is.

You heard me. What's more, not a single solitary soul ever sees her – except one poor damned photographer, who's making more money off her than he ever hoped to in his life and who's scared and miserable as Hell every minute of the day.

No, I haven't the faintest idea who he is or where he has his studio. But I know there has to be such a man and I'm morally certain he feels just like I said.

Yes, I might be able to find her, if I tried. I'm not sure though – by now she probably has other safeguards. Besides, I don't want to.

Oh, I'm off my rocker, am I? That sort of thing can't happen in the Era of the Atom? People can't keep out of sight that way, not even Garbo?

Well I happen to know they can, because last year I was that poor damned photographer I was telling you about. Yes, last year, when the Girl made her first poisonous splash right here in this big little city of ours.

Yes, I know you weren't here last year and you don't know about it. Even the Girl had to start small. But if you hunted through the files of the local newspapers, you'd find some ads, and I might be able to locate you some of the old displays – I think Lovelybelt is still using one of them. I used to have a mountain of photos myself, until I burned them.

Yes, I made my cut off her. Nothing like what that other photographer must be making, but enough so it still bought this whisky. She was funny about money. I'll tell you about that.

But first picture me then. I had a fourth-floor studio in that rathole the Hauser Building, not far from Ardleigh Park.

I'd been working at the Marsh-Mason studios until I'd

236

gotten my bellyful of it and decided to start in for myself. The Hauser Building was awful – I'll never forget how the stairs creaked – but it was cheap and there was a skylight.

Business was lousy. I kept making the rounds of all the advertisers and agencies, and some of them didn't object to me too much personally, but my stuff never clicked. I was pretty near broke. I was behind on my rent. Hell, I didn't even have enough money to have a girl.

It was one of those dark, grey afternoons. The building was very quiet – I'd just finished developing some pix I was doing on speculation for Lovelybelt Girdles and Budford's Pool and Playground. My model had left. A Miss Leon. She was a civics teacher at one of the high schools and modelled for me on the side, just lately on speculation, too. After one look at the prints, I decided that Miss Leon probably wasn't just what Lovelybelt was looking for – or my photography either. I was about to call it a day.

And then the street door slammed four storeys down and there were steps on the stairs and she came in.

She was wearing a cheap, shiny black dress. Black pumps. No stockings. And except that she had a grey cloth coat over one of them, those skinny arms of hers were bare. Her arms are pretty skinny, you know, or can't you see things like that any more?

And then the thin neck, the slightly gaunt, almost prim face, the tumbling mass of dark hair, and looking out from under it the hungriest eyes in the world.

That's the real reason she's plastered all over the country to-day, you know – those eyes. Nothing vulgar, but just the same they're looking at you with a hunger that's all sex and something more than sex. That's what everybody's been looking for since the Year One – something a little more than sex.

Well, boys, there I was, alone with the Girl, in an office that was getting shadowy, in a nearly empty building. A situation

237

that a million male Americans have undoubtedly pictured to themselves with various lush details. How was I feeling? Scared.

I know sex can be frightening. That cold heart-thumping when you're alone with a girl and feel you're going to touch her. But if it was sex this time, it was overlaid with something else.

At least I wasn't thinking about sex.

I remember that I took a backward step and that my hand jerked so that the photos I was looking at sailed to the floor.

There was the faintest dizzy feeling like something was being drawn out of me. Just a little bit.

That was all. Then she opened her mouth and everything was back to normal for a while.

'I see you're a photographer, mister,' she said. 'Could you use a model?'

Her voice wasn't very cultivated.

'I doubt it,' I told her, picking up the pix. You see, I wasn't impressed. The commercial possibilities of her eyes hadn't registered on me yet, by a long shot. 'What have you done?'

Well, she gave me a vague sort of story and I began to check her knowledge of model agencies and studios and rates and what not and pretty soon I said to her, 'Look here, you never modelled for a photographer in your life. You just walked in here cold.'

Well, she admitted that was more or less so.

All along through our talk I got the idea she was feeling her way, like someone in a strange place. Not that she was uncertain of herself, or of me, but just of the general situation.

'And you think anyone can model?' I asked her pityingly.

'Sure,' she said.

'Look,' I said, 'a photographer can waste a dozen negatives

trying to get one halfway human photo of an average woman. How many do you think he'd have to waste before he got a real catchy, glamorous photo of her?'

'I think I could do it,' she said.

Well, I should have kicked her out right then. Maybe I admired the cool way she stuck to her dumb little guns. Maybe I was touched by her underfed look. More likely I was feeling mean on account of the way my pictures had been snubbed by everybody and I wanted to take it out on her by showing her up.

'Okay, I'm going to put you on the spot,' I told her. 'I'm going to try a couple of shots of you. Understand it's strictly on spec. If somebody should ever want to use a photo of you, which is about one chance in two million, I'll pay you regular rates for your time. Not otherwise.'

She gave me a smile. The first. 'That's swell by me,' she said.

Well, I took three or four shots, close-ups of her face since I didn't fancy her cheap dress, and at least she stood up to my sarcasm. Then I remembered I still had the Lovelybelt stuff and I guess the meanness was still working in me because I handed her a girdle and told her to go behind the screen and get into it and she did, without getting flustered as I'd expected, and since we'd gone that far, I figured we might as well shoot the beach scene to round it out, and that was that.

All this time I wasn't feeling anything particular one way or the other, except every once in a while I'd get one of those faint dizzy flashes and wonder if there was something wrong with my stomach or if I could have been a bit careless with my chemicals.

Still, you know, I think the uneasiness was in me all the while.

I tossed her a card and pencil. 'Write your name and address and phone,' I told her and made for the dark-room.

A little later she walked out. I didn't call any goodbyes. I was irked because she hadn't fussed around or seemed anxious about her poses, or even thanked me, except for that one smile.

I finished developing the negatives, made some prints, glanced at them, decided they weren't a great deal worse than Miss Leon. On an impulse I slipped them in with the pictures I was going to take on the rounds next morning.

By now I'd worked long enough, so I was a bit fagged and nervous, but I didn't dare waste enough money on liquor to help that. I wasn't very hungry. I think I went to a cheap movie.

I didn't think of the Girl at all, except maybe to wonder faintly why in my present womanless state I hadn't made a pass at her. She had seemed to belong to a – well, distinctly more approachable social strata than Miss Leon. But then, of course, there were all sorts of arguable reasons for my not doing that.

Next morning I made the rounds. My first step was Munsch's Brewery. They were looking for a 'Munsch Girl'. Papa Munsch had a sort of affection for me, though he razzed my photography. He had a good natural judgment about that, too. Fifty years ago he might have been one of the shoe-string boys who made Hollywood.

Right now he was out in the plant pursuing his favourite occupation. He put down the beaded schooner, smacked his lips, gabbled something technical to someone about hops, wiped his fat hands on the big apron he was wearing, and grabbed my thin stack of pictures.

He was about halfway through, making noises with his tongue and teeth, when he came to her. I kicked myself for even having stuck her in.

'That's her,' he said. 'The photography's not so hot, but that's the girl.'

It was all decided. I wonder now why Papa Munsch sensed

what the Girl had right away, while I didn't. I think it was because I saw her first in the flesh, if that's the right word.

At the time I just felt faint.

'Who is she?' he said.

'One of my new models.' I tried to make it casual.

'Bring her out tomorrow morning,' he told me. 'And your stuff. We'll photograph her here.'

'Here, don't look so sick,' he added. 'Have some beer.'

Well, I went away telling myself it was just a fluke, so that she'd probably blow it tomorrow with her inexperience, and so on.

Just the same, when I reverently laid my next stack of pictures on Mr Fitch, of Lovelybelt's, rose-coloured blotter, I had hers on top.

Mr Fitch went through the motions of being an art critic. He leaned over backwards, squinted his eyes, waved his long fingers, and said, 'Hmm. What do you think, Miss Willow? Here, in this light, of course, the photograph doesn't show the bias cut. And perhaps we should use the Lovelybelt Imp instead of the Angel. Still, the girl. . . . Come over here, Binns.' More finger-waving. 'I want a married man's reaction.'

He couldn't hide the fact that he was hooked.

Exactly the same thing happened at Budford's Pool and Playground, except that Da Costa didn't need a married man's say-so.

'Hot stuff,' he said, sucking his lips. 'Oh boy, you photographers!'

I hot-footed it back to the office and grabbed up the card I'd given her to put down her name and address.

It was blank.

I don't mind telling you that the next five days were about the worst I ever went through, in an ordinary way. When next morning rolled around and I still hadn't got hold of her, I had to start stalling.

'She's sick,' I told Papa Munsch over the phone.

'She at a hospital?' he asked me.

'Nothing that serious,' I told him.

'Get her out here then. What's a little headache?'

'Sorry, I can't.'

Papa Munsch got suspicious. 'You really got this girl?'

'Of course I have.'

'Well, I don't know. I'd think it was some New York model, except I recognised your lousy photography.'

I laughed.

'Well look, you get her here tomorrow morning, you hear?'

'I'll try.'

'Try nothing. You get her out here.'

He didn't know half of what I tried. I went around to all the model and employment agencies. I did some slick detective work at the photographic and art studios. I used up some of my last dimes putting advertisements in all three papers. I looked at high-school year-books and at employee photos in local house organs. I went to restaurants and drugstores, looking at waitresses, and to dime stores and department stores, looking at clerks. I watched the crowds coming out of movie theatres. I roamed the streets.

Evenings, I spent quite a bit of time along Pick-up Row. Somehow that seemed the right place.

The fifth afternoon I knew I was licked. Papa Munsch's deadline – he'd given me several, but this was it – was due to run out at six o'clock. Mr Fitch had already cancelled.

I was at the studio window, looking out at Ardleigh Park.

She walked in.

I'd gone over this moment so often in my mind that I had no trouble putting on my act. Even the faint dizzy feeling didn't throw me off.

'Hello,' I said, hardly looking at her.

'Hello,' she said.

'Not discouraged yet?'

'No.' It didn't sound uneasy or defiant. It was just a statement.

I snapped a look at my watch, got up and said curtly, 'Look here, I'm going to give you a chance. There's a client of mine looking for a girl your general type. If you do a real good job you might break into the modelling business.'

'We can see him this afternoon if we hurry,' I said. I picked up my stuff. 'Come on. And next time if you expect favours, don't forget to leave your phone number.'

'Uh, uh,' she said, not moving.

'What do you mean?' I said.

'I'm not going out to see any client of yours.'

'The hell you aren't,' I said. 'You little nut, I'm giving you a break.'

She shook her head slowly. 'You're not fooling me, baby, you're not fooling me at all. They want me.' And she gave me the second smile.

At the time I thought she must have seen my newspaper ad. Now I'm not so sure.

'And now I'll tell you how we're going to work,' she went on. 'You aren't going to have my name or address or phone number. Nobody is. And we're going to do all the pictures right here. Just you and me.'

You can imagine the roar I raised at that. I was everything – angry, sarcastic, patiently explanatory, off my nut, threatening, pleading.

I would have slapped her face off, except it was photographic capital.

In the end all I could do was phone Papa Munsch and tell him her conditions. I knew I didn't have a chance, but I had to take it.

He gave me a really angry bawling out, said 'no' several times and hung up.

243

It didn't worry her. 'We'll start shooting at ten o'clock to-morrow,' she said.

It was just like her, using that corny line from the movie magazines.

About midnight Papa Munsch called me up.

'I don't know what insane asylum you're renting this girl from,' he said, 'but I'll take her. Come round tomorrow morning and I'll try to get it through your head just how I want the pictures. And I'm glad I got you out of bed!'

After that it was a breeze. Even Mr Fitch reconsidered and after taking two days to tell me it was quite impossible, he accepted the conditions too.

Of course you're all under the spell of the Girl, so you can't understand how much self-sacrifice it represented on Mr Fitch's part when he agreed to forego supervising the photography of my model in the Lovelybelt Imp or Vixen or whatever it was we finally used.

Next morning she turned up on time according to her schedule, and we went to work. I'll say one thing for her, she never got tired and she never kicked at the way I fussed over shots. I got along okay, except I still had that feeling of something being shoved away gently. Maybe you've felt it just a little, looking at her picture.

When we finished I found out there were still more rules. It was about the middle of the afternoon. I started with her to get a sandwich and coffee.

'Uh, uh,' she said, 'I'm going down alone. And look, baby, if you ever try to follow me, if you ever so much as stick your head out of that window when I go, you can hire yourself another model.'

You can imagine how all this crazy stuff strained my temper – and my imagination. I remember opening the window after she was gone – I waited a few minutes first – and standing there getting some fresh air and trying to figure out what could be behind it, whether she was hiding from the police, or was somebody's ruined daughter, or maybe had got the idea it was smart to be temperamental, or more likely Papa Munsch was right and she was partly nuts.

But I had my pictures to finish up.

Looking back it's amazing to think how fast her magic began to take hold of the city after that. Remembering what came after, I'm frightened of what's happening to the whole country – and maybe the world. Yesterday I read something in *Time* about the Girl's picture turning up on billboards in Egypt.

The rest of my story will help show you why I'm frightened in that big, general way. But I have a theory, too, that helps explain, though it's one of those things that's beyond that 'certain point'. It's about the Girl. I'll give it to you in a few words.

You know how modern advertising gets everybody's mind set in the same direction, wanting the same things, imagining the same things. And you know the psychologists aren't so sceptical of telepathy as they used to be.

Add up the two ideas. Suppose the identical desires of millions of people focussed on one telepathic person. Say a girl. Shaped her in their image.

Imagine her knowing the hiddenmost hungers of millions of men. Imagine her seeing deeper into those hungers than the people that had them, seeing the hatred and the wish for death behind the lust. Imagine her shaping herself in that complete image, keeping herself as aloof as marble. Yet imagine the hunger she might feel in answer to their hunger.

But that's getting a long way from the facts of my story. And some of those facts are darn solid. Like money. We made money.

That was the funny thing I was going to tell you. I was afraid the Girl was going to hold me up. She really had me over a barrel, you know.

But she didn't ask for anything but the regular rates. Later on I insisted on pushing more money at her, a whole lot. But she always took it with that same contemptuous look, as if she were going to toss it down the first drain when she got outside.

Maybe she did.

At any rate, I had money. For the first time in months I had money enough to get drunk, buy new clothes, take taxicabs. I could make a play for any girl I wanted to. I only had to pick.

And so of course I had to go and pick . . .

But first let me tell you about Papa Munsch.

Papa Munsch wasn't the first of the boys to try to meet my model but I think he was the first to really go soft on her. I could watch the change in his eyes as he looked at her pictures. They began to get sentimental, reverent. Mama Munsch had been dead for two years.

He was smart about the way he planned it. He got me to drop some information which told him when she came to work, and then one morning he came pounding up the stairs a few minutes before.

'I've got to see her, Dave,' he told me.

I argued with him, I kidded him, I explained he didn't know just how serious she was about her crazy ideas. I even pointed out he was cutting both our throats. I even amazed myself by bawling him out

He didn't take any of it in his usual way. He just kept repeating, 'But, Dave, I've got to see her.'

The street door slammed.

'That's her,' I said, lowering my voice. 'You've got to get out.'

He wouldn't, so I shoved him in the dark-room, 'And keep quiet,' I whispered. 'I'll tell her I can't work today.'

I knew he'd try to look at her and probably come busting in, but there wasn't anything else I could do.

The footsteps came to the fourth floor. But she never showed at the door. I got uneasy.

'Get that bum out of there!' she yelled suddenly from beyond the door. Not very loud, but in her commonest voice.

'I'm going up to the next landing,' she said. 'And if that fat-bellied bum doesn't march straight down to the street, he'll never get another picture of me except spitting in his lousy beer.'

Papa Munsch came out of the dark-room. He was white. He didn't look at me as he went out. He never looked at her pictures in front of me again.

That was Papa Munsch. Now it's me I'm telling about. I talked around the subject with her, I hinted, eventually I made my pass.

She lifted my hand off her as if it were a damp rag.

'No, baby,' she said. 'This is working time.'

'But afterwards . . .' I pressed.

'The rules still hold.' And I got what I think was the fifth smile.

It's hard to believe, but she never budged an inch from that crazy line. I mustn't make a pass at her in the office, because our work was very important and she loved it and there mustn't be any distractions. And I couldn't see her anywhere else, because if I tried to, I'd never snap another picture of her – and all this with more money coming in all the time and me never so stupid as to think my photography had anything to do with it.

Of course I wouldn't have been human if I hadn't made more passes. But they always got the wet-rag treatment and there weren't any more smiles.

I changed. I went sort of crazy and light-headed – only sometimes I felt my head was going to burst. And I started to talk to her all the time. About myself.

It was like being in a constant delirium that never interfered with business. I didn't pay any attention to the dizzy feeling. It seemed natural.

I'd walk around and for a moment the reflector would look like a sheet of white-hot steel, or the shadows would seem like armies of moths, or the camera would be a big black coal car. But the next instant they'd come all right again.

I think sometimes I was scared to death of her. She'd seem the strangest, most horrible person in the world. But other times. . . .

And I talked. It didn't matter what I was doing – lighting her, posing her, fussing with props, snapping my pictures – or where she was – on the platform, behind the screen, relaxing with a magazine – I kept up a steady gab.

I told her everything I knew about myself. I told her about my first girl. I told her about my brother Bob's bicycle. I told her about running away on a freight, and the licking Pa gave me when I came home. I told her about shipping to South America and the blue sky at night. I told her about Betty. I told her about my mother dying of cancer. I told her about being beaten up in a fight in an alley behind a bar. I told her about Mildred. I told her about the first picture I ever sold. I told her how Chicago looked from a sailboat. I told her about the longest drunk I was ever on. I told her about Marsh-Mason. I told her about Gwen. I told her about how I met Papa Munsch. I told her about hunting her. I told her about how I felt now.

She never paid the slightest attention to what I said. I couldn't even tell if she heard me.

It was when we were getting our first nibble from national advertisers that I decided to follow her when she went home.

Wait, I can place it better than that. Something you'll remember from the out-of-town papers – those maybe murders I mentioned. I think there were six.

I say 'maybe' because the police could never be sure they weren't heart attacks. But there's bound to be suspicion when attacks happen to people whose hearts have been okay, and always at night when they're alone and away from home and there's a question of what they were doing.

The six deaths created one of those 'mystery poisoner' scares. And afterwards there was a feeling that they hadn't really stopped, but were being continued in a less suspicious way.

That's one of the things that scares me now.

But at that time my only feeling was relief that I'd decided to follow her.

I made her work until dark one afternoon. I didn't need any excuses, we were snowed under with orders. I waited until the street door slammed, then I ran down. I was wearing rubber-soled shoes. I'd slipped on a dark coat she'd never seen me in, and a dark hat.

I stood in the doorway until I spotted her. She was walking by Ardleigh Park towards the heart of town. It was one of those warm fall nights. I followed her on the other side of the street. My idea for tonight was just to find out where she lived. That would give me a hold on her.

She stopped in front of a display window of Everley's department store, standing back from the flow. She stood there looking in.

I remembered we'd done a big photograph of her for Everley's, to make a flat model for a lingerie display. That was what she was looking at.

At the time it seemed all right to me that she should adore herself, if that was what she was doing.

When people passed she'd turn away a little or drift back further into the shadows.

Then a man came by alone. I couldn't see his face very well, but he looked middle-aged. He stopped and stood looking in the window.

249

She came out of the shadows and stepped up beside him.

How would you boys feel if you were looking at a poster of the Girl and suddenly she was there beside you, her arm linked with yours?

This fellow's reaction showed plain as day. A crazy dream had come to life for him.

They talked for a moment. Then he waved a taxi to the kerb. They got in and drove off.

I got drunk that night. It was almost as if she'd known I was following her and had picked that way to hurt me. Maybe she had. Maybe this was the finish.

But the next morning she turned up at the usual time and I was back in the delirium, only now with some new angles added.

That night when I followed her she picked a spot under a street lamp, opposite one of the Munsch Girl billboards.

Now it frightens me to think of her lurking that way.

After about twenty minutes a convertible slowed down going past her, backed up, swung into the kerb.

I was closer this time. I got a good look at the fellow's face. He was a little younger, about my age.

Next morning the same face looked up at me from the front page of the paper. The convertible had been found parked on a side street. He had been in it. As in the other maybe-murders, the cause of death was uncertain.

All kinds of thoughts were spinning in my head that day, but there were only two things I knew for sure. That I'd got the first real offer from a national advertiser, and that I was going to take the Girl's arm and walk down the stairs with her when we quit work.

She didn't seem surprised. 'You know what you're doing?' she said.

'I know.'

She smiled. 'I was wondering when you'd get around to it.'

I began to feel good. I was kissing everything goodbye, but I had my arm around hers.

It was another of those warm fall evenings. We cut across into Ardleigh Park. It was dark there, but all around the sky was a sallow pink from the advertising signs.

We walked for a long time in the park. She didn't say anything and she didn't look at me, but I could see her lips twitching and after a while her hand tightened on my arm.

We stopped. We'd been walking across the grass. She dropped down and pulled me after her. She put her hands on my shoulders. I was looking down at her face. It was the faintest sallow pink from the glow in the sky. The hungry eyes were dark smudges.

I was fumbling with her blouse. She took my hand away, not like she had in the studio. 'I don't want that,' she said.

First I'll tell you what I did afterwards. Then I'll tell you why I did it. Then I'll tell you what she said.

What I did was run away. I don't remember all of that because I was dizzy, and the pink sky was swinging against the dark trees. But after a while I staggered into the lights of the street. The next day I closed up the studio. The telephone was ringing when I locked the door and there were unopened letters on the floor. I never saw the Girl again in the flesh, if that's the right word.

I did it because I didn't want to die. I didn't want the life drawn out of me. There are vampires and vampires, and the ones that suck blood aren't the worst. If it hadn't been for the warning of those dizzy flashes, and Papa Munsch and the face in the morning paper, I'd have gone the way the others did. But I realised what I was up against while there was still time to tear myself away. I realised that wherever she came from, whatever shaped her, she's the quintessence of the horror behind the bright billboard. She's the smile that tricks you into throwing away your money and your life. She's the eyes that lead you on and on, and then show you death. She's the creature you give everything for and never really get. She's the being that takes everything you've got and gives nothing in return. When you yearn towards her face on the billboards, remember that. She's the lure. She's the bait. She's the Girl.

And this is what she said, 'I want you. I want your high spots. I want everything that's made you happy and everything that's hurt you bad. I want your first girl. I want that shiny bicycle. I want that licking. I want that pinhole camera. I want Betty's legs. I want the blue sky filled with stars. I want your mother's death. I want your blood on the cobblestones. I want Mildred's mouth. I want the first picture you sold. I want the lights of Chicago. I want the gin. I want Gwen's hands. I want your wanting me. I want your life. Feed me, baby, feed me.'

Postscript

CASES of vampirism may be said to be in our time a rare occult phenomenon. Yet whether we are justified in supposing that they are less frequent today than in past centuries I am far from certain. One thing is plain – not that they do not occur but that they are carefully hushed up and stifled. More than one such instance has come to my own notice.

'A Mrs Hayes informs me of a vampiric experience which befell her only some ten years ago, but happily in this case no actual harm was done, perhaps because the evil force (although none the less dangerous in intent) was something old and waning and had not at the time collected a sufficient reserve of that new strength for which it was so eagerly athirst in order that it might manifest itself more potently and with intensely active malice.

'It chanced that Mrs Hayes took a small house at Penlee, South Devon, not far from Dartmouth. She writes:

' "I had a friend staying with me, but otherwise we were quite alone in the place. One morning we came down to find in the middle of the parquet floor of the sitting-room the mark of a single cloven hoof in mud. The house and windows were very small, so it was quite impossible for an animal to have got in, nor indeed were such the case could it have managed so as to leave one single footprint. We hunted everywhere for a second trace but without success. For several nights I had most unpleasant and frightening experiences with an invisible but perfectly tangible being. I had no peace until I had hung the place with garlic, which acted like a charm. I tried it as a last resource."

'In a recent book, *Oddities*, Commander Gould has spoken

of the Devil's Footsteps that have from time to time appeared in South Devon, and it might very well be thought that the haunting at Penlee was the evocation of demonism whose energies persist, that formerly Satanists dwelt or assembled on the spot and diabolic rites were celebrated, but the purgation of the house by garlic unmistakably betrays that the horror was due to a definite vampiric origin. I have no doubt that there are many localities similarly infested, and that from time to time the vampire manifests in a greater or less degree, but the exact nature of these molestations is unrecognised and the happenings unrecorded.

'In 1924 the Hon. Ralph Shirley wrote: "It may be doubted indeed, in spite of the lack of records, whether vampirism in one form or another is quite as absent from the conditions of modern civilisation as is commonly supposed. Although we are not today familiar with the Slavonic type of vampire that sucks the blood of its victims, producing death in two or three days time, strange cases come to light occasionally when people are the victims, by their own confession, of something of a very similar nature, the vampire in these cases being an entity in human form who indulges in intercourse with someone of the opposite sex. Such cases are today, generally speaking, promptly consigned to one of our lunatic asylums and do not reach the public ear. I happened, however, quite recently to hear an instance of the kind. The victim had been engaged to a young man, the family on account of the man's antecedents, not approving of the engagement, but not being actively hostile. The man died suddenly, and the girl was prostrated with grief. Shortly after, however, she recovered her normal cheerfulness, and somewhat later confessed to her mother that she was visited by her former lover in physical form. She subsequently became engaged to another man, but owing to threats, as he said, of her deceased lover, the engagement was broken off. The last time I heard of the young lady in question she was stated o be consumptive. Naturally, these things do not get into the papers, and obviously the ordinary medical man will put down instances of the kind as pure hallucination. Still, if we have any belief in the philosophy of the occultist, they are bound to give us pause and make us hesitate before saying that vampirism is entirely a thing of the past."

'Such cases, in truth, are happening every day, and I have met with not a few instances in my own experience.'

MONTAGUE SUMMERS
(*The Vampire in Europe*)

Warner now offers an exciting range of quality titles by both established and new authors. All of the books in this series are available from:
Little, Brown and Company (UK) Limited,
P.O. Box 11,
Falmouth,
Cornwall TR10 9EN.

Alternatively you may fax your order to the above address. Fax No. 0326 376423.

Payments can be made as follows: Cheque, postal order (payable to Little, Brown and Company) or by credit cards, Visa/Access. Do not send cash or currency. UK customers: and B.F.P.O.: please send a cheque or postal order (no currency) and allow £1.00 for postage and packing for the first book, plus 50p for the second book, plus 30p for each additional book up to a maximum charge of £3.00 (7 books plus).

Overseas customers including Ireland, please allow £2.00 for postage and packing for the first book, plus £1.00 for the second book, plus 50p for each additional book.

NAME (Block Letters) ....

ADDRESS...

....

☐ I enclose my remittance for _____

☐ I wish to pay by Access/Visa Card

Number ☐☐☐☐☐☐☐☐☐☐☐☐☐☐☐☐

Card Expiry Date ☐☐☐☐